CW01262388

# DREAMS

## C.D. FOX

ArrowGate

Published by Arrow Gate Publishing Ltd
London

Copyright © C.D. Fox 2022

19 18 17 15 14 13 12 11 10 9

C. D. Fox has asserted his rights under the Copyright, Designs and Patent Act 1998 to be identified as the author of this work.

This book is sold subject to the condition that it shall not, by way of trade or otherwise, be lent, resold, hired out, or otherwise circulated without the publisher's prior consent in any form of binding or cover other than that in which it is published and without similar condition including this condition being imposed on the subsequent purchaser

Arrow Gate Publishing's titles may be purchased in bulk for educational, business, fundraising, or sales promotional use. For information, please email info@arrowgatepublishing.com

A CIP catalogue record for this book is available from the British Library

ISBN 978-1-913142-24-7

www.arrowgatepublishing.com

Arrow Gate Publishing Ltd Reg. No. 8376606

Arrow Gate Publishing Ltd's policy is to use papers that are natural, renewable, and recyclable products and made from wood grown in sustainable forests. The logging and manufacturing processes are expected to conform to the environmental regulations of the country of origin

## ACKNOWLEDGEMENTS

*Writing the first book is a secretive undertaking, and few people knew I was working on Dreams until the manuscript was close to completion. I would like to thank friends David Cunningham and Simon Drew, whose helpful suggestions and words of encouragement gave me the confidence to push on with the first draft and polish it into a final version. I am indebted to Sandra David and the entire team at Arrow Gate Publishing for believing in this book; without them, Dreams would not have come to fruition. Lastly, I would like to thank my parents, David and Stella Fox, who first heard about my writing aspirations when I told them I'd signed a Publishing Agreement. They may not have helped with the book, but they have contributed in countless other ways since day one.*

*When, leaning on your faithless breast,*
*Wrapped in security and rest,*
*Soft kindness all my powers did move,*
*And reason lay dissolved in love!*

—FROM 'A Ramble in St. James's Park',
John Wilmot, 2nd Earl of Rochester: 1672.

• CHAPTER 1 •

She closed her eyes as a breath of wind kissed her cheek. The evening was warm and replete with kind comforts. Insects hummed their busy tunes in the meadow's long grass and wildflowers. Birdsong played like a symphony from the hidden depths of the bramble thickets. In the distance, the faint sound of church bells drifted across the landscape, their ghostly toll complementing the evening melody of nature.

Deep in thought, she sat on the grass and gazed at the stream, its languid flow enchanting her. Eyes wide and semi-hypnotised, she watched as a pair of dragonflies pranced across her line of sight, chasing each other like courting lovers. Suddenly a small fish, perhaps a minnow, broke the surface and rolled before disappearing beneath the shifting glints of sunlit water.

Yet the woman barely noticed nature's circus tricks and playful games; instead, her blue eyes remained fixed in a forward focus, mesmerised by the ceaseless flow of the stream.

The meadow was a beautiful spot all year round. The balmy days of summer had given way to autumn, but the vicinity's radiance was undiminished on a mild evening like this. She gazed up at the boundless blue expanse above her head, its shade now deepening in the fading light. Like a spotlight low on the horizon, the lingering sun illuminated the meadow and drenched it in a honey-sweet golden hue. On the bank of the stream, between the bulrushes, a spider's web sparkled as it caught the sunlight and shimmered in the lazy breeze.

As she pondered the meadow's natural artwork, meditating on its serene splendour, time itself seemed to melt away into the evening stillness. This was the woman's private place. She didn't own it, for the meadow was common land, yet no other folk ever seemed to venture there. The overgrown footpaths guarded a secret paradise long since forgotten by the dog walkers and blackberry pickers of the Kentish Weald. Each visit offered her solitude, and she would sit, sometimes for hours, and allow her thoughts to swirl in a maelstrom of aching memories.

For the meadow's peace contrasted with a tempest that howled in her mind. A storm that ravaged her senses, it was a tumult she tried to escape from…

…The despairing echo of her past.

She held a spliff to her lips, struck a match, and took one, very long, drag. Her eyes closed as relaxation flooded her body and mind, soothing her thoughts almost instantly. The anguish was still there, spinning and churning in her head like cement in a mixer, but the drug provided a hazy veil that made it feel remote and detached.

How had it come to this? She was thirty-two years old, but like the terrifying lunge of a ghoulish black shuck, her past had warped her life into a waking nightmare. What had she done to deserve it? Each day, those terrible memories pounded away at her psyche. If sanity was the dam that held back a reservoir of madness, it felt like the walls were about to be breached.

And cannabis was her prime weapon in the fight to remain sane – the only thing that could help shore up that straining, crumbling structure. What a paradox, she thought, that a drug used to craze the mind should instead be employed as a fortress – the last line of defence against the dark spectre of insanity. It was an unenviable dichotomy – and one that she hated! But at least it offered her some solace, and she was not in a position to refuse that smallest of mercies.

The poor, dejected woman felt her eyes begin to well. Nevertheless, when the tear broke ranks, she did not move to wipe it. Instead, it rolled down her cheek, pausing for a moment at the bottom of her chin before dropping to the earth like a hesitant skydiver leaping from a plane.

She took another drag on the spliff, a shorter one this time. As she exhaled, she let go a sigh that hinted at her sadness and wandering melancholy. For the secrets she kept were so twisted and rotten that they must always remain guarded from the scrutiny of others. And yet, they were forever with her, pervading her thoughts like an invasive, smothering illness. Inside, she felt her usual stoicism eroding. The time had come to stop this parasite from feeding on her emotions any longer.

As the shadows lengthened that evening, her feelings darkened in a mirror image of the physical world around her. Her cannabis-induced high could not shield her forever. The whirlpool of torment began to rotate as her blurred mind struggled to make sense of her internal musings. All she could discern was the ever-creeping tide of depression, its hands clasped tightly around her throat.

And it appeared this dark assailant was finally to be the architect of her demise, that she would, at last, succumb to its asphyxiating grip. She felt weak and unable to fight any longer. Her mind and body conveyed a willingness to capitulate. Fluent thoughts began to race in her otherwise clouded mind with breath-taking clarity. She could not…she *would* not…live like this any longer. It was time to escape her secrets. It was time for decisive, *ultimate* action.

As she contemplated release from the pain, a brief anticipation enveloped her. Alone in the meadow, her suicidal thoughts crystallised. It was getting dark, and the twilight chorus played like music in her ears. Encased in the dim weariness of an emotional prison, she lay down and rested the back of her head on the grass. With thoughts of impending oblivion still whirring through her mind, she closed her eyes and drifted into a restless, dope-fuelled sleep.

• CHAPTER 2 •

Professor Rupert Swann sat with his legs crossed. Even after a hard day's work, the psychiatrist retained a dignified posture as he relaxed in the living room of his Ealing home. On the little table next to his armchair was an elegant looking crystal-cut whisky glass. The handsome receptacle was a quarter filled with brown liquid. Dark brown, to be precise: the whisky it contained had been matured in its barrel for a long time. It was a good whisky, a *very* good one.

Swann was a man with high standards, unprepared to compromise on quality. His Edwardian three-bed London semi was furnished to the highest standards of upper-middle-class taste and discretion. The room's dominant feature was the original cast-iron fireplace, painted black. Above it hung an elegant mirror that complemented the charm of a building constructed in 1909. His television was smaller than average and was relegated to the corner to avoid dominating things in the way they too often do in less discerning abodes. Eleven years earlier, Swann had agonised over whether to carpet his home or install oak flooring. In the end, he'd opted for carpet, deep cream in colour, and it remained pristine to this day.

A quick look at his watch told him it was nine-thirty. Uncrossing his legs and relaxing deeper into the chair, he took hold of his whisky and moved it towards his lips. Immediately, a shrill noise made him jump. A small amount of liquid spilt from his glass and into his lap.

The professor glanced angrily at his iPhone as if the device itself were to blame for intruding on his peaceful evening with its impertinent blaring. His first thought was to ignore it, so he dabbed at the wet patch between his legs and took another sip of whisky.

But despite being aggravated, something inside urged him to check who was phoning, so he flicked his eyes to the screen and read the name. His mood changed instantly: it was his son calling.

'Dad...it's me'. The voice was timid but had a caring softness about it.

'Hugo!' boomed the professor, rising to his feet and grinning at hearing his son's voice. 'How have your first couple of weeks been? Oxford's been treating you well, I trust?'

'Well, it's hard work, to be honest, Dad. But I guess that's what I'm here for. It's good fun, too, though. I'm enjoying it.'

The pair had conversed only via text in the first fortnight of Hugo Swann's new chapter as an eighteen-year-old undergraduate at Oriel College, Oxford. Their relationship could be fraught at times, and Hugo had been putting the phone call off. Now it was happening, the teenager knew his father would take control of the conversation.

'Superb!' exclaimed the older man. 'And the tutorials are going well, I trust?'

'Absolutely fine. In this morning's we—'

'Glad to hear it,' said Swann, somewhat dismissively and without the faintest flicker of interest in the content of Hugo's English tutorials. He was far more keen to discuss other aspects of his son's first couple of weeks at university. 'Clubs and societies. Tell me which ones you've joined, then.'

The haughty man sat back in his seat and began to reminisce. 'Yes, I remember my days at Cambridge. Within twenty minutes of arriving, I'd joined the boat club, the cricket club and the college rugger team. Those were the days, all right. God, I miss them sometimes. Well, boy, speak up. What clubs and societies have you joined?'

Hugo's stammer indicated he had little to share with his father in that regard. Nervously, he attempted to dodge the question. 'Well...I've been very busy with work, and—'

'You mean you haven't joined any sports clubs?' Swann's mood had changed again, this time to one of frustration. He jumped up from his seat and threw his free hand into the air in irritation, narrowly missing the cut-glass chandelier-style light fitting that hung in the centre of his living room. 'What the devil's wrong with you, boy? University is meant to be an all-round experience!'

Hugo squirmed on the other end of the line. 'Like I say, the reading list is very long…and we have deadlines every—'

'Debating. That's what you need if you want to be a barrister. Make sure you join the debating society. You're lacking confidence, lad. Sharp thinking and confidence. Precisely the skills you're going to need in the courtroom one day. Debating will help you acquire them. Are you listening, Hugo?'

Hugo was thankful he was talking to his father on the phone and not via FaceTime. He rolled his eyes, then silently puffed his cheeks as the old man exhorted. In fact, Hugo had never wanted to be a barrister at all. A career in Law didn't interest him, and besides, he knew he possessed nothing of the ruthlessness required for success in that profession.

Instead, Hugo dreamed of becoming an English teacher. In his mind, it was the natural ambition given his love of literature and caring disposition. The psychiatrist, however, so keen to live vicariously through his son, had initially torpedoed the idea. *I have a Gray's Inn friend*, Hugo remembered his father announce during his Lower Sixth year. *I'm sure he'll be able to sort you some work experience in chambers.*

Nevertheless, Hugo had persisted cunningly. He had told the medic he aimed to secure a position in one of London's most prestigious schools. Westminster, or Harrow, perhaps. He had even hinted at becoming a headmaster one day. Indeed, his lies had resulted in partial success. Whilst Hugo would, in truth, have preferred an obscure career making a difference to the lives of state school pupils, Professor Swann had gradually warmed to the idea of his son rising to the very top in private education.

Still, the legal profession was never too far from the psychiatrist's mind, especially when he had a whisky in his hand. Hugo, as usual, was forced to play along.

'Actually, Dad, there's a public speaking competition coming up at Oriel,' he lied, knowing it would calm his capricious father's exasperation. 'I was thinking of entering. It can't hurt to give it a go.'

'Well, that's just excellent,' beamed Swann as he settled back down in his chair. Again he reached for his glass, but this time he swirled the contents before taking a sip, then stole a moment to appreciate the decorative shadows cast on the ceiling and walls by the soft glow from the light fitting. 'Now then,' he pried, keen to sniff out the real gossip. 'How are things going with the fillies?'

'The fillies?'

'The *women*, Hugo!'

'Oh, I see.' *Good Lord, the man must be on his second whisky.*

'I'm asking whether you've found yourself a girlfriend yet.'

'Well...'

'You *need* to find yourself a girlfriend,' Swann insisted. 'University is as much a preparation for life as it is about getting a degree, you know...'

Hugo prepared himself for another rambling monologue.

'Yes, back in my day, we all had a splendid time. Lord knows how we ever made any of our morning supervisions, but we worked just as hard as we played, to be fair. In fact, the girls were the ones who kept us on the straight and narrow. Made men of us. As for you, Hugo...well, I suppose you'll just have to do your best, won't you? You might have failed with the girls at school, but you can at least make *some* effort now you're at Oxford.'

Hugo allowed the remark to wash over him and simply waited until his father had ceased pontificating. 'But that's what I'm ringing to tell you, Dad. I have found a girlfriend.'

The professor's jaw hung loose in astonishment.

'That was my reason for calling you. I wanted to tell you I've met someone. Her name's Alice and she's a very nice girl. An Experimental Psychology student. At Wadham.'

Hugo's pleasure in informing his father was palpable. Swann's response was one of pride in his son. 'I knew it!' he exclaimed, wagging his finger in the air. 'I knew Oxford would be the making of you.'

This time, he took a big gulp of whisky before leaning back in his comfortably upholstered armchair. 'Well, you be sure to bring her here for a visit,' he said in an almost friendly tone. 'Perhaps one weekend. In between assignments, maybe. Obviously not when you're preparing for that public speaking competition you're entering...'

'*Might* be entering.' Hugo couldn't help but roll his eyes again. 'It's only an option at this stage, Dad. Maybe I'll do it, maybe not.'

'Whatever. The point is I want to meet her. Sooner rather than later.'

'One weekend then. As you suggest.'

'Excellent man! Well, you enjoy yourself. And good luck with the public speaking,' Swann said dismissively, urging his son off the phone so he could return to the remnants of his whisky.

'Oh, one more thing, Dad,' said Hugo, before the medic could terminate the conversation.

'What's that?'

'Nothing really. It's just been good to hear your voice again, that's all.'

'Hmm. Yours too,' was all that was offered in return. A curt click indicated his father had hung up.

Hugo had never been a confident boy. He was shy and reserved by nature and, much to his father's consternation, had never been popular at school. *He's hardly a chip off the old block,* he'd once heard Swann tell his mother after complaining to her about bullying. *Why, when I was his age, no trouble ever came my way. He ought to stand up for himself a bit better.*

His lack of sporting ability had compounded matters. Last to be picked for everything on the games field, Hugo despised competition. But he had never dared ask mummy for a note to be excused. Not when there was a chance his father, who had captained his school's rugby team, might find out. Hugo remembered the old man's sporting rants with revulsion: *jolly good batsman I was, too. There were never any close fielders for me when I was at the crease.*

And then there was Hugo's general mien. One look at him signalled his difference from the others. He had worn the same uniform, but he was a different kind of person from *them*. His pale skin and bony face contrasted starkly with the chiselled looks that *they* possessed. His mousy hair was lank and dull – nothing like the luxurious mops that paraded proudly above *their* foppish features. He may have attended the same expensive school as his peers, but he did not occupy the same niche. He simply did not share *their* posh school vibe. In so many respects, he was the complete opposite of his father.

A further misfortune lay in his name: *Hugo* Swann. He had hated it at first and had even called himself 'Henry' at prep school to avoid being teased. He'd always known his mother had named him after Victor Hugo, but it wasn't until he'd read *Les Miserables* at fourteen that he'd begun to embrace the name, eventually wearing it as a badge of honour once he'd finished *The Hunchback of Notre Dame*.

With so many tribulations, Hugo had instead found solace in painting – his only real hobby – and in his studies. He was a bright rather than brilliant academic but had worked hard to secure his place at Oriel College, Oxford, to read English. His dream of studying at the oldest university in the English-speaking world, the one dream his father had actually approved of, had finally come to fruition.

And no one at Oxford knew of the difficulties he'd encountered at school and at home. He could thus begin afresh and with a clean slate. His chance to shine and come of age had finally arrived. Hugo Swann could at last take flight.

'I see you've got into bed then. Was that your dad on the phone?' queried Alice as she stepped back through from the ensuite shower. A damp towel wrapped around her body maintained her modesty.

Hugo's Grade A room in the Third Quad of Oriel College wasn't massive, but it was large enough to accommodate a small double bed in its own little alcove at one end. Cocooned under the covers, the English undergraduate peered out, the walls of the alcove acting like blinkers and tunnelling his vision towards Alice at the far end of the room.

Before him lay a sea of pastel colours: a blue square-armed sofa lay flush against a baby-blue painted wall on the right-hand side. On the left, by the window, was a little timber desk with a lamp and a blue upholstered study seat tucked underneath it. Framing the window above the desk were two checked curtains, their peach and lavender colour scheme slightly faded from exposure to sunlight.

'He says he wants to meet you,' admitted Hugo, pushing his spectacles up the bridge of his nose in a coy disclosure of his father's request. Skittishly, he buried himself a little deeper beneath the covers.

Alice's response made him feel better. 'Great,' she replied, casually dropping her towel and letting it land in a heap on the turquoise carpet. 'So, when are we going to go? A weekend at yours in London would be a welcome relief from all this study. It's only been a fortnight, and I feel like I'm drowning already.'

Hugo channelled all his efforts into maintaining eye contact, desperately trying not to gawk at Alice's naked body as she stood conversing nonchalantly in front of him. To his left and right, the alcove walls felt like they were closing in on him, reducing his peripheral vision and focusing his eyes laser-like on the unclothed student in front of him. She was the first girl he had ever seen naked. He had only lost his virginity to her a couple of nights before, and here she was again, nude and entirely uninhibited.

'We...we can visit whenever you like,' he replied, clearing his throat to regain his composure. 'He definitely wants to meet you.'

The effort was all too much, and Hugo couldn't help but flick his eyes south to steal a glimpse of her breasts. Alice noticed but pretended not to; the power of her nudity was a turn-on for her.

'Remind me what your father does?' she enquired, tying her dark curly hair into a bun.

Her casual nakedness and carefree conversation formed an erotic juxtaposition in Hugo's mind that drove him to exquisite distraction. 'Psychiatrist,' he stammered, his embarrassed eyes shooting up to meet hers. 'Quite a prominent one. He's done a lot of pioneering work in the field of mental health.'

'Sounds quite a person, your dad.'

'It's an irony how someone so lacking in emotional intelligence chose the career he did and had so much success with it.'

Alice cocked her head to the left and frowned at his cold comments. 'It sounds almost as if you resent him.'

'No, not at all. That sounded callous, didn't it? The truth is, I love him dearly. He can be a difficult person, but he means well. He's always wanted the best for me. It's just his expectations can be a little high at times. We're patently different people.'

'How very intriguing,' she commented with a playful arch of her eyebrows. She began moving towards the bed, and Hugo felt his veins burn as testosterone flooded his system.

With a flick of her wrist, she pulled back the duvet and climbed in next to him. Her hot breath, like air rushing through a blast furnace, excited the skin on his neck. He sensed her flesh meet his as she drew her body closer and entwined him in her arms. As their lips met, he felt her hand move slowly and intimately down and across his torso. In silent prayer, he offered a brief 'thank you,' for the bliss he had waited so long to experience.

• CHAPTER 3 •

She woke with a start, wondering what had disturbed her slumber. The chilly draught caused her to curl into the foetal position. As the woman's mind returned to reality, the cause of her waking became apparent. A large raindrop splashed her earlobe, immediately followed by another, which struck the bridge of her nose.

Slowly, the fog in her mind began to wash away as her skin grew moist, baptised by the cold precipitation striking it. She rubbed her eyes and squinted at the sky above. It was not yet fully light, but she could see enough to make out the ominous black cumulonimbus that had replaced the cotton wool cumulous of the evening before. How long had she been asleep? Her watch told her it was quarter-to-six in the morning. She had been unconscious for hours.

The rain began to intensify. Coming to, she lay still for a moment as large drops pounded against her forehead. Like the tears of heaven, they ran down her cheeks and the back of her neck, prompting her to rise from the soggy discomfort. A chilly gust from the west ruffled her hair and made her shiver.

The unpropitious atmospherics were dampening her body, but not the fire in her mind. Oblivion was calling her, but it was a sweet-scented beckon. A soft rumble of thunder in the distance urged her to move forwards. It was time to head for home.

She set off at pace across the green expanse. By the time she reached the far side of the meadow, her feet were cold and sodden, her porous trainers absorbing a good deal of moisture. As she entered the overgrown footpath that led back to civilisation, her surface temperature was dropping like a stone. With blood beginning to pull from her extremities, she folded her arms to keep them warm, bowing her head and fixing her eyes on the floor as she trudged. At least the autumn-yellowed canopy of trees now shielded her from the worst of the rain.

Eventually, she emerged onto the little country lane that wound back up the hill towards her home. The gentle Wealden slope was slippery, and the wind began to gust a little more as she ascended it. Out in the open, she felt the full force of the elements again. A proper storm was on its way.

Tucking her hands under her armpits, she glanced to her left as she walked. Low hedgerows surrounded the field beyond the lane, enclosing a single patch of countryside in the wider Kentish quilt. In the centre, a few nervous sheep huddled under an oak tree that sprang from the lush, undulating pasture. A solitary crow was perched on one of the branches, and a few leaves fell like snow in the autumn gusts.

Turning her head, she peered right. Stretching for miles ahead lay the Weald, its rolling beauty shadowed by the dark clouds that hung overhead like a threat from Thor himself. Wet and miserable, she quickened her pace, knowing that sanctuary lay within striking distance.

At the crest of the hill, the landscape flattened, and the hedges on either side of the lane grew taller, obscuring the fields and Wealden landscape beyond them. The village itself lay under a mile ahead but, before the first houses and parked cars honed into view, the woman turned right off the tarmac. Heading perpendicular, she walked the final few yards along the potholed lane that led to her secluded, redbrick cottage.

Back home, and protected from the elements by three-hundred-year-old walls and a steep pitched roof, her steadfast conviction increased. Goose pimples sprang from her skin as she stripped from her sodden clothing. She grabbed a towel and rubbed vigorously at her wet hair and clammy body.

As her hands rubbed, her mind pulsated. The plot she'd formed was morbid and demanded swift resolution. Thus, with skin now dry but hair still damp, she began rifling through her kitchen cupboards.

She smiled as she located the first item she was looking for: a bottle of vodka standing proudly in front of her, almost full. As she pulled the bottle from the cupboard, the clear liquid inside seemed to grin as it glinted in the brightness of the kitchen light. She placed it down on the worktop before her fingers, rodent-like in their probing, found what they were fumbling for in one of the drawers: two packs of pills. Not enough to finish the job, but most of the ingredients for her very special recipe were in place. Now it was simply a case of waiting.

She wouldn't do it at home among the mundane items of functional existence. Only one place could offer her the setting that such an undertaking deserved; a place where she could feel at one with the elements; where the story of her life could culminate in comfort. That place was the meadow. It was too early to head back there yet. The shops had not yet opened, and she knew she would have to buy more pills if her macabre plans were to be fulfilled. And besides, the weather was far too inclement to return just yet. Thus, with some time to pass, she got dressed and made a start on the vodka.

The alcohol pierced her bloodstream and cooled her mind's inferno. As she sat on the sofa in her living room, the thoughts of her past began to dredge. Ever since those events...*those dirty little events*...she had failed to function properly. She had been so young when it happened. Why her? For what purpose?

But once upon a time, things had been different. Things had been perfect. Picture postcard perfect. Momentarily, her vodka dampened brain propelled her back to that utopia, and scenes began to play out in her mind's eye. For the second time in a day, she sighed as she contemplated the alternative route her life might have taken.

A bittersweet history called her name, and she could not help but gaze back at it. Memories of a glorious childhood glided through her thoughts — a childhood cruelly stolen. Today, however, the vicious circle would be broken. Death would be a cure to nigh on twenty years of poisoned existence. She allowed herself to look forward to it.

But thoughts of her imminent future ceased when she realised what was happening in the present. *Jesus Christ! What the bloody hell is happening?*

It was occurring outside her window.

And what she saw astonished her.

• CHAPTER 4 •

A hospital consultation room was the last place Mike Buckland expected to find himself that October morning.

Buckland hated hospitals, especially London ones with their drab interiors and staff who were all from abroad. Still, at least the nurse was pretty. He guessed her to be Filipino. She was short in stature, but he reckoned she had a nice bosom hidden beneath her uniform.

Buckland ogled the contours as she leaned in and tightened the sling that held his freshly broken arm in place. He grimaced as another wave of pain ricocheted along his right forelimb. His naturally ruddy face grew even redder from the discomfort.

'I'll sue that bastard,' he swore. 'I'll take him to the cleaners. You wait and see!'

The nurse didn't engage with his vitriol. 'There you go, Mr Buckland,' she said. 'You're all fixed up now and ready to leave. Just be sure to give that arm a rest in the coming days. We'll have you back in a few weeks to check how it's healing.'

'The story will have broken by then,' said Buckland, his eyes narrowing with spite. 'That'll hit him where it hurts. Almost literally.'

'I'm afraid I don't know very much about football,' replied the nurse, wheeling her chair away to fill in some paperwork.

'Neither do I. But, the England football captain sleeping with the manager's daughter – that's a big story. And not something the skipper wants plastered all over the news. No wonder his minder pushed me into those iron railings when I ambushed him for a comment.' Buckland couldn't help but press the matter. 'We journos have to put our safety on the line in pursuit of the public interest. It's all part of the service, you see.'

The man's self-importance was nothing short of startling.

'So I'll be reading about this footballer in the news?' asked the nurse, humouring him. Having finished her notes, she rose to her feet and was ready to usher him out.

'Or watch it,' said Buckland, who also rose and began moving towards the door. 'My reports are frequently televised. In fact, you probably recognise me.'

She looked vacant.

Buckland was an intriguing creature with features difficult to pinpoint. He was a little shorter than average at five-foot-nine, but people often guessed him to be taller than that. At fifty, he retained a full head of side-parted hair that was beginning to look a little wispy now. Under bright lights, it looked decidedly ginger but appeared light brown if the conditions outside were right. A permanent film of sweat gave him a dishevelled appearance, and his hair was invariably plastered against his scalp. A double chin hung below his jaw and wobbled when he spoke.

But when he spoke, his voice was beautiful. Deep in tone and precise in tempo, Buckland's received pronunciation was exquisite – like Richard Burton with an English accent.

The newsman wore a creased blazer and a collared shirt with the top button undone. He always kept a tie in his blazer pocket should his look need professionalising at short notice: those big stories had a habit of cropping up at the most unexpected moments!

'Thank you for sorting this out for me,' he said, pointing to the sling as he hung in the doorway.

'You're very welcome,' replied the nurse, mistaking his sleaze for politeness.

He looked at her chest for one last time before he left. 'I sure hope you're the one who does the check-up when I come back in a few weeks.'

With that, he exited the consultation room and slithered back off to Reception.

• CHAPTER 5 •

Hugo's head hurt, and he felt groggy. 'What the hell are you doing?' he groaned, annoyed at having been woken.

'Getting up,' replied Alice, hauling herself out of bed and shuffling beyond the alcove.

'Getting up?'

'I have a tutorial this morning. I told you so last night.'

He squinted in the semi-darkness and rolled onto his back. 'There's no way it can be morning yet,' he complained.

'Hugo, it's half-past nine.'

He thought back to yesterday evening, bits of which were missing from his memory. His head was pounding, so he pressed at his temples with the thumb and index finger of his right hand. Alice turned the light on.

'Aaarrgghh!' he whinnied. 'Turn it off, will you!'

'Sorry.'

She flicked the switch and the was room returned to shade.

They hadn't drunk that much. Or had they? Maybe they had. Either way, Hugo's hangover felt totally disproportionate. He'd been on the beer all night and hadn't mixed his drinks. No shots, no champagne. Just beer.

They'd made love in Hugo's bed following Alice's shower and had expected to sleep soon after. But an insistent text from a friend meant they'd risen and headed out for what was billed as a couple of quiet beers.

It was a heavier session than that, though.

'Don't you have a headache?' he strained in a hoarser voice than usual.

'A bit. But yours is clearly worse than mine. Shall I open the curtains? The natural light will be less severe for you. I think it's pretty grey outside.'

He nodded.

'Bloody hell,' said Alice, pulling the curtains apart. 'It's absolutely bucketing down.'

Hugo sat up in the bed and rubbed his eyes. It was still pretty gloomy, even with the curtains open. *No wonder I thought it was the middle of the night.*

'Aren't you going to have a shower?' he asked, seeing her reach for her shoes and coat.

'There's no time for that. I'm late already. I had one last night anyway.'

She glanced out of the window. The sky above the Third Quad was black as the rain beat down. Below, the little tree on the manicured grass looked forlorn. In the summertime, students would sit in its shade and revise while games of croquet thwacked around them. Not this morning, though. That lawn was taking a drenching.

'Looks like I'll be showering as I walk,' she said. 'Thank God this coat's got a hood.'

She departed Hugo's room and left him in solitude. At least his own tutorial wasn't 'til eleven. Desperate for water, he got out of bed, feeling sick for a moment as he stood up. A stray tumbler lay on his desk by the window. He grabbed it, then wandered through to the ensuite and filled it at the sink.

Utterly parched, he took a big gulp. It quenched his thirst, but he still felt queasy. He gave it a moment, then took a smaller sip before wiping his mouth. Looking up, he gazed into the mirror above the sink.

His light-featured reflection appeared worse than usual, given the hangover. Even without his spectacles, he could see it clearly enough through the blur. He was distinctly unphotogenic, although certainly not ugly. Sparse eyebrows sat above blue-grey eyes while large nostrils dominated his aquiline nose. At five-foot-ten, he was rather skinny: slender shouldered, and lacking in poise. Pasty white skin stretched across a bony face, and his mousy hair was lacking in style. *How have I ended up with Alice? She's far too good for me!*

• CHAPTER 6 •

She heard it before she saw it: a thunderous roar, yet constant – like the bellow of a Spitfire's Merlin engine.

Through the cottage window, her eyes were met with an incredible sight. She jumped out of her chair and moved to investigate properly, taking another swig of vodka.

The torrent of water lashing from above provided a startling spectacle. Enormous drops hurled down from the heavens and sprang back up when they hit the ground. A lightning bolt, bright and brilliant, engulfed the vicinity in a luminescent flash, swiftly followed by the deep and breathless purr of the thunderclap as it rumbled through the atmosphere in pursuit of its quicker cousin.

Thick with descending liquid, the charged air felt agitated as the storm spoke its soliloquy. On the ground below, roads ran like rivers as sheets of water cascaded across the path outside her home. So violent was the force with which the clouds expelled their cargo that she could barely make out the trees across the valley. Had she ever seen it rain like this before? Certainly not in England.

Conditions meant her plans to return to the meadow were temporarily halted. She couldn't help but feel disappointed at the postponement of her final journey, but a little bad weather would not thwart her for long. She had waited twenty long years; a few more hours wouldn't harm her. Heaven would have to wait until the first break in the weather.

But the delay was longer than she expected.

It was late afternoon when light finally poured into the woman's living room. From behind the clouds, a watery sun peered nervously. It hadn't stopped raining completely – a fine drizzle now fell from above like diamond dust, each crystal-like droplet sparkling in the sunlight.

The storm had lasted all day and had resulted in an unsolicited stay of execution, but intuition informed her that things would move quickly now. Peeking through the window, she looked upwards. The black clouds had become grey, and pockets of swirling blue smiled down at her. This was the break in the weather she'd been waiting for.

She didn't bother to lock her front door or even take her house key. Such items would be redundant in the place she was planning to visit. Instead, her knuckles whitened around one object in particular. Most of the contents had gone, but she clutched the bottle tightly anyway.

Outside, it still felt cold and blustery, the west wind licking her cheeks with spite as she traipsed towards the village to buy the additional pills. At least she was wearing a thick coat, although the gloveless fingers of her right hand became numb as they gripped the neck of the vodka bottle.

The village was quite large and home to over two thousand people. Had it been located in the Cotswolds or Yorkshire, it would probably have been designated a small market town. She often thought of it as 'the metropolis', so starkly did it contrast with the peace of her own cottage just a few hundred metres away, secluded in its position from the hustle and bustle of village life. Each visit reminded her of just how busy the Kent commuter belt could be.

Several shops and a couple of pubs offered plenty of local amenities for the residents, but for all the settlement's charm, it suffered from horrendous traffic problems. The quiet country lane up which she'd walked ended at a T-junction with the main road from Tunbridge Wells, which ran right through the heart of the village and off into the countryside beyond.

At its centre, a village green provided the focal point. Two weeping willows and a pond formed an idyllic oasis at one end. In the spring, clumps of daffodils embellished the scene, but today, the only adornments were a couple of empty benches.

As she wandered down the road, the carriageway narrowed. Parked cars outside the houses littered both sides of the street, causing a backlog of traffic in both directions. Each time a car pulled into a gap to let another pass, great splashes spewed up from the puddles left by the earlier rain. She had to keep her wits about her to avoid them.

Eventually, she reached the pond, framed on its far side by pretty weatherboarded cottages, their outlines reflecting lazily in the water. Her target was a little minimart in the far corner of the green. A bit unsteady on her feet, she entered it.

'Got a headache, love?' asked the attendant behind the counter.

The woman offered a vacant smile but did not reply as she exchanged some money for the pills.

'You do look a bit unwell,' said the attendant, who recognised her but didn't know her name. 'Get well soon, you poor thing.'

She simpered, then left the store in silence.

At the T-junction, it was like crossing into another realm as she turned back onto the country lane, the noise of passing engines receding with every step. Continuing beyond the turning to her cottage, she meandered down the hill towards the overgrown path that led to the meadow.

The woman's heart leapt with glee when she reached her destination. To die surrounded by nature's tranquil architecture felt fitting. But the journey back to paradise had been arduous. The little footpath, still dry underfoot when she'd returned home earlier, had since been reduced to a quagmire. Thick mud now covered her shoes and dirty specks had splashed up her jeans. The meadow itself, unable to absorb the earlier deluge, was now sodden and marshy underfoot. But the woman remained unperturbed.

She positioned herself under the sprawling canopy of her favourite oak tree and sat at its base. Wet mud oozed up around her, and the damp bark moistened her back as she rested against the trunk. Placing the vodka down by her side, she pulled the packs of pills from her pocket and began to shiver once more from the cold.

She pressed each pill through the packets' perforations until she held the lot of them loose in her right hand. With her left, she gripped the neck of the vodka bottle. The act she was about to commit was seismic, so she stole a moment in mental preparation by closing her eyes and drawing a deep breath.

On widening her lids, she struggled to regain her focus, her brain confused by the alcohol that saturated it. Then, as sharpness returned to her vision, she noticed it.

It had not been immediately apparent when she'd arrived, but she could see it clearly now. Down at the stream, a change had occurred, which begged her to inspect it closer. With drink churning through her senses, she almost stumbled as she approached it.

The stream's calm and soothing flow had been replaced by the surging rush of a muddy torrent. It had not burst its banks, but it swept along angrily in its channel.

The woman surveyed the stream as it seethed and roiled in its wrath, her eyes following tatty clumps of debris as they washed downstream remorselessly. But the frantic flow and hypnotic swirls only added to her intoxication. In visual confusion, her eyes closed, and she lost her focus. Instinctively, she shifted her balance by thrusting a foot forwards as she began to topple. But the boggy ground afforded her too little grip. She felt herself collapsing, so flailed out her right arm to break her fall, dropping the pills in the process.

Her next sensation was one of shock and terror. Rather than striking the muddy bank, her wrist plunged straight into the raging hell beneath her. A mixture of gravity and current took over, hauling the rest of her body into the all-consuming water. Dragged below by the tempestuous flow, murky fluid began invading her body, filling first her stomach, before, alas, decanting into her lungs.

Submerged and horror-stricken, she spluttered beneath the surface, but the panic simply caused her to inhale more of the brown filth that had consumed her. She strained for the surface, but to no avail.

As her oxygen-depleted brain began to fade, her final lucid thought turned to the bottle of vodka she was still clutching in her left hand. It had seemed so precious just a few moments earlier, but she had no use for it now. Resigned to her fate, she let it go, the indefatigable torrent sweeping the bottle along its turbulent journey to God-knows-where while her body tumbled down a separate path to the same inevitable destination.

• CHAPTER 7 •

Nina Patel sat at the kitchen table in her open-plan London flat. Dinner was cooking and the smell of risotto permeated the air, causing her stomach to rumble.

It was dinner for one.

Her phone's battery was running low, but she kept the dating app open. More often than not, she swiped left; it was becoming something of a ritual now. Only occasionally did someone have the credentials to pique her interest, and swiping right was a rare thing of late.

Suddenly her screen began to flash as the FaceTime ringtone sounded. Her colleague was calling her.

'Hi, Gaby, what's up?'

Her colleague was also her closest friend.

'Hey babe, just calling to see how you are?'

A look of mischief sparkled in her eyes. Nina and Gaby were known as the 'terrible twosome', always getting into scrapes and playing practical jokes on friends.

'Just got some risotto on,' said Nina. 'Doing a spot of swiping as well.'

'Any luck?'

'No.' She wrinkled her nose in disappointment. 'Will you wait one second, babe? My battery's running low and I need to grab my charger. Be right back.'

The first floor flat was bright and modern. The thirty-three-year-old had bought it four years earlier, straight off the plan before the block was even finished. She wasn't the tidiest individual, and clothes and books were strewn all over the place. The flat was clean, though. Nina Patel had an aversion to dirt and was obsessed with the dwelling's cleanliness. There wasn't a speck of dust or grime in sight.

On the table, some flowers stood in a jug of water. Nina loved plants but without a garden, she was limited in what she could do. Still, the flat did have a tiny balcony. In the summer, she would fill it with pots, although her work hours meant she struggled to keep on top of the watering.

She located the charger and plugged it in at the wall. Her battery icon went green as fresh life breathed back into it. Settling again at the table, she looked at her friend, eager to hear the latest news and gossip.

'You won't need to worry about your matches for too much longer,' said Gaby, who cut straight to the chase. 'Tomasz has been asking after you. Which is a bit of a surprise given your behaviour at the Halloween party.'

Nina blushed. 'Oh, Lord, I wish I hadn't drunk so much tequila. I'm getting too old for that sort of thing.'

'You and me both, hun. But with a new month comes new opportunity. What are you doing this Saturday?'

'Why's that?' she asked, worried she'd be pressganged into yet another night out. She *was* getting too old for such misdemeanours.

'Robert and I are having a little fireworks get together,' said Gaby. 'Drinks, nibbles – that sort of thing.'

'Sounds nice.'

Gaby smiled. 'And guess who else is coming...'

'Tomasz? You're serious?' Nina's eyes brightened.

'I wanted to be sure he could make it before telling you,' said Gaby, savouring her friend's excitement. 'Perhaps you'll finally be able to delete those dating apps.'

Tomasz was handsome. Tall and strong-jawed, his Eastern European accent really did it for her. 'Let's not get too carried away,' Nina cautioned her. 'Are you sure he was asking after me?'

'Of course,' said Gaby. 'You're the reason he's coming on Saturday. I told him you couldn't resist a party.'

'That's true enough,' giggled Nina.

'Listen, if you play your cards right, this could be your last risotto for a while. It might be Polish bigos stew from next weekend if you're lucky.'

Both women laughed before Gaby moved things forward. 'Hey,' she said. 'That's not the only reason I'm calling, though. I've got to tell you what happened at work today after your shift ended. It all got very weird.'

'Really? What happened?'

'Well, you'd better prepare yourself,' said Gaby. 'You'll be the one dealing with the fallout tomorrow...'

## CHAPTER 8

Hugo shifted in his seat as the train shuddered into movement. 'He can be a blunt man, but he'll definitely like you. He mentions your name every time I ring him.'

'I just worry I won't quite measure up,' replied Alice. 'You've made him out to be so...so *demanding*.'

Her trepidation was obvious. Hugo could almost taste it. 'He has high standards, that's all. But there's nothing to worry about.'

As the train gathered speed, the platform at Oxford station started winding past the window. 'High standards sound daunting,' said Alice, unconvinced by his reassurances.

'High standards means he'll like *you*,' came the charming riposte. Hugo surprised himself at the sweetness he'd managed to conjure, and Alice rewarded him with a brief kiss on the lips.

As the dreaming spires receded, the landscape morphed into a rewinding sea of green fields. It was Friday afternoon, and the long-awaited weekend in Ealing had finally arrived. Both students were a little nervous about what might lie ahead.

'You have a lot of respect for your father, don't you?'

'It's hard not to have,' he admitted with semi-sigh. 'You can't argue with the success he's had.'

Hugo turned his head and gazed at the grey November landscape as it whizzed past the window. The rat-a-tat-tat of wheels on the track only added to the monotony of the rail journey. A few silent moments passed before Alice gave his blue jumper a tug. He turned his head and looked her in the eye.

She peered back at him through a pair of oversized glasses that made her large, brown eyes look even bigger. Mixed race, her dominant feature was a thick head of tightly curled hair. Beneath it, her skin seemed to glow with life as her bright eyes bore into his. To Hugo, she was just about the prettiest thing he'd ever seen with her rounded face and neat little nose.

'Tell me about your mother,' she said, still gazing at him.

He shifted again in his seat, only this time more uncomfortably. 'What do you want to know?' he replied.

'Anything at all. I've told you everything about mine.'

'Your father's second wife, you said. The first was an Ethiopian he'd met on business, but your mum's a British lawyer with St. Lucian and Jamaican roots.'

'Dearest daddy certainly has a thing for Black women,' she joked. 'But don't change the subject. I want to know about *your* mother. Are your dad and her still together?'

Hugo shook his head sorrowfully. 'She died,' he admitted. 'It was very sad.'

Alice's features contorted in a mix of sympathy and embarrassment, but Hugo grasped the opportunity to confide.

'It was cancer,' he continued. 'She passed away about nine months ago. It was the slow degradation that was the worst part. Bloody awful, to be honest with you. It hit my father particularly hard. She was his soulmate.'

'I'm so sorry,' Alice said sheepishly. 'That must have been terrible for you both.'

In loving affection, she placed her arm around his shoulder. Hugo removed it and held her hand instead. 'I still don't think Dad's recovered,' he said.

The train arrived at Paddington, and the pair disembarked into the crisp autumn air. London's noisy claustrophobia clashed with the quaintness they'd become accustomed to in Oxford. In the encroaching dusk, they battled their way to Ealing on public transport and arrived at the Edwardian semi with a due sense of relief.

Alice looked up at the handsome building in front of her. A white door lay directly ahead, with a large bay window to the left. A little sloping roof jutted out above the door, with a decorative white fascia running parallel to the ground. On the second storey, a white-clad dormer pointed to the sky on the bay window side, its vertical timbers completing the elegant feel.

The front garden was small and neat, well-stocked with still-flowering asters and salvias.

'Mum was the gardener really,' Hugo said as they stepped onto the little mosaicked path that led to the front door. 'Dad keeps it neat and tidy in her memory.'

They walked up to the door and knocked. 'He doesn't trust me with my own house key,' explained Hugo. Alice blinked in surprise.

A sound stirred inside the house, and Alice's heartbeat quickened as she prepared to meet the professor she had heard so much about.

• CHAPTER 9 •

It was down the hospital corridor, away from the hustle and bustle of Reception, that a woman lay prostrate in a private room. Pain burned inside her chest, each breath a fresh dagger-slash at her water-damaged lungs. She opened her eyes, still groggy from the morphine.

Above her, two large eyes gazed into hers. Big and brown, they exuded kindness and caring sympathy. The figure wore a blue tunic, and the woman regarded the NHS lanyard that dangled from her neck. The name on the lanyard read: Dr Nina Patel.

The woman couldn't remember much, but she knew this hospital was different from the one she'd woken up in. Then, ever so slowly, things began to return. *Of course: they moved me up to London last night.*

A different doctor had seen her last night. Another woman. Young, like the one in front of her now. She hadn't answered *her* questions either. Perhaps that was why they'd sent that man through earlier. He was older than they were. A different kind of doctor altogether. *Why can't they all just leave me alone? I don't want their care.*

'Are you feeling any better?' asked Patel.

Silence.

'You're bound to feel woozy from the drugs,' she continued. 'You need morphine for pain relief while your lungs continue to heal. But it really would help if we knew who you were.'

The medic turned her head to take a reading from one of the instruments that monitored the patient. Patel's long black hair was tied back in a neat ponytail. Her frame was slight, but she was strong and graceful in her movements.

'The good news is you're making excellent physical progress,' said Patel, showing a perfect set of white teeth as she smiled.

Still silence. The woman simply closed her eyes. *Not quite the physical progress I'd intended, though.*

'Perhaps you can tell us your name, at least? You must have family who are worried about you.'

Nothing.

'Well, it won't be long until you're fully healed,' chirped Patel. 'Your brain came through unscathed, and your lungs will be as right as rain before you know it.'

*Right as rain. Not the best choice of words there, Doctor.*

'It's your mental health that concerns us now. If you don't speak, we can't assess how vulnerable you are. That's why my colleague visited you this afternoon. He'll be back on Monday, I'd have thought.'

*Why couldn't you people just let me die in peace? Was that too much to ask?*

The woman surveyed the dismal room she lay in. Its whitewashed walls and smell of disinfectant felt like a prison. If she wasn't careful, it might become one.

Patel leant in a bit closer. 'It would make things so much easier if you said something to us.'

## CHAPTER 10

A tall man with a strong build answered the door. His receding hairline was dark but greying, and his spectacles gave him an intellectual appearance. Alice guessed him to be in his late fifties. Curiously, his forehead was furrowed with permanent wrinkles, but the skin around them retained an air of youthfulness. The breadth of the man's shoulders disguised the prominence with which his stomach had begun to protrude. He was dressed tastefully for a man of his age in a collared shirt, cashmere jumper and dark-coloured chinos.

'Come in, come in,' he said enthusiastically, shaking Hugo's hand.

'Dad, this is Alice.'

'I've heard so much about you, Alice.' The professor shook her hand too. 'I've been so looking forward to meeting Hugo's first girlfriend.'

'I'm the first?' she said, playfully teasing her boyfriend.

Hugo flushed.

'Of course, you're his first,' scoffed the professor. 'Now tell me what you'd like to drink.'

'Ooo, white wine, please,' said Alice, who reasoned that alcohol would be a useful ally if she wanted to survive the weekend with her sanity intact.

'White wine it is. Whisky Hugo?'

'I'm all right, thanks.'

'Oh, for God's sake, man, have a whisky!'

Hugo thought better than to offer further protest. 'Okay, Dad, I'll have a whisky with you.'

'Splendid,' said Swann. 'Now make yourselves at home in the living room. We've so much to talk about.'

Alice and Hugo sat on the sofa. As they waited for the professor's return, they looked like a pair of naughty school pupils dumped outside the headmaster's office.

'I like that light fitting,' said Alice.

'It casts nice patterns on the walls and ceiling,' agreed Hugo.

Swann seemed to take an age pouring the drinks, but the television in the corner had been left on, and both students focused on the 'Breaking News.' It seemed the England football captain had been playing away in more ways than one and enjoying a bit of extra time with the manager's daughter. The red-faced, potbellied reporter was conjecturing whether the manager or the player would vacate their position first.

Swann re-entered the room with a couple of drinks glasses. 'I can't stand that odious little creature,' he said, pointing at the TV and turning it off.

'Buckland or the skipper?' joked Alice.

Swann threw his head back and roared with laughter, almost spilling the drinks on his cream-coloured carpet. Hugo couldn't help but smile. The weekend had got off to a good start with the jest.

As the light faded that evening, the conversation remained light-hearted, if a little one way. The professor laughed heartily as he regaled them with tales of his youth, some of which were genuinely amusing.

Then, unexpectedly, and totally without warning, a mood change conquered him. Immediately, Alice understood what Hugo meant when he spoke of his father's caprices and sudden shifts of temper.

'What a shame your mother can't be with us,' the old man lamented. 'Seeing the three of us here, laughing and joking like this. Witnessing her son come of age, studying at Oxford, girlfriend in tow. Such a pity.' He shook his head glumly.

'Tell Alice about your days as an oarsman at Cambridge,' said Hugo, who watched his father's eyes light up at the suggestion. Swann's excitement radiated from every pore as he narrated the story of his rowing credentials, and how he would certainly have won a Blue had it not been for a bout of glandular fever in his final year.

The evening concluded mirthfully.

'He's certainly quite a character,' admitted Alice as she clambered into bed next to Hugo. 'I see what you mean about his moods.'

Hugo's bedroom was at the very top of the house in the part that included the dormer. His bed was a large single positioned under the window, and a study desk lay flush against the wall on the far side. Pleasant free-standing wardrobes lined the wall opposite the door, and the room was immaculately tidy. Entirely congruous with the rest of the house, it still seemed rather odd. There was nothing of Hugo's personality: no posters, no mess and none of his artwork. It was more like a guest room than a teenage boy's. Alice wondered whether the professor had chosen the décor instead of Hugo.

'He's always been like that,' said Hugo. 'But it got much worse when Mum died. Sometimes I think he's the one who ought to see a psychiatrist.'

'He's very proud of you,' she said, snuggling close to him.

'You think so?'

'Definitely.'

'What makes you say that?'

'The way he revels in your Oxford education. And in the fact that we're together, you and I. He's happy for you.' She gave him a quick kiss to show her pride in him too.

'I don't think it's pride,' Hugo dissented. 'He wants me to be like *him*, that's all. To follow in his social, sporting and professional footsteps. But I can't be like him. We're such very different people. Sometimes, I don't think he gets that.'

Slumber followed swiftly that night, the journey from Oxford having caught up with them. Hugo rolled over and, before long, his worn out mind carried him to the tender realm of sleep…

*Laughter rang like church bells as he peered through nighttime's portal. The dreamscape transported him to an attractive suburban garden, where a young family – a mother, father and daughter – played together in peaceful joy.*

*It was summertime, and a generous sun shone down from a gin-clear sky. Bees and butterflies danced among the garden's flowers, midges hovered in the shade under a cherry tree and choirs of blackbirds, blue tits, and sparrows sang amidst the pretty flora.*

*In the centre of the lawn, a little girl, perhaps ten years old, splashed and giggled with her father in a paddling pool. The mother chortled blissfully in a chair as she enjoyed the carefree delight of her daughter's fun and frolics from a distance.*

*The joyful scene captivated Hugo, and he could not stifle a smile of his own. 'What a beautiful home and garden,' Hugo said to the man. 'How long have you lived here?'*

*But no response was forthcoming. The man did not look up; he just continued playing with his daughter in the pool. The woman, too, was oblivious, and laughed along from her posi-*

tion in the chair – Hugo was a ghost to her as well. Even the little girl could not discern his presence. He remained unseen and undetectable to all.

It didn't matter to Hugo; he was more than happy to play the part of the invisible observer. He was simply enjoying the sense of love and joy that had inexplicably overwhelmed him. It was as if he were absorbing it directly from the family; it was a most curious sensation indeed.

A few moments passed before the father and mother went inside, leaving the girl alone in the pool. She continued splashing and seemed completely at peace, but with her parents' departure, a sudden blackness struck Hugo's emotions. Gone was the joy and the euphoria of earlier; instead, dark feelings of dread and doom rushed in. He couldn't explain his horror; neither had he experienced anything quite like it before. The sensation was sheer terror – like a premonition of some impending fate. He couldn't help but shudder.

His unease was tempered by a distraction on his forehead. It was coming from the waking world...

Hugo woke in terror. He opened his eyes and saw Alice was already alert and looking at him. She was stroking his forehead and fringe with her hand.

'Nightmare, babe?' Alice's face exuded concern as she tried to soothe his distress. Her stroking became more fervent.

Hugo said nothing, but gripped her hand to arrest its motion. Alice pursed her lips in sympathy. 'What's the matter, babe?'

'Nothing...I just...' Hugo's mind was a million miles away. His heart raced, and his breathing quickened. Words wouldn't come while he struggled to make sense of his night-time experience.

Alice stroked his sweat-moistened forehead again.

'*No!*' barked Hugo, swatting her hand away from him.

Alice was taken aback.

Hugo knew he'd offended her and attempted an explanation. 'I had a dream,' he said. 'A really vivid one. The sort you wake up from and it's kind of still there.'

'Tell me about it.' The offence in her eyes was replaced with sympathetic intrigue.

'It's difficult to explain,' he said. 'There was a girl...'

'A girl?' Alice feigned a look of jealousy to inject a touch of light-heartedness.

'A *little* girl,' he explained. 'A mother and father, too. I can see it all so clearly, even now I've woken. The house, the garden. Everything.'

He sprang out of bed and began to get dressed.

Alice remained perplexed.

'Come on, let's go down and get some breakfast,' he said.

'Fine,' she replied before pulling on her underwear.

Downstairs, the table was already set. Professor Swann sipped quietly on a cup of tea while tucking into some porridge. Alice helped herself to some toast and marmalade. Hugo sat down but remained motionless, uninterested in the food on offer.

'What the bloody hell's wrong with you, boy?' blurted Swann. 'Get some breakfast inside you.' The outburst failed to draw any words.

'Babe?' prompted Alice.

'I'm sorry. I'm just not feeling very hungry this morning.'

He leapt salmon-like from the table and went back up the stairs, leaving Alice and the professor to exchange quizzical looks.

'I'll go after him,' she said before following Hugo up. Swann just raised an eyebrow and took another sip of his tea.

She entered Hugo's room to find him sitting on the bed with his head in his hands and index fingers wedged in his ears. When he spoke, he didn't look up at her. 'I don't understand,' he complained. 'It just won't go away.'

'What won't go away?'

She sat next to him on the bed and placed her arm around his shoulder.

'The dream,' he said. 'I don't get it. They normally fade once you've been awake for a few minutes, but this one's still really clear. I can still see that little girl's face. The emotions I felt were so intense. And so contrasting, too. They're still with me, Alice. Even now, I can feel them.'

Alice consoled him. 'It was just a bad dream,' she said, stroking the back of his head with her thumb.

'But it's the *sound*,' he protested. 'It's so persistent. It's like when you leave a nightclub and can still hear the music ringing in your ears hours later.'

'What sound? What can you hear?'

'The little girl's laughter. It won't go away. I can hear it as if she were with us in this very room.'

'Look,' she replied, trying to soothe his temper. 'You've been under a lot of stress with assignments, not to mention bringing me back here to meet your father. It's no surprise your mind's playing tricks on you.'

'I know. I'll be fine, honestly. As you say, it was just a bad dream.'

Alice kissed his cheek.

'And dreams are only imaginary, Hugo. They aren't for real.'

• CHAPTER 11 •

Monday morning howled with dark ferocity. Alice and Hugo had departed for Oxford late on Sunday evening, and the rigours of a new working week lay ahead for Professor Swann.

The alarm had sounded loud and clear. The clock on the bedside table showed it was six-thirty in the morning, yet the room's darkness provided an illusion that it was still the middle of the night. Swann hesitated to get out of bed; outside, he could hear the wind whistle like a squealing battle cry, the gusts blasting droplets of rain against his bedroom window like a hail of arrows striking the shields of medieval soldiers.

Defiantly, he rolled over and screwed his eyes shut before pulling the duvet over his head to prevent the harassing chill from penetrating the cocoon he had fashioned. But coming to beneath the sheets, the professor's mind began to stir. He opened his eyes and stretched before one piercing thought thrust through his brain like a sword.

He flung the sheets away and sat bolt upright, barely noticing the incipient onslaught of cold air as it began laying siege to his skin. He grinned, then jumped out of bed like a teenager as he remembered what lay ahead.

That morning, his work would take him away from the mundane consultations at his usual surgery. Doctors at a London hospital had sought his expertise in aiding them with a very unusual patient. Swann had already become fascinated with the case on a preliminary visit on Friday afternoon. An unidentified woman who couldn't (or wouldn't) speak had required psychiatric assessment. Oozing fervour, he readied himself to meet her again.

It was still dark when he left the house. He fought to raise his umbrella, but the November wind rendered it impossible to control, so he folded it back up and employed it as a makeshift walking stick instead.

He pulled his collar up and strolled in a sprightly fashion, whistling a tune and intermittently flicking his umbrella up as he paced along the pavement. Invisible drops of rain, occasionally transfigured into silver darts or tiny beads of mercury by the headlamps of passing cars, splashed against his skin and ran down his cheeks like streaming tears. Yet Swann remained filled with zeal as he approached the public transport services.

He arrived at the hospital in a buoyant mood and was finally shown along the corridor to a small, whitewashed room. On the bed in front of him, a woman lay flat on her back. 'Good morning,' smiled the professor. 'My name is Rupert Swann. Do you remember me? I visited you here on Friday afternoon?'

The woman turned her head but stayed silent and avoided eye contact. Her long, dark blonde hair was draped across her shoulders, and her eyes, a brilliant, yet haunted shade of blue, gazed off into the infinite distance beyond him.

She had pale skin and seemed neatly put together. Her mouth and nose were unremarkable and her forehead appeared decidedly average. There were no freckles or birthmarks to speak of; indeed, her face was largely forgettable. Except, that is, for those haunting blue eyes – the most extraordinary features the professor thought he'd ever seen.

Her silence didn't perturb him. Swann had come prepared having seen these sorts of cases before. He reached for a blank piece of paper and a selection of coloured pencils he'd brought and laid them out in front of her with an inviting gesture. 'I'm going to head off for a while,' he explained. 'I'll leave these here for when you feel ready.'

His words were met with pure vacancy, but he was not deterred. The professor felt sure she would express herself and jot a few words when the time felt right. He offered a reassuring smile and then withdrew from her proximity.

Twenty minutes later, Rupert Swann sat in a small office and watched as a doctor returned with a cup of coffee in each hand. She took a swig from one of the plastic cups and then placed the other on the table in front of him.

'I know we've been through this already, Dr Patel, but I want to be sure I haven't missed anything,' said Swann. 'I want every little detail you have.'

Dr Patel raised her eyebrows and puffed her cheeks. 'She was transferred here from the Kent and Sussex hospital's A&E department in Tunbridge Wells,' she began. 'They stabilised her before she was moved here to complete her recovery. She's been with us for a couple of days now.'

'What happened?'

'They found a large quantity of alcohol in her system. Our best guess is that she fell in while drunk. A passer-by found her and dialled 999 after providing CPR.'

Swann listened with interest, furrowing his brow and accentuating the wrinkles on his forehead. He went to take a swig of coffee but the heat burnt his tongue. Placing it back on the table, he tried not to grimace.

'She was very lucky,' Patel continued. 'The current had washed her body onto a beach area. Thankfully, the man who found her was in the right place at the right time. He was first aid trained, too.'

'Very lucky indeed,' concurred Swann. 'What was her condition upon arrival at the Kent and Sussex?'

'Unconscious and suffering from hypothermia. They estimated her to have been in the water for about two to three minutes. She didn't say anything to *them* either.' Patel took another swig of her coffee. Swann mirrored her, determined to ignore the scolding sensation in his mouth.

'And you're certain there's been no brain damage?' asked the psychiatrist.

'No physical damage whatsoever. We've done all the necessary scans. As far as we can tell, she's *choosing* not to speak. Until she does, we've got no way of identifying her.'

Swann pursed his lips and looked deeper into the doctor's eyes. 'Two or three minutes is a long time,' he commented. 'Upwards of four minutes, and she would surely have drowned. And yet you say there's no brain damage at all.'

'I agree it's a long time. But under the right conditions, the brain can make a full recovery. The main problem was the amount of water she'd ingested and inhaled. We've been monitoring the damage to her lungs and treating her, but she's on the mend now.'

Patel began to play with her coffee by rotating it round and round on the table in a manner that irritated the professor. 'Have you attempted any other identification methods?' he asked, failing to prevent a 'tut' at the end of his question.

'We've tried everything we can think of,' said Patel, pretending not to notice his rudeness. 'Unfortunately, she had no documentation with her. The police were informed immediately, but no one matching her description has been reported missing.'

'And nobody has contacted the hospital to see if a loved one is residing with you?'

'No one. Neither have they contacted any other hospitals, including the Kent and Sussex. We just don't have any leads at all.'

'I see,' nodded Swann, his face a picture of intrigue.

Patel, on the other hand, looked confused. 'Professor, why won't she speak to us? There's nothing physically wrong with her as far as we can tell. If she doesn't speak English, she would surely have found a way of letting us know. Could it be that she's still in shock, do you think?'

'It's too soon to say,' Swann stated with an authoritarian shake of his head. 'But I've left her some paper and coloured pencils – I'm sure she'll communicate in her own time and on her own terms. These sorts of people usually write something down in the end. I'll check if any progress has been made before I leave, but it'll probably be a few days at least until she's ready.'

Swann was true to his word. Before he left, he made his way back along the corridor to the woman's room.

On entering, he prepared to speak but was instantly lost for words when he saw what lay before him. Dumfounded, the professor stared in disbelief.

• CHAPTER 12 •

Mike Buckland was disappointed. He'd been hoping the sling on his arm would be off by now. It was awfully bothersome and a pain in the neck for day-to-day living. It also hampered his work, making it difficult to take notes or thrust a microphone in someone's face.

He was also disappointed with the nurse who'd attended him. That Filipino – or wherever she was from – was nowhere to be seen. Not to worry, he hadn't really expected that particular lightning to strike twice. Nevertheless, to be seen by a *male* nurse. *Just my bloody luck.*

Buckland had been asked to take a seat in Reception. His arm was healing, but not as quickly as expected. A reassessment was necessary, possibly even a fresh cast. Somebody would be with him soon, he was told.

He watched the comings and goings from his seat in Reception. Corridors ran off in different directions, with the names of various departments displayed on hanging signage. He hoped he'd be seen quickly. Frankly, he couldn't wait to leave and be on his merry way.

The newsman observed the other patients with disdain: infirm geriatrics that stunk of piss and shit; young mothers with numerous offspring and big hooped earrings; endless obese people.

Worst of all was the coughing. As soon as one culprit stopped, another would begin. *It's like fucking Whac-a-Mole in here!* Even the staff provided little relief as they scuttled past and were rushed off their feet.

As Buckland waited, his boredom grew. After a while, he stood up to stretch his legs. He'd been sitting with them crossed in the same position for too long, and pins and needles had started. Limping a little, he took a few paces to walk off the discomfort, his asymmetry making him fit right in with the invalids.

After a few moments of pacing, the blood began to return to his lower limbs. Feeling better, he wandered over to one of the notice boards and read the posters – tips for a healthy heart and how to spot signs of cancer. *God, hospitals are depressing. I wonder whether there are any vending machines down one of those corridors?*

• CHAPTER 13 •

Swann's eyes fixed on the paper he'd left her. No longer was it a blank and lifeless sheet. In his absence, it had been transformed into a work of art: a meadow with trees, flowers, grass and a delightful looking chalk stream. The light and shadows had been captured stupendously; the emotiveness depicted was tangible in its expression. It was as if the picture had a soul of its very own.

As Swann marvelled, he noticed an arrangement of sixteen capital letters in the bottom right-hand corner. The woman had signed her name: ELIZABETH RITCHIE.

'Well done, Professor. We have a name at last,' beamed Patel as she congratulated him in a meeting room just off from Reception. The door was slightly ajar as they conversed across a plastic-topped industrial table.

'It's only a partial breakthrough,' Swann cautioned her. 'There's still an awful lot of work to do. This is just the beginning.'

'So what happens next?' The young doctor's eyes betrayed her eagerness.

'We give her some more paper. See if there's anything else she wishes to communicate.'

'You think she might write something else?'

'I didn't say she'd *write* anything.'

Patel shook her head in bafflement. 'But you just said she wrote her name on the paper you left her.'

'Indeed,' said the professor with a knowing smile. 'But that's not all she did.'

He produced Elizabeth's artwork and showed her. Patel was astonished. 'Wow!' she exclaimed. 'Not too shabby for twenty minutes' work. Looks like we might have a professional on our hands.'

'Who knows?' replied Swann. He passed the picture to her side of the table and gestured. It was an instruction for her to keep hold of it.

'As things move forward, we want her to graduate to full-on speech,' he said. 'It'll be baby steps at first, but I'm sure we'll get there. Today's development is important.'

'Thank you, Professor. You've been such a great source of help. We're making real progress now, aren't we?'

'Just make sure she has plenty of paper and coloured pencils to express herself,' said Swann, rising from his seat. 'A biro, too, in case she wants to write anything. I'll return in the morning to re-examine the patient.'

The two shook hands before Swann departed. Patel remained in the meeting room to finish some notes and admire the artwork for a few more minutes. Upon her exit, a short, red-faced man confronted her. He was eating a chocolate bar.

'Doctor...' said the man as he sidled towards her. 'Forgive me, Doctor. I couldn't help but overhear your conversation with that other professional. It does indeed sound a fascinating case.'

'Were you listening in on a private conversation?' Patel's question was brusque. She was discombobulated by the rudeness of this slithering creature in front of her. She noticed he had his arm in a sling. 'I'm afraid you'll have to wait for one of the nurses to look at that. I'm not available right now.'

'Oh, I understand that,' he laughed. 'I just want to talk to you about this special patient of yours.'

'I'm afraid that won't be possible,' said Patel. 'Do I recognise you from somewhere?'

'I shouldn't think so.'

Patel turned and made to move off.

'Doctor, please don't go,' the man implored. 'I can help you. I can help identify this woman.'

Patel paused, her inquisitiveness getting the better of her. 'And how can you do that, exactly?' With a sceptical look, she turned to face him again.

'Forgive me,' he said, flashing a disarming smile that revealed a yellowing set of teeth. 'Allow me to introduce myself properly. My name is Mike Buckland. I'm a journalist.'

*I knew I recognised you from somewhere.* Patel folded her arms and rolled her eyes.

Buckland could tell he needed to move quickly before the medic had him escorted off-site. 'Just think about it, Doctor, er...'

'Patel.'

'Doctor Patel. This isn't just a medical case; it's so much more than that. This case is a *story*. Consider it for one little moment. A woman turns up in a hospital. She's unable to speak and no one can identify her. She's given a piece of paper and a selection of coloured pencils in the hope she might write something. But instead of jotting a few words, she produces an artistic masterpiece. It's a *sensational* story. The sort they turn into a film a few years down the line.'

'You said you could help identify her,' said Patel. It was an invitation to cut to the chase.

'And I can,' claimed Buckland. 'With your kind permission, Doctor, I would like to broadcast this picture along with a photograph of your patient. If I can tell this story to the nation, someone is bound to recognise her and get in touch with you. A friend or family member, perhaps.'

Patel narrowed her eyes and chewed Buckland's words with caution. The little specimen in front of her reeked of ill motive.

The journalist sensed her hesitation. 'You do want this woman to be identified, Doctor?'

The medic wrestled with her conscience before answering. 'I'm afraid I cannot allow it,' she said decisively. 'It would be a breach of the patient's confidence. And in any case, she's in no condition to—'

'Why don't we ask the patient herself?' suggested Buckland. 'She's a grown woman. Surely the decision is hers? If she says no or shows signs of distress, then I'll simply be on my way.'

Patel shook her head. 'I'm afraid not,' she repeated. 'I cannot breach her—'

'How about the artwork on its own, then?' said Buckland. 'That way, the patient can remain anonymous.'

The doctor's guard lowered. 'Very well,' she said hesitantly, hoping it would be enough to slake the newsman and send him on his way. 'You can photograph the picture and use it in your broadcast. But you're not to speak with the patient. Her condition is too vulnerable at present. At this stage, I can't vouch for her state of mind.'

'Perfectly understandable,' said Buckland enthusiastically. 'It's the picture alone then.'

She led the journalist into the meeting room and placed Elizabeth's drawing back on the table. Buckland nodded his head in admiration. 'Outstanding,' he remarked, as he fumbled for his phone in his pocket.

'I must insist you blur the signature,' said Patel. 'Leaving it visible for the broadcast would be a breach of—'

'I know, I know — her confidence,' Buckland interjected. 'No problem, Doctor. Of course, we'll blur it for the broadcast.'

He switched the device to camera mode and the shutter sound clicked as he took a quick snap.

'There. All done.' He flicked the phone to silent and placed it back in his pocket.

'Satisfied?' enquired Patel, her arms folded and face impatient.

'Yes, Doctor. And thank you. But may I ask one last favour?'

'And what is that, precisely?' She was becoming exasperated now.

'May I *view* the patient? I understand why you won't allow a picture or an interview. You've explained that very clearly…'

'Then why do you want to see her?'

Buckland used his palm to mop at the film of sweat on his forehead. It gave him time to choose his next words carefully. 'The artwork on its own won't pique anyone's interest,' he explained. 'The audience needs to make a connection with the person at the centre of things. I'll need to provide a physical description in my report. Please, Doctor, just let me see her with my own eyes to put a face to the image. No picture, I promise. Just a description for the audience.'

Patel shifted uneasily. 'We'll have to be very brief,' she said. 'Just a glimpse. No more than a few seconds.'

She led him down the corridor, conflicted over whether this course of action was sensible. 'Down here on the left,' she said.

'Thank you. Just give me a moment before we go in. I need to forward that snap of the artwork to my editor.'

'Remember to blur the signature,' she reminded him.

Buckland nodded.

Patel watched him locate the image on his camera roll and send it to his boss. Then, she turned her head and opened the door to Elizabeth's room.

'I don't want us to go fully in,' she said in a hushed whisper. 'She mustn't be upset or overwhelmed by our presence. *I'll go a few steps in, but I want you to stay behind and keep by the door. You'll have to observe from a distance.*'

'I will,' said Buckland in a whisper of his own. 'Here at the entrance is perfectly fine. Just give me a moment to see her in the flesh. Then we can leave.'

Patel entered, but the journalist remained back and sneakily returned his phone to camera mode. With a quick glance down, he positioned it so Elizabeth's features were in shot. When she flicked her eyes in his direction, he took a surreptitious photo. And with his phone on 'silent', Patel never noticed the misdemeanour.

'Well, I think I've seen enough,' said Buckland. 'Many thanks for your time. I'll be on my way now.' He'd scurried halfway down the corridor before the doctor could offer a reply.

Patel had barely collected her thoughts when a second voice piped up. Her head shot round as Elizabeth spoke.

'Who the hell was that?' the patient demanded. 'He wasn't a doctor. Who was he?'

'*My God!*' exclaimed Patel. 'You're talking!' Bewildered at the unexpected outburst, she looked like a rabbit in headlights.

'*WHO WAS HE*?' Elizabeth's raised voice caused Patel to panic.

'A journalist...' she blurted before curtailing the rest of the sentence. She knew it was a mistake as soon as she'd said it, but in her state of shock, the admission came out accidentally.

Elizabeth's eyes widened in horror. 'A journalist...' she repeated in a tone now hushed and fearful.

The two watched each other like neighbourhood cats, each waiting for the other to make the first move.

Elizabeth spoke up first. 'Please, Doctor,' she implored, looking Patel in the eye. 'You have to stop it from happening.

## CHAPTER 14

In his living room, Swann sank back in his armchair. The evening had come, and it was time for a whisky after the day's work. He was pleased with his earlier achievements at the hospital and thought back fondly.

*Elizabeth Ritchie*. He wondered who she was and what her story might be. No doubt he'd find out just as soon as he could get her talking.

He'd discovered her name quicker than expected, but her reaction bemused him nonetheless. He thought she'd have written her name or a few sentences at most. But to have produced an artwork! The case was more intriguing than he'd first realised. As contentment flowed through his heart, he sipped his whisky and grabbed the remote control to begin channel surfing.

Contentment turned to irritation when he failed to find a documentary he cared to watch. Instead, he settled for the insipid white noise of one of the news channels. He closed his eyes and almost nodded off as the reporters pontificated, each rambling piece more monotonous than the last. After a while, their words seemed to merge into a single tedious lyric that carried him close to slumber. With eyes beginning to droop, he relaxed deeper and deeper into his chair. But half an ear dredged the anchor's next words from the precipice of oblivion and delivered them plainly into his reckoning:

*'Now it sounds like a story from a Hollywood blockbuster,'* the anchor began. *'A woman is pulled unconscious from a swollen river. On arrival at the hospital, she's unable to speak. Not even her own name…'*

Swann's eyes flicked open and alertness returned to his mind with a vengeance.

*'Without any information to go on, doctors were at a loss to confirm the woman's identity. Nevertheless, they hatched a plan involving a piece of paper and some coloured pencils. And as you're about to see, the results were nothing short of astounding. Mike Buckland has the details…'*

Swann's fingers tightened around his whisky as the camera cut to a red-faced reporter with his arm in a sling. Buckland looked rather smug as he stood outside the London hospital. Powerless to intervene, Swann awaited the inevitable.

*'The doctors had exhausted every line of enquiry,'* said Buckland. *'Without any leads to go on, they had no way of determining who she was. So with a final throw of the dice, they*

*provided her with a piece of paper in the hope she'd express herself in her own manner. They thought she might write her name or a few words. But what she came up with instead startled everyone...'*

As Buckland's resonant voice continued, the camera cut to a close-up of Elizabeth's picture, its swirling colours radiating from the TV screen. Swann's grip on the glass was so tight that his hand had begun to shake. The whisky inside quivered in response.

*'Her doctors were stunned at what she produced in just twenty minutes. There's even been speculation that the patient might be a professional artist. But a stunning drawing wasn't the only thing she left them with: notice how the picture is clearly signed with the name 'Elizabeth Ritchie' in capital letters at the bottom.'*

The camera then cut from the artwork, and Elizabeth's face was emblazoned across the screen as Buckland approached the end of his piece.

*'The race is now on to identify this mystery woman with the shining talent for art. And something tells me the filmmakers will be keeping an eye on this one. You can bet Hollywood will come calling at some point! We'll bring you the very latest on this story as we receive it.'*

Swann nearly jumped out of his skin as his phone began to shriek. He didn't recognise the number, but he answered the call with a bark.

'Swann...' His irritation was palpable.

'Professor...it's me. Doctor Patel...from the hospital. I'm sorry to be calling you so late, but something terrible has happened.'

'Our patient is all over the news,' he responded with an icy chill. It sounded ominous and was an attempt to veil the rage that burned inside him.

'Professor?'

'I said...SHE'S ALL OVER THE BLOODY NEWS,' he yelled, his boiling rage spewing forth on Doctor Patel, who swallowed nervously on the other end. 'How did this happen?' His voice was now calm and seemingly unflappable once more.

'I...I imagined I was doing the right thing,' she explained. 'If the journalist had the picture and knew the story, I thought the exposure and publicity could help us discover Elizabeth's identity.'

Patel shivered as Swann finished his whisky with a single gulp. 'In hindsight, I know it was idiotic,' she said. 'But he was so persistent. And so very convincing with his arguments. But I see now how I was duped. I'm so very sorry, Professor.'

Swann rose from his seat and shook his head in disbelief. 'Do you have the slightest inkling of what you've done?' he snapped. 'Allowing her case to be broadcast to the nation like that! The psychological damage this could cause is incalculable. And bloody Buckland, too. Surely you know the man's reputation!'

'He tricked me,' she protested. 'I didn't give him permission to photograph the patient. Only the picture she drew. I told him to blur—'

'Incredible that you failed to see through him.'

'It all happened out of context...'

'That hardly matters now, does it! The damage is done.'

Swann looked at his walls and ceiling. The shadows cast by the soft lighting looked like an abstract mural. Small and sharp-patterned near the light fitting, they were larger and fuzzy-edged at a distance. They calmed his mood and he sat back down.

'I shudder to think about the legal ramifications,' continued Swann. 'This was highly unprofessional behaviour and it happened on your watch. I suggest you write everything up and document what happened. You'll need a proper report. The General Medical Council will undoubtedly get involved in this. Make sure they know he tricked you. The fact you're a first-year medic won't wash if they think you breached her confidence on purpose.'

'Yes,' said Patel, her voice trembling at the thought. 'I'll get everything together as a matter of urgency. But Professor...'

'What is it?'

She hesitated for a moment.

'...I have another reason for ringing. I'm afraid there's something else I need to tell you.'

Now it was Swann's turn to feel nervous. 'Something else?' he repeated, his words expressing his worry. 'You'd better get on and say it then.'

Patel's voice stuck in her throat as she spoke. 'She's started talking. She realised what Buckland did and is terrified of the story going public. We need to act, Professor. We need to act fast.'

• CHAPTER 15 •

Hugo sat defiantly on the blue, square-armed sofa in his room at Oriel. Next to him, Alice repeated her invitation.

'How about we go to a house party later?'

He crossed his arms and shook his head from side to side like a five-year-old having a tantrum.

'No,' he scowled, screwing his features as if he'd just ingested a tumbler of vinegar. 'I'm not in the mood for it.'

'Oh Hugo, don't be so wet,' she teased him.

'What's wrong with a nice, quiet evening in the pub?' he complained, throwing his arms in the air in protest. 'I don't want to go to a house party.'

'Come on, it'll be *fun*,' she insisted.

'It'd be more fun down the pub.' He stuck his bottom lip out and sulked. Alice tried not to laugh at him.

'How about we compromise?' she said. 'We can go to the pub first for a bit, just you and me. Then, after a few drinks, we can head to the party. Fair deal.'

'Hardly.'

It was already dark outside the window, so he stomped over to close the curtains.

'Come on,' she persisted. 'You know you'll enjoy it when you get there. It's not even far. Just off the Cowley Road.'

Hugo sat back down on the sofa. He knew there was little point in arguing – Alice always got her way in the end. 'Okay, let's do it,' he sighed petulantly. 'Pub first, though.'

In truth, Hugo was shy. Large crowds always made him nervous, especially when he didn't know the people there. He thought back to his leavers' ball at school just a few months before. One of only four boys to attend date-less, he'd felt awkward and embarrassed throughout. In the end, he'd finished the evening completely alone. It would be a similar story at this party, no doubt.

After a few drinks at the pub, they arrived at the party. Hugo glanced at the attendees, who seemed different from most of the Oxford students he'd met thus far. The ubiquitous Etonians and Wykehamists, with their confident swaggers and entitled perspectives, were not in attendance here. Neither could he see any expensive champagne, for that matter. There was plenty of beer, though.

The guests were mainly T-shirt wearers. Some had dyed hair, and there were numerous tattoos on view. Hugo felt rather stiff

## DREAMS

in his ill-fitting checked shirt. *Why are these people so much cooler than me?* Even their spectacles were trendier than his.

'Relax, they're normal people,' said Alice, who perceived his discomfort.

The party was in a large student house, and each room had a different vibe with different music. An amateur DJ had decks set up in the living room, with cheap lighting providing a nightclub feel. Upstairs, the bedrooms were given over to various themes and musical tastes, with waifs and strays cluttering the landing and stairs like abandoned animals.

But the most popular room was the kitchen. Under the glare of a flickering strip light, bodies sat on worktops and hovered around the fridge. Despite the warm temperature, one boy insisted on wearing his oversized coat all evening as he stood and conversed in the same spot by the oven. On the floor next to him, a plastic bin was filled with ice and water. In it, bottles and cans of beer lay submerged.

Alice and Hugo were still in the hall when a tall boy approached them. He had an eyebrow piercing and a perfectly gelled quiff. His eyebrows were thick and his cheekbones high.

'Great to see you, Alice,' said the boy. 'I'm so glad you could make it.' His accent was Welsh and he spoke from a full-lipped mouth.

'Hi Owen,' she replied with a diffident giggle. She hugged him and allowed him to kiss her on the cheek. 'This is Hugo.'

'Nice to meet you, Hugo.' The pair shook hands.

'Owen's from Wadham too,' explained Alice. 'He's on my course as well.'

The friendly Welshman grabbed a couple of beers and passed them to the young couple. 'Just help yourselves when you're ready for more,' he said.

They took him at his word and did precisely that. Whenever their bottles depleted, they went and fetched some more. The beer did its job that night and lubricated Hugo's savoir-faire. The more he imbibed, the more he seemed to fit in.

Gradually, his grip on Alice's hand loosened and he began to speak more confidentially. A couple of beers later, and he even left her side to converse with people independently. His inhibitions were lifting and he started to relax and enjoy himself, laughing at their jokes and attempting a few of his own. He was no longer an isolated pariah – just another ordinary student, like everyone else. Oxford was treating him very differently from the way that school had done.

Later, with the party in full flow, Hugo found himself sitting with a small group of boys on the floor of one of the bedrooms. The music had a distinct 'chill out' vibe and a loose floorboard creaked under his backside as he shifted his weight on the carpet. A single bed lay in one corner, and soft toys were strewn here and there. Photographs of nights out decorated the walls, with laughing women in each of them.

Owen sat on the floor next to him. Downstairs, Alice was still in the kitchen talking to friends. In her absence, Hugo observed the Welshman, who'd begun regaling the group with a story about a girl he knew. He was wearing a Wales rugby shirt that accentuated the dark glow of his eyes. He was very good-looking and, as a Glamorgan native, his voice had a deep, musical intonation.

But Hugo's thoughts swiftly turned to what Owen was doing with his fingers. Transfixed, he stared as Owen constructed a small tube-like creation, white in colour. He knew what it was immediately. He wasn't so naive that he couldn't recognise a spliff, but he had never seen one this close before.

Several boys at school had been cannabis users, or 'tokers', as they often referred to themselves. Like packs of dogs, they would escape the boarding houses and congregate unseen in the woods, moving only under the cover of darkness. In the dead of night, they would drink and smoke before returning ghostlike to their termly dwellings, hoping to avoid the masters' detection.

Hugo had been a 'flexi-boarder', only sleeping on-site a couple of nights a week. Even so, he'd never dared engage in such risky behaviour. Every so often, one reeking unfortunate would be caught sneaking back in, prompting a search of clothing or dorm. He'd seen many a tearful mother or irate father summoned to collect their rumbled progeny, sometimes for good. He couldn't bear the thought of his own father arriving under those circumstances and had calculated that such extracurricular activities weren't worth the peril.

But this situation was different. This was an undergraduate party in Oxford. There were no prying schoolmasters here, no disapproving father breathing down his neck, ready to drag him away in disappointment. Here, he could experiment in safety.

Owen put the spliff to his lips, struck a match and inhaled. Hugo watched as he held the smoke in his lungs for a moment before expelling it through his nose.

He felt nervous. He knew what was coming once Owen had taken a couple more drags. He dithered and considered declining the invitation. In his mind's eye, he could see his father's face rage at the proceedings.

*Fuck you*, he thought, putting the spliff between his lips and sucking. The smoke rushed over his tongue and stuck at the back of his throat, smothering his windpipe. Immediately, he coughed and gasped for air, his lungs recoiling from the invasive fog.

'Oh my God, you're a *VIRGIN!*'

Owen's ridicule made him blush. The other boys in the group laughed as the Welshman pointed and chuckled.

'Yeah, it's my first time,' Hugo admitted, his voice lost at the back of his burning throat.

'Don't worry, we've all been there. Have a gulp or two of beer.'

Hugo tipped his head back and poured some booze down his gullet. His breath remained short and raspy.

'Better?' enquired Owen.

'Not really.'

'Here's a tip. Try taking shorter drags to begin with and hold the smoke in your mouth. When you're ready to take it down, do it slowly and try sucking in some external air at the same time. It'll be easier on your lungs.'

The advice worked, and Hugo's choking organs grudgingly accepted their new pollutant. A sudden rush pervaded his body as he sank back and rested against the wall behind him. The light-headed warmth was like a hot water bottle on a cold winter's night. It removed his burdens and enveloped his senses. His mind was clouded but felt expanded by the chemicals in his bloodstream. No longer was he shackled by the manacles of dull sobriety.

The spliff circulated the little group two or three more times before running down. Each toke pulled Hugo deeper into his bubble of floating ecstasy. As the minutes ticked by, his conversation felt increasingly profound and enlightened; in truth, it was nothing more than a superficial gobbledegook that disconnected him further from reality. The more he inhaled, the more his eyelids began to droop.

As the spliff's THC worked its soporific magic, he cocked his head against the wall and closed his eyes. Before long, he drifted off and surrendered his mind to weed-fuelled slumber.

*Hugo clambered through sleep's gateway and into the world of dreams. Transported to the living room of a suburban home, the family he saw was familiar. He recognised them immediately from the garden and the occasion by the paddling pool on a summer's day.*

*But now, the season was different. It was pitch dark outside, and the curtains on both sides of the dual aspect room were closed. Soft artificial light illuminated the room, and a decorated tree stood in front of one set of curtains.*

It was Christmas Eve, and the family was consumed with festive spirit. The man was sat on the floor by the tree, trying to mend the fairy lights with a screwdriver. Meanwhile, the woman dressed her ten-year-old daughter in a warm coat and handed her some mittens. Hugo's attempts at communication failed. As before, he was totally unobservable to the family.

The woman and girl waved goodbye to the man and exited the house. Hugo wondered where they were going and followed them out of the door. On his way, he turned to see the man fiddling with a plug socket. As he wandered away, Hugo thought he looked increasingly exasperated with the broken down electrics.

It was early evening, and they walked briskly, their steamy white breath hanging ghostlike in the air before dissolving away into nothingness. The air was crisp, and stars shone down like pinpricks of light from the milky heavens above them. Beneath their feet, the ground was hard, with mud and leaves frost-fixed as they trudged.

After some minutes, a church honed into view, its spire piercing the velvet sky like a giant knitting needle. Taking refuge from the chill, they entered the building and sat in a pew, ready for the Candlelight service.

Prayers were said, carols were sung and a little nativity scene was performed by a few of the children. Hugo listened intently as the priest delivered his sermon, aimed specifically at the congregation's youngsters.

After the service, they left the church and began walking home. Hugo looked at the Christingle the girl was holding and *felt serene. Shielded from visibility, he listened to the pair's conversation. The talk of Santa and snowballs, of stockings and presents, of turkey and Christmas pudding reminded him of his own Christmases as a child at home with his father and mother. His smile was sweet but tinged with the pain of his mother's untimely death.*

*The screaming sirens of an ambulance, its blue lights pulsing as it approached from behind, jolted him away from such sentimentality. He wondered where it was heading and who had the need for it. Momentarily, he felt troubled, with anguish replacing his earlier feeling of warmth. It was the same shift that had occurred in the garden during his previous dream.*

*As they drew closer to the house, Hugo saw that the woman had grown anxious too. Something had changed in the air.*

*'I can smell bonfires,' said the girl, still absorbed in the Christmas spirit and oblivious to the altered mood. 'It's meant to be Christmas Eve, not Bonfire Night!'*

*The woman didn't reply. Instead, she quickened her pace and rounded the next corner. Behind the row of homes in the foreground, a thick plume of acrid smoke billowed into the cold night air.*

*'House fire!' exclaimed the woman. She took hold of her daughter's hand and began running, eager to turn the final corner. Hugo was forced into a jog to keep up.*

*As they emerged onto their street, the full horror became apparent. A sea of dazzling blue lights mesmerised them. Water gushed from the hoses of two fire engines, and the ambulance from before lay sandwiched between the pair of giant red trucks.*

*'OH, JESUS CHRIST!' yelled the woman, realising it was her own home that had gone up in flames. She let go of her daughter's hand and began sprinting towards the scene, but was prevented from getting too close by a sturdy fireman, who gathered her in his arms. Hugo looked on from a distance as flames licked the side of the building and danced along the roofline.*

*'My husband!' wailed the woman as she struggled to free herself from the fireman's grip. 'Let me go,' she implored. 'My husband's in there. You have to let me through.'*

*She called his name: 'Jim...JIIIIIIIIIIIIMM!'*

*'Daddy!' cried the girl.*

*But what happened next froze the pair of them solid. With a spine-chilling fusion of thundering roar and haunting creek, the building's roof collapsed and crashed onto the rest of the house below. Hugo, too, stood motionless and watched as the scene played out.*

*A crowd of bystanders had gathered in the street to witness the chaos unfold. One woman broke ranks and approached. 'Sandra,' cried the neighbour. 'Oh Sandra, how terrible for you. I rang the emergency services straight away.'*

*'My house!' she howled. 'What the hell happened here?'*

*'I don't know. It looked like an explosion. An electrical explosion. I saw the flames and dialled 999 immediately.'*

*'And Jim? Is he okay? What news do you have of my husband?'*

'I... I don't know,' stuttered the neighbour. 'I've been here since the beginning, but...I haven't seen him.'

Also desperate for news of Jim, Hugo peered through the haze. Then, as the acrid clouds of smoke began to part, ghostly shadows stirred in the blackness. As the shapes sharpened in front of him, he saw a stretcher being carried by four firefighters. On it lay a body – there was only one possible explanation.

Hugo was as unseen to the emergency workers and bystanders as he was to the suburban family. Impelled by inquisitiveness, he stepped forward and passed through the midst of them, his heart beating a little quicker as he approached the stretcher.

The person was burnt beyond visible recognition, yet Hugo knew who it was. It was the man whose name he now knew to be Jim, the husband of Sandra and father of the little girl.

Jim's skin had become dark and leathery. Thin wisps of smoke rose from his charred clothing, and his blackened face was shrivelled and contorted.

But most harrowing of all was the faint moaning that rose from the stretcher. Poor Jim was still alive.

His scream was so loud it woke him, and an overpowering sickness caused him to tilt his head forwards. With a heaving rush, he vomited the contents of his stomach over the carpet.

Upon finishing, he screamed again. Breathless, heart pounding, he opened his eyes to find himself in the real world.

The little gathering around Hugo was not amused.

'Jesus, man!' Owen spat without a hint of sympathy. 'I can't believe you just did that!' He was riled by the vomit that had splashed against his rugby shirt and stormed away with a look of scorn on his face.

The remaining members of the group also began moving away from the culprit. Hugo looked up to see the other guests' reactions. Some were amused. Others displayed contempt. One had a look of thunder as she approached...

Alice grabbed his arm and hauled him to his feet. The girl whose room it was stood next to her and looked even less amused. They had arrived from the kitchen just in time to witness the spectacle.

'You're a drunken idiot!' said Alice, castigating him.

'You don't understand,' he slurred. 'It was the dream again! That little girl! Her parents! They were back!'

Alice shot him a withering look. 'Hugo, we're heading off,' she said, giving him a yank and dragging him out of the bedroom.

'There was a house fire!' cried Hugo as they disappeared down the landing to fits of laughter behind them. 'He was burnt black! He's on the stretcher! I can still see him...'

Alice rolled her eyes as she led him through the front door and onto the street. 'Just stop talking,' she ordered him, still clutching his arm and shepherding him back onto Cowley Road. 'We're going straight to bed when we're back. Honestly, the tiniest bit of weed and you're acting like a total moron. Do you realise how embarrassing you've been tonight?'

Hugo said nothing but followed along in silence.

• CHAPTER 16 •

Back at Oriel, Alice flared her nostrils and sniffed as she got into bed. The walk back had sobered them up a little, and Hugo plunged them into blackness by turning off the light. Fumbling blind for the alcove wall, he located his bed and stumbled into it. 'I made a complete arse of myself, didn't I?'

'Yes,' replied Alice, sounding tired and distinctly unsympathetic. 'It's a pity. You were getting on so well with everyone.'

'And now they all think I'm a total idiot.' He sighed and rolled onto his back, trying to make out the ceiling as his eyes began to adjust.

'Don't worry, Owen's cool. He won't hold it against you.' She turned onto her side and faced away from him.

Hugo had perceived the frostiness in her voice. Now she had her back to him too. 'I'm sorry, Alice. It's just this bloody dream.' He coughed and felt a little trapped smoke escape his lungs. 'I don't know what's causing it.'

'I know it's been upsetting you. But the weed will have exacerbated things. Made it seem more potent.'

'It's so vivid when it happens,' he explained, putting his arm around her shoulder. She removed it and pushed it firmly into the mattress by her side.

Alice looked at her watch and was just able to perceive the time. 'Christ, Hugo. It's nearly 4 AM. We really ought to get some sleep.'

Before long, he heard her snoring, but Hugo resolved to remain awake. He feared what another round of slumber might bring, and wakefulness was his shield against any torment he might experience should his guard lower. And besides, Alice's coldness had left him feeling alert, so he rolled back over and pondered what their future as a couple might hold.

But he couldn't fight sleep forever. In the end, exhaustion won, and he, too, drifted into unconsciousness.

It was precisely 11 AM when Hugo's eyes opened. The sunshine streaming through the window had woken him, and he strained to recollect the next details of the dream. What had happened to poor Jim? Surely the next instalment had been delivered while he slept. He racked his brains...

Nothing.

Vague snippets of an unconnected dream bobbed to the surface of his mind, then receded again rapidly. It was surreal, amorphous, and it was fading fast from his memory. It had been a normal night-time dream. Jim's fate remained a mystery.

He shifted his head to survey the room. Alice was already up and sitting at his desk by the window. She'd opened the curtains, and an autumn sun now burned at the pastel wall behind her. Steam rose from a coffee cup and her mobile phone was in her hand. She was reading something on the screen.

'Welcome back to the world of the living,' she said without looking up. 'Headache?'

'A bit.'

'The kettle's still hot. Grab a coffee if you want one.'

'Thanks.'

He got out of bed and went to kiss her good morning. As his lips approached hers, she pushed him away. 'And brush your teeth as well,' she said, contorting her features. 'You reek of beer and weed.'

Hugo did as he was bid, brushing his teeth and grabbing a quick shower while waiting for his coffee to cool to a drinkable temperature. The shower left him feeling refreshed, cleansed both physically and mentally. On returning from the ensuite, he joined her at the desk to drink his morning coffee.

'Have a look at this article I was reading while you were getting out of bed and showering,' she said, handing him her iPhone. A tabloid news app was already open.

'What is it?' he asked, taking hold of the phone.

'Read it. You used to do a bit of painting, didn't you? You still haven't shown me any of your work.' Her tone wasn't especially friendly. She still sounded vexed from last night.

'I haven't done anything for ages,' he mumbled. 'I think they're all…oh, this is interesting – "Mystery Woman Found on Riverbank,"' he said, repeating the headline to her.

Alice glanced over. Hugo sipped his coffee, then used his thumb and index finger to enlarge the text.

'Keep reading,' she urged him. 'As a psychology student, this fascinated me. I bet your dad's noticed it too.'

'My dad's a psychiatrist, not a psychologist. He treats people with complex mental illnesses as opposed to…'

He didn't complete the sentence. Instead, his eyes fastened on the meadow picture, its *Elizabeth Ritchie* signature plain to see on the left of a split-screen photo. Hugo thought the piece wouldn't look out of place in a gallery. After a moment's appreciation, he looked to the right and regarded the artist's face.

Was it her blue eyes that made his heart skip a beat? She wasn't beautiful, but he couldn't look away.

'Why does this case ring a bell?' he wondered out loud.

'Piano Man,' replied Alice, as if she'd been anticipating his question.

He looked at her blankly. 'Who's Piano Man?'

'Happened back in 2005. I read about it in a psychology journal only last week. A guy was found walking the streets of Sheerness in Kent wearing a soaking wet suit and tie—'

'This woman's from Kent,' he interjected. 'Sorry. Carry on.' He picked up his coffee and took a big gulp, which curbed his urge to interrupt.

Alice continued. 'They tried doctors, psychologists, interpreters – a whole array of professionals. But whatever they did, nobody could get him to speak.'

'So what happened?'

'They left him a piece of paper and hoped he'd write his name. But instead of writing, he drew a picture of a grand piano. You can probably work out what happened next.'

'Let me guess,' said Hugo, still holding his coffee. 'They sat him down at a piano, and he started playing?'

'Got it in one,' said Alice, who smiled for the first time that morning. 'All sorts of stuff, from classical to pop. He'd play for hours and hours. That was why the press dubbed him Piano Man.'

'Did they find out who he was?'

Her smile faded, and she was matter-of-fact once more. 'It went on for about four months and made headlines around the world,' she told him. 'They sent notes to orchestras in various countries. Media agencies, too. They weren't sure if he was neurodivergent or scarred psychologically. In the end, it turns out he was a twenty-year-old German guy called Andreas. And that was the end of the story. Some people think it was a hoax.'

Hugo looked down at the phone and saw the screen had gone dark. He switched it back on, almost forgetting Alice's coldness as he stared at Elizabeth's face, her eyes boring into his like a couple of blue lasers. For some reason, he felt a sudden and inexplicable captivation for this woman's story. And for her.

• CHAPTER 17 •

Professor Swann's rage boiled inside him. *How could Patel have been so stupid?*

Repairing the patient's damaged trust would be difficult, impossible even. Still, he had to try, so he'd arranged a meeting with colleagues for the afternoon. Time, however, was short, and with Elizabeth lying in front of him, he kept his anger concealed.

This particular visit was unplanned. There was no psychiatric diagnosis, and, apart from a name, they were no closer to discovering her identity. Given Patel's idiocy, he knew he had to move quickly: the patient had to be stopped from absconding.

He'd started by apologising to Elizabeth on behalf of the hospital and explained that the journalist had been cunning, tricking the young doctor. Permission to take the picture had certainly not been granted. He would, he assured her, do everything he could to prevent the story from going any further.

In return, she'd told him about the suicide bid and how she'd planned to do it with vodka and pills at the meadow. But those pills had never been taken; instead, she'd fallen into the swollen stream while drunk.

'You're doing very well,' said Swann as Elizabeth elucidated the details. Even at this early stage, he felt psychotic episodes or personality disorders were less likely. Depression brought on by previous traumatic events was far more plausible.

The whitewashed room still reeked of disinfectant, but most of the monitoring equipment had been removed now that the patient was out of physical danger. A sink was installed at the far end, with a giant roll of blue paper towels on top of it. Next to the bed, Swann sat cross-legged on a plastic chair, the room's only other item of furniture. He spoke softly, but his deep voice still echoed in the utilitarian chamber.

'But why?' he asked her. 'Why try to end your life? What sorts of things were going through your mind?'

'Things from my past,' she admitted, casting her blue eyes to the ceiling and away from his.

'Such as?'

'I don't want to say.'

Swann didn't relent. 'These *things* you speak of. You wanted release from them?'

Elizabeth nodded.

'I understand,' he said. 'Sometimes our feelings can overwhelm us.'

She turned even further away from him.

The psychiatrist was satisfied with his conclusions: this was a case for a trained counsellor, and urgent professional therapy was required. Fortunately, he had plenty of contacts on that front. Referring her would be a straightforward matter.

'Before I leave, there's one other thing I need to ask,' he continued. 'Why did you remain silent for so long?'

She puffed her cheeks and looked at the sink before turning her eyes on him. Again, Swann was struck by their blueness.

'It was the failure,' she said. 'I'd expected to die at the meadow only to wake up and find myself in hospital. Tunbridge Wells first, then here. I guess I just withdrew into my own little world.'

She was beginning to talk lucidly and Swann couldn't help but press things. 'But then you started speaking. And very suddenly too, I might add.' His curiosity was getting the better of him.

'Because of that *journalist!*' she hissed. 'You have to understand — there are people out there who know about my past. People who will come looking for me if they hear about my story in the news.'

Swann watched as her eyes began to moisten from the stress. She used a sleeve to wipe them, then snorted up the mucus she'd secreted. He could tell it was time to stop — further questions would be counterproductive right now, so he prepared to leave her in peace. But the woman was clearly unstable. His afternoon meeting couldn't come quickly enough.

Swann fortified himself with a light lunch: a cheese sandwich and a latte. He knew he'd bent the rules with his unofficial visit to Elizabeth that morning, but the intervention had been necessary. Nina Patel had been right on the phone – they'd had to act fast, so he'd seized the initiative and been in to see her. As a result, he was much better prepared for the meeting and knew exactly what he would recommend.

Realising that time was critical, Swann had arrived five minutes early. As he hustled down the corridor towards the meeting room, two figures stood outside as he approached. He recognised Doctor Patel; the other was a social worker. The pair were waiting for him.

'Greetings,' said Swann, pleased to see they'd also arrived early. 'I'm glad you both recognise the urgency of this meeting. Let's go in and get started.'

Patel raised a hand to stop him in his tracks. 'Professor, please wait a moment.' The doctor's expression was troubled. Something was wrong, and Swann sensed it.

'What on earth's the matter?' he demanded, his pulse quickening with apprehension.

'It's Elizabeth,' she explained. 'I'm afraid something's happened to her. Something terrible.'

• CHAPTER 18 •

Hugo's heart sank a notch. Why hadn't Alice replied to his WhatsApp messages? At the bottom of his screen, a couple of blue ticks indicated she'd read them, but still no response had come through.

After discussing Elizabeth's story and its resemblance to the 2005 case of Piano Man, she'd left his room and disappeared on the pretext of working on a group project with some friends at Wadham. No doubt Owen would be there, and Hugo knew the previous evening's misfortune wouldn't escape mention. He hoped any ridicule wouldn't be too severe in his absence.

But it was the *manner* of her departure that was most troubling for him. She'd been so frosty in bed the night before and had been civil rather than affectionate in the morning. Were things cooling between them? Had his shenanigans at the party annoyed her more than he'd first thought?

Her lack of communication was disquieting, so he pulled his phone from his pocket and opened WhatsApp.

Still nothing. *For fuck's sake!*

Coming to the end of his tether he pressed the telephone icon to make a voice call. Frustrated, he waited for the tone to sound.

The ringing went on and on. Was she ignoring him? Surely not! Maybe she just had her phone on silent. It seemed to take an age, but finally the call connected and he heard her voice.

'Hi.' It was a statement rather than a greeting.

'Alice!' he exclaimed. 'For a minute, I thought you weren't picking up.'

'Sorry, I was busy working.' She didn't sound particularly apologetic. 'What are you up to?' There was no warmth in her voice. Only civility.

'Just back at my room having had a bit of lunch,' said Hugo, moving to the window and staring across the quad. Grey clouds had replaced the earlier sunshine and the breeze had picked up a little. 'I'm going to the library this afternoon,' he continued, 'so I thought I'd call you before heading out.'

'Okay...'

She was being very cagey. Disconcertingly so.

'Do we have a plan for this evening?' he asked, trying to sound ebullient and ignoring her lack of reciprocity. 'I could come over to Wadham if you like. We could get a pizza and watch a film together.'

The silence only lasted a couple of seconds, but it was plain nonetheless.

'Alice?' he prompted her.

'Sorry, I was miles away for a moment.'

'So what do you think? Pizza and a film?'

There was another short silence before she mustered an answer. 'The thing is…I'll be working quite late into the evening. I wonder whether it's worth it tonight.'

'Think of it as a reward,' he said, pressing the issue like a dog with a bone. 'Something to look forward to when you're done working.'

The next pause was a little longer. 'Listen,' she countered, sounding more alert this time. 'I'm not going to promise anything, but why don't you give me a ring a bit later?'

Her lack of clarity was disgruntling. 'Why later?' he queried.

'Cos, I'm working, Hugo!' Her indecision was morphing into irritation now. 'Look, maybe we should just leave it this evening. I'm bound to be tired and ratty later. I doubt I'll be very good company.'

There was little point in continuing when she was in this sort of mood. 'Fine,' he yielded. 'When's a good time to ring later?'

'Dunno. Maybe early evening or something.'

He rolled his eyes and shook his head. It was obvious she wanted him off the line, so he said his goodbyes and hung up. He placed his phone back in his pocket and puffed his cheeks. An ominous feeling stirred as he sat back down on the sofa. The grey clouds outside his window seemed portentous all of a sudden.

*Fuck me, this isn't looking good.*

• CHAPTER 19 •

Swann's eyes flicked between the two figures in front of him. 'What do you mean something's happened to her?' he barked.

'She's discharged herself,' said the social worker, taking over from Patel. 'Following an impromptu discussion with *you*.'

Swann's blood began to pump and beads of sweat appeared on his forehead. This meeting was scheduled to discuss whether Elizabeth should be sectioned for the next twenty-eight days under the Mental Health Act of 1983.

She'd initially been sectioned for 72 hours as an emergency case upon her arrival. But once that period had elapsed, she had resided at the hospital voluntarily. Swann knew the legislation required three professionals to meet and make a combined judgement. He also knew how pressing things were:

without sectioning, she was free to leave whenever she chose to.

Given what he'd surmised during their chat, he was of the strongest opinion that she ought to remain in medical care. But with her self-discharge, it seemed his visit had backfired. *Who's the unprofessional one now?*

The professor's head began to spin. With only a name to go on, tracing her would take time. And goodness knew what she might do before they could get to her. If only he'd waited and followed proper protocol.

He looked at Patel, whose features oozed contempt. She folded her arms, then spoke patronisingly. 'I suggest you write things up, Professor…'

The doctor was enjoying her moment of revenge, and Swann knew it.

'…Make sure you've got everything documented. You'll need a proper record for the General Medical Council. No doubt they'll get involved in this.'

Meanwhile, in St. James's Park, a lone woman sat opposite the lake on a bench. Cradled in the grey embrace of autumn, an overcast sky mirrored the blistering thoughts in her head. A soft, swirling breeze gnawed at her skin and manipulated the lake into a magic-eye puzzle of rolling waves, its reflections ever-shifting like the to and fro of a fly fisherman's cast.

The incongruity of the pelicans on Duck Island echoed the pathos of Elizabeth's new setting: for all its metropolitan loveliness, St. James's Park was no Kentish meadow. She gazed to her right and saw a carefree squirrel prance insouciantly across the ground, its mouth stuffed with an acorn. On the path in front of her, a young boy sped by on his bicycle, music blaring from a speaker he was holding. In the distance, a police siren screeched for what seemed an age before fading like music into the constant hum of traffic.

Elizabeth's mind felt cleansed now her ordeal at the hospital was over. There would be no more questions and no further tests. Absconding had returned her liberty and rewarded her with the opportunity to slip back into prosaic anonymity. But with her freedom came an unfettered urgency: she had no money, no purse, and was wearing only the hospital's clothes. She looked up as the remnants of daylight began to fade. It was still dry, but the leaden sky looked threatening. As night chipped away at day, she knew she needed shelter and more appropriate attire.

She rose from the bench and rambled to the park's exit, eager to set a brisk pace in the encroaching chill. The city streets felt foreboding, but she expunged any fearful thoughts and focused her mind. She needed a plan: how, exactly, was she going to raise the price of a train ticket back to Kent?

Trafalgar Square was still quite busy when she happened upon it after a few minutes of walking. A fine drizzle now hung in the air like scattered pollen, the tiny droplets dispersed in all directions by the swirling grey wind. The bustle of the square offered scant comfort as the drizzle intensified into light rain.

Looking towards the northeast corner, Elizabeth noticed the neoclassical spire of St-Martin-in-the-Fields and made her way towards it. Like Jonah by the whale, she felt consumed as she passed under the enormous supporting columns and into the building's belly. At least it offered a safe place to sit and think. It was also warm and dry.

Inside, there were plenty of folk still present. Most were tourists, dazzled by the church's splendour, their cameras primed and ready for action. A smattering of worshippers dotted the pews, and two clergymen stood at the far end of the nave. However, six souls in particular caught her eye.

These six people, all men, were scattered at various points throughout the church. Each sat motionless as if contemplating life's lottery. Elizabeth was aware of St-Martin-in-the-Fields' charity work with the homeless, and the starkness of their presence made her ponder her own lot.

Perhaps it was the religious setting, but suddenly she felt thankful. Was her life really so bad when compared to the experiences of these poor souls? Despite the horrors of her past, she had her own home in the Kent countryside and a warm bed in which to sleep. Their misfortune provided pause for thought. It also gave her an idea.

• CHAPTER 20 •

True to his word, Hugo spent that afternoon in the library working on a Chaucer essay. By evening, his mind was saturated, and he was ready to unwind and relax. He'd given Alice another call. Two calls, actually – she hadn't answered the first. During the second, she'd invited him to Wadham having caved in to his suggestion about pizza and a film.

But convincing her had been hard. She had taken some serious persuading. Despite relenting, there was no doubt about it: she didn't really want to see him.

Alice's room had magnolia walls, with a large single bed at one end. There were no ensuite facilities, but a washbasin was plumbed in at the wall. Beside it, her study desk was replete with books and folders, with more packed onto the shelving above it. A new magenta carpet added a touch of luxury to the otherwise tired looking room.

Facing the door, they perched on a dilapidated purple sofa in the middle of the room. On a little table in front of them, an open laptop played a film. An empty pizza box was discarded next to the sofa.

The pepperoni pizza was delicious, but the film was interminable; indeed, they'd almost fallen asleep before the end and were glad to be heading to bed when the credits finally rolled. Alice was first to brush her teeth at the basin, and Hugo did likewise straight after.

As Alice plumped up the pillows, Hugo noticed her smother an item of jewellery. She smiled coyly, then placed it in one of the drawers by her bed. Her behaviour seemed strange but he was far too tired to press the matter. *It must be one of her earrings.*

Once they were prostrate, sleep was quick to follow. Neither student attempted intimacy and neither was disappointed at being denied it. Instead, they closed their eyes and waited for slumber. It wasn't long in coming.

*Hugo found himself in the visitors' area of a hospital. It was the dead of night, and a clock on the wall informed him it was two-forty-five in the morning. In front of him, a pair of worried faces looked desperate for news of a loved one.*

*Before long, a medic appeared and began a conversation with Sandra. He looked sombre, and Hugo was filled with dread.*

*He tried to listen but couldn't make anything out. It didn't matter: Sandra's actions confirmed his fears.*

*She gathered her daughter in her arms and the pair began to sob. Hugo, too, was overcome with grief at the news of Jim's passing. It was the expected conclusion given what he'd seen on the stretcher, but his head still spun with horror. Jim's life had been cruelly extinguished, snatched away in the most agonising circumstances. A fault in the fairy lights had electrocuted him, and he'd passed out with the shock. The subsequent fire had quickly taken hold and the unconscious Jim was caught in its trap. Hugo felt his own fire rage at the injustice. With anger burning in his heart, he withdrew from Sandra and the girl.*

*Led by instinct, he headed down the corridor, his pulse quickening as he approached Jim's room. He stole a nervous pause before entering, then choked back vomit at what he saw on crossing the threshold.*

*On the bed before him, Jim's charred body lay stiff and lifeless. The man he'd seen at the suburban home was no longer a man at all. All that remained was a desiccated corpse, human in the past tense only. He moved in to regard his first dead body more closely. The face was crisped and blackened, the features fixed and contorted. Hugo shuddered at the agony in which poor Jim must have died. Gazing down, he took one last look at that perpetual, silent scream...*

His own scream was not silent. Alice woke at the noise and grunted in displeasure.

The sheets were soaked with cold sweat and his head felt like he'd been kicked. He puffed his cheeks to control his breathing; then, as his heart rate slowed, he opened his eyes.

The room was still black, with no natural light penetrating from outside. He turned his head and glanced at the clock on the bedside table. He screamed again when he saw what it read: *two-forty-five*.

'*Shit!*' he shouted, his voice a notch higher than usual. He threw the covers back and leapt out of bed. *Two-forty-five*: it was the same time he'd seen on the hospital clock. The time of Jim's death.

He took a couple of bounds across the room and banged into the study desk. The sound of items crashing to the floor was amplified in the darkness.

'*What the hell, Hugo!*' Alice's voice was muffled by the pillow, but there was no mistaking her irritability.

'I'm sorry,' he whimpered. 'The time on your clock. It's the same time I saw in my dream!'

Alice sighed and rolled over. 'Not this bloody dream again!' She buried herself deeper under the covers and muttered something under her breath.

'I can't stay here,' he whispered. 'I have to go.' He began fumbling for his clothes like a rodent ferreting in the blackness.

Alice sat bolt upright. 'What do you mean you have to go?' she protested, throwing her arms in the air. 'Where are you going to go? It's the middle of the fucking night, Hugo!'

'Back to Oriel,' he declared. 'I need to get my head together.'

The door clunked as Hugo closed it and left. Alice grabbed a pillow and hurled it after him.

His dream remained vivid as he journeyed back to Oriel, his quest for solitude stymied by Oxford's usual presence of late-night revellers and homeless people. Only when back in his room did he finally find tranquillity, and he embraced it like a long-lost friend.

He wandered to the window, opened the curtains and gazed across the darkened quad. He stood motionless for an hour or so, trying to untangle the seething knot of thoughts in his head. But despite his best efforts, the nocturnal visions refused to subside. Thus, with Jim's contorted face still fixed in his mind's eye, he returned to the alcove and climbed into bed.

Too charged to sleep, too shattered to stay awake, he propped himself up and leaned his head against the wall. There he stayed until a grey dawn crept ever so slowly from behind the blanket of night. The next morning had arrived.

• CHAPTER 21 •

London was dank and grey that Thursday morning and the pavements were still wet following the previous evening's rain. The grey sky mirrored the grey of the buildings and streets below. Even the air seemed grey, thickened into a light blanket somewhere between mist and fog.

Trafalgar Square was already quite busy as Elizabeth sat on the steps of the National Gallery. In front of her, Nelson's Column thrust skyward like a giant sea stack rising from the waves. The square's few trees were now semi-naked, their leaves half shed in the grey November gloom. And by God, was she cold on those steps!

Her priority was to find some warmer clothing. She'd noted a charity shop last evening as she'd walked up from St. James's Park. Once she'd raised sufficient funds, it would definitely be worth a look. There was bound to be a bargain inside.

The disposable coffee cup she'd found on the floor would serve her purposes nicely. She'd washed it in one of the square's fountains and was ready to use it as a money-making tool. Pretending to be homeless and begging didn't sit comfortably, but she had little choice in the circumstances. A tenner should buy some warm clothes, and twenty pounds should secure a train ticket from Charing Cross to Tunbridge Wells. A few hours among the throngs of tourists ought to do it.

She began quite passively, tipping her cup towards those who passed by. Now and again, she'd engage them verbally, an awkward 'spare any change?' passing her lips. Fifteen minutes later, the first coins were tossed her way by an American tourist: two five-pence pieces and a U.S. dime.

By mid-morning, she was freezing and had barely a fiver to show for her endeavours. It wouldn't buy her much, and things were becoming desperate: she was shivering and needed to find some suitable clothing.

A wall of warmth enveloped her as she walked through the charity shop door. An older woman behind the counter smiled as she entered. Elizabeth returned the expression, then started browsing. She took longer than necessary, trying on a few bits and taking her time while her temperature rose. In the end, she settled on a beanie and a pair of gloves. They were all she could afford with her meagre resources.

She paid for the items, despondent at having just fifty pence left from her previous labours. As she prepared to leave, a coat near the doorway beckoned seductively. She'd tried it on earlier, but it was way out of her price range at eight pounds.

Turning her head, she noticed the attendant had stepped into the back room. A sudden rush of guilt ran through her but she quickly pushed it aside. Careful to remain unheard, Elizabeth took the coat off its hanger and slipped quietly from the shop without paying for it.

Out on the street, she put the garments on. Her conscience disapproved, but at least she was warm as she trudged back up to Trafalgar Square. At the National Gallery, she sat on the steps and resumed begging, desperate to raise the price of a train ticket home.

It was mid-morning in Oxford, too, when Hugo's iPhone sounded. Incoming was a FaceTime call from Alice. This was going to be interesting. He knew his two-forty-five departure must have seemed strange, and he cringed when he saw her name on the screen.

'Hi, Alice.' He could barely have sounded more sheepish as he sat, feet up, on his sofa.

'How are you feeling today?' she asked.

'I'm okay,' he replied. 'Just very, very tired.'

She looked pensive, and he could tell these early exchanges were merely preparatory to something else. 'That was a pretty hasty exit last night,' she said, continuing the small talk.

'I know. I owe you an apology for that. It must have seemed —'

'Hugo,' she said, cutting him off mid-flow. 'I think we should stop seeing each other.'

He knew it. He knew this was why she'd called. Nevertheless, the abruptness shocked him like a blow to the head. For a moment, he was lost for words, and he swivelled to sit more upright.

'Look,' he murmured, grappling for cogency of thought. 'I'm sorry about last night. It won't happen again, I promise.'

He could tell she was at her study desk with the phone tilted slightly above her head. Behind her, last night's pizza box was still lying by the sofa where he'd left it. Hugo regarded it wistfully.

'It's not just about last night,' she told him, the brightness of her study lamp reflecting in her glasses.

'I know these dreams—'

'It's not the dreams either,' she explained, cutting him off once more. She looked away for a moment before re-engaging him. What she said next was difficult to listen to. 'The thing is, Hugo...there's someone else.'

She let that sink in for a second or two. In response, Hugo rose to his feet and stood rigid. He knew they'd been drifting, but he hadn't suspected a rival. 'Who is it?' he demanded.

'Does it matter?'

'Of course, it matters!' he exclaimed, clenching his free fist by his side.

He watched her shift nervously in her seat. 'Alice...' he demanded.

'It's Owen,' she admitted. 'We've spent so much time working together, and one thing just led to another...'

'Fucking hell!' he swore. 'That was his eyebrow stud on the pillow, wasn't it? Not one of your earrings.'

She looked remorseful. 'I'm sorry, Hugo. You're a great guy. Perhaps we can stay friends when the dust has settled on this. I'd like that...'

'Just save it, Alice.'

And with that, he hung up. He felt foolish for doing so but was frustrated with the turn of events. He wandered to the window and looked out of it, struggling to comprehend his emotions.

There was shock, certainly. Betrayal too. Alice had told him she'd been working yesterday, but she'd actually been making love with Owen on her bed. The same bed Hugo had slept in just hours later. No wonder she'd ignored the first of his WhatsApp calls. No wonder she'd been so reluctant to see him full stop.

Alice had dumped him for the much more handsome Owen. Jealousy burned in Hugo, but the aching sorrow he'd expected in his *heart* wasn't there. His love for Alice had been less deep than he'd thought. Their break-up wasn't the hammer blow he'd expected.

By evening, Elizabeth's heart was heavy. The day had come and gone, but she had very little fruit for her labours. The clink of coins had been steady but not from the one and two-pound pieces she'd been hoping for. As darkness fell, the crowds began to thin.

She poured out her cash and counted. Not even half of what she needed to get home. Amassing the required sums would take at least another day. A cold and potentially dangerous night on London's streets was looming. She rubbed her face and pondered what to do.

Last night had been easy. She'd fought off sleep with a mix of adrenaline and fear, walking the streets before finding a place to sit and wish the darkness away in wide-eyed monotony.

This evening would be different. She was cold, damp and hopelessly fatigued. She was also famished. Her last food had been back at the hospital and the pangs of hunger had become intolerable. She gazed down at her little coffee cup and exhaled at the weight of her decision.

If she chose to sleep hungry, there was a chance, but not a guarantee, that she would make sufficient money to return to Kent the following day (provided nobody robbed her in the night). But if she chose to sate her hunger, it would mean starting the begging process afresh in the morning.

Her stomach growled as if casting a vote. She *needed* to find food.

Feeling slightly dizzy through lack of nutrition, she got up and started moving. Three or four pounds should buy her an evening meal from a newsagent's. Perhaps there'd even be a little something leftover for breakfast. She would save the remaining money and put it towards her ticket in the morning. Aware she was resetting the clock on her endeavours to get home, she walked off in search of sustenance.

• CHAPTER 22 •

Grateful his sleep had not been haunted by suburban ghosts, Hugo woke refreshed. It was Friday morning, and, without tutorials, the day ahead was his. His spirits dipped a little as he thought of Alice, the returning familiarity of singledom hitting him like a train crashing through buffers. They fell even further when he remembered the three essays he needed to do that week.

He dragged himself out of bed and splashed some water on his face in the ensuite. The coolness revived him and infused his thinking with clarity. He glanced at the mirror; as usual, the reflection displeased him.

Returning through, he sat on his sofa and watched dust motes dance in the morning light of his bedroom. Cushioned in tranquillity, ideas began to develop in his head. He felt stifled and strangulated in Oxford, as though the city had somehow pulled him underwater and left him struggling beneath the surface. He felt he couldn't breathe. What he needed was a change – of image as well as location.

He began with a haircut in Oxford's covered market, requesting more than his usual scissors trim. This time, he insisted on a blade around the back and sides. Not too much off the top, though – just the excess length snipping away.

'Any gel or wax, sir?' asked the barber. It was a formality that Hugo usually turned down.

Not today.

'Yes, please,' he nodded. 'Gel it into a quiff.'

While the barber was working, Hugo was thinking and plotting his next move. He knew it was a bad idea, but he was in an impulsive mood. He could always take it out if he didn't like it.

Consequently, he wandered along the High Street, down St Aldates and into a little tattoo and piercing parlour on Folly Bridge above the Thames. It was less painful than he'd expected, but the area around his left eye had swollen up a little. Indeed, the new eyebrow stud felt clunky and cumbersome at first. It also had an annoying habit of catching against the rim of his glasses. Nevertheless, he thought it gave him an edge he'd been lacking, even if it did look incongruous on a face like his.

Goodness knew what his father would say that evening when he saw it. Hugo wondered if he'd insist on its removal before allowing him to set foot in the house. He hadn't yet told Swann he was returning for the weekend; he'd do that later on, and certainly not before he'd spent the day indulging his artistic passions in the capital. Thus, when back on the High Street, he boarded one of the London-bound coach services and left Oxford behind.

He arrived later that morning and made straight for Trafalgar Square. As he ascended the steps of the National Gallery, he fished a fifty-pence-piece from his pocket and gave it to the beggar woman on the steps. He couldn't help but notice how cold and dishevelled she looked, her hair a knotted mess as it protruded from under her beanie.

'Thank you,' she said, acknowledging his generosity as the coin dropped into her cup. A blue flash, like a couple of darting kingfishers, met his gaze as the woman looked up.

And that was when it hit him.

Stunned, he stood still for a moment, thoughts racing, heart palpitating. For all the world, it was like being shot in the chest when her eyes met his. He'd seen those blue flashes before – staring up from an iPhone screen.

'Hello, Elizabeth...' It was little more than a reflex born from pure shock.

She dropped the coffee cup, and Hugo watched its contents spill over the floor. Some of the coins began rolling down the steps towards the grey square below. Elizabeth scrambled to gather them up again.

'Who the hell are *you*?' Her tone was accusatory.

He raised both hands in a *calm down* gesture, painfully aware of the communal setting. 'It's okay,' he said, keeping his voice to a whisper. 'My name's Hugo. I'm a university student.'

'So how do you know *my* name?' she snapped back. A couple of passers-by turned their heads at the outburst.

Fearing a public commotion, Hugo began to sweat. He felt caught in the spotlight, like an actor in front of an audience. He cleared his throat and spoke softly. 'I saw your meadow drawing,' he explained. 'I saw it in a news article. You signed it *Elizabeth Ritchie*. There was a picture of your face, too...'

'That *BASTARD!*' she spat. 'I knew he was full of bullshit. He *promised* me he'd stop things going any further.'

Hugo grew more uncomfortable as a couple more people turned around. 'Who did?' he whispered. 'I don't understand what you mean.'

'That *doctor!*' she hissed. 'He assured me he'd do what he could to stop this becoming news.'

She started backing away, and Hugo watched her descend a couple of steps in reverse.

'He even told me his colleague was duped by the journalist,' she continued, still heading down the steps and away from him. 'Yet she was the one who brought him to my room in the first place. Those total *FUCKING BASTARDS!*'

Fucking bastards. She spat those words with extraordinary venom. More people turned to look at the pair, and Hugo felt their glares like daggers. She was almost at the bottom now. If he wasn't careful, she'd be gone for good, so he rushed down the steps to keep pace with her.

'Please, let me help you,' he pleaded, finally drawing level at the base of the steps. It was an effort not to grab her arm to stop her escaping.

'Help me?' she scoffed. 'And how can you do that, exactly?'

She turned and began marching across the square. Hugo was forced into a semi jog to keep up. They were almost level with one of the giant lions that guarded Nelson's Column when she stopped.

'Why do you care anyway?' she said, flipping to face him and rooting herself to the spot.

The question was rhetorical, but a faint hint of curiosity lurked in her eyes. Hugo sensed his way in. He *did* care. He didn't know why, but he'd been intrigued since he'd first seen her face on Alice's iPhone.

Perhaps it was the creative energy of the meadow drawing. Or the mystery of her riverbank discovery. Or was it those blue eyes that held such fascination for him? He couldn't explain it, but he felt a powerful draw to this woman.

She was still looking his way and her face demanded an explanation. Fumbling for words, he attempted one. 'Your meadow picture,' he began. 'That's why I care. As soon as I saw it, I was captivated.'

'You're an Art student?'

'No. I study English. But art is a passion of mine.' He turned and gestured to the vast neoclassical museum behind him. 'In fact, I was just on my way up to the National Gallery.'

His statement conveyed sincerity and her features softened slightly. 'But how did you know it was *me*?' she asked, intrigue replacing the cynicism of before.

'Your blue eyes,' he replied. 'The second you looked up, I knew it was you.'

Once again, he regarded her. She seemed so cold and unkempt. 'So why don't you tell me,' he continued, holding her gaze. 'How can I help you?'

Those words disarmed Elizabeth and her guard lowered at his kindness.

'You really want to help?' she asked in a quiet voice. She was beginning to trust him now.

'Of course. Just tell me how.'

She took a step to the side and leant her back against the plinth the lion stood on. Hugo detected a pleading look in her eyes as she spoke her next words.

'Help me get home,' she implored. 'I left the hospital two nights ago. Since then, I've been on the streets trying to beg enough money for a train ticket back to Kent.' She looked down in shame. 'It's not going very well,' she added, showing him the half-empty cup.

Hugo understood what she was asking and nodded. 'Okay,' he agreed. 'I'll pay for your ticket home.'

Elizabeth's eyes lit up like torches. 'Thank you!' she said. 'Thank you so much!' The relief on her face was palpable, and Hugo couldn't help but smile.

'But there is one condition,' he added insistently.

She looked wary for a moment. 'What is it?'

'Let me buy you a proper lunch first. You look like you could do with one.'

• CHAPTER 23 •

They headed east from Trafalgar Square and made the short walk to Charing Cross. Right next to the station was the Ship and Shovell public house. They entered, and Elizabeth made straight for the ladies' room to freshen up. She removed the beanie, scratched her scalp and used her fingers as a makeshift comb to untangle the knots in her hair. Just a couple of nights on London's streets had left her feeling a decade older, a sensation not gainsaid by the mirror when she caught sight of her reflection.

Upon her return, Hugo felt self-conscious. He wondered what an odd couple they must seem to the other drinkers and diners. Despite freshening up, she looked like she'd just been pulled from a swamp. The contrast with his own change of image was an irony not lost on him. He surveyed the pub, but no one was paying attention.

Looking around, his eyes were met with copious amounts of oak. Oak panelling on the walls, oak booths, and oak flooring. Even the bar was made of oak, with an oak pillar rising from one end.

Elizabeth felt peculiar as she watched him order a couple of burgers and two soft drinks. This young man, little more than a boy, had a bewildering effect on her. She felt warm and safe in his presence, yet couldn't put her finger on why. There was something about him that made her feel strangely at ease. To her surprise, she was the one who initiated a conversation.

'Which uni are you at?' she asked as a waitress placed the food in front of them.

'Oxford,' he replied, fiddling with his paper napkin and laying it on his lap. 'I'm back in London for the weekend. Which reminds me, I ought to tell my father at some point.'

'He doesn't know you're back?'

'He can be a difficult man.'

Hugo left it at that and took a sip of his drink. Elizabeth looked puzzled but didn't pursue things. She had a far more pressing question gnawing away at her. She took a couple of bites of food and then washed them down with a swig of cola. 'That news article,' she began, wiping her mouth with her napkin. 'What did it say?'

Hugo saw her squirm as she asked the question. He could tell she was trying to keep a lid on her emotions.

'It was titled "Mystery Woman Found on Riverbank,"' he explained, cutting to the chase straight away. 'It said you were pulled from a swollen stream and that no one could get you to speak. You had no identification, so nobody knew who you were.' He bit into his burger and started munching. 'There was a picture of your drawing at the top of the article. Your face, too.'

'May I see the article?'

'Sure. Let me look for it.' He pulled his phone from his pocket and typed the headline into Google. It soon came up. 'There,' he said, handing her the phone.

Elizabeth took it and perused the story. She read it, then waved the phone in front of him. 'This is the reason I was on the streets,' she said.

'The article?'

'The *journalist*. He was the reason I started talking.' She picked up a chip and bit it in half before squishing the remnants between her thumb and forefinger.

'You said the doctors invited him in?' probed Hugo.

'Yes. Dr Patel was her name. But the other one—'

'Promised he'd keep it out of the news,' said Hugo, finishing her sentence for her. 'Or so you said in the square.'

'That's right. And yet there's an article right here on your phone.' She handed the device back, and he put it away in his pocket. 'Clearly that doctor was lying.'

'I haven't seen any further reports,' said Hugo. 'Maybe he was true to his word but wasn't in time to stop this first one.'

A flicker in her eyes suggested she hadn't thought of that.

'In any case,' he continued. 'how did the journalist's actions result in you being on the streets of London?'

She put the rest of the squashed chip in her mouth and followed it with another sip of cola. 'I discharged myself,' she told him, bemused at how openly she was revealing information.

'Discharged yourself? Why?'

'Because I knew what would happen if I didn't.' She pushed her plate away and leaned in a little. Hugo did likewise, sensing something big was coming. 'They were going to section me,' she explained in a whisper. 'That second doctor – the one who said he'd keep the story out of the news – he wasn't an ordinary hospital doctor. He was a psychiatrist, you see. And he kept asking all these probing questions. I had to get out of there, Hugo. I had to escape, or the hospital would have become my prison. And all because Rupert Swann thought I needed sectioning.'

Hugo's blood froze solid. *What did she just say?*

• CHAPTER 24 •

Satisfied with their lovemaking, Owen collapsed on the bed next to Alice. She had invited him round for a bite to eat before they began a project together. But carnal desires had taken over, and the pair were naked not ten minutes after his arrival.

Owen smiled across at her. 'Did Hugo make you scream like that?'

Alice rebuked him with a frown. 'Leave him alone,' she said, giving him a tap on the hip with the outside of her right hand. 'He wasn't as experienced as you are. I was the first girl he slept with.'

'I don't mean him any disrespect,' said Owen, hoping he hadn't offended her. 'I just never quite knew what you saw in him.' He took a moment to regard her. 'You're way out of his league, surely.'

The compliment didn't stop her from defending Hugo. 'It's not just about looks,' she replied, drawing the duvet down to avoid overheating. 'He's very clever too.'

'Come on,' Owen jested, flashing his teeth and smiling cheekily. 'You're saying you're a sapiosexual now?' His eyes roved south to ogle her body.

Alice enjoyed his gawking and let him look. 'I know we weren't right as a couple, but I'd like to stay friends with him. We're on the same wavelength. I just hope he agrees when he's over the break-up.' She flipped onto her side and rested her head on her elbow. Owen was forced to lift his gaze. 'Does that bother you, Owen?'

'Not at all,' he breezed indifferently.

Owen was speaking the truth: her remarks didn't worry him in the slightest. As far as he was concerned, Hugo didn't cut it as a rival. Their friendship was acceptable to him.

He flashed her one last smile, then got up and headed to the bathroom. Alice remained on the bed and waited for him to return.

• CHAPTER 25 •

Hugo's head became an instant jumble of chaos as Elizabeth's words sunk in. *My father was one of the doctors treating her?* His face flushed and his fingers started to tremble with the adrenaline. The dizziness was almost overpowering.

'Are you okay?' she asked, sensing his incipient nausea.

This time it was Hugo who pushed his plate away. 'Will you excuse me a moment?' He rose to his feet. 'I just need to visit the lavatory.'

He burst through the door and made straight for the sink, placing a hand on either side to prop himself up. His legs were like jelly and could scarcely bear his weight as they trembled. His breathing had become short and shallow. When he looked into the mirror, he saw his quiff had sagged from the accumulation of sweat on his scalp, and perspiration glistened like cooking oil on his forehead. Above his left eye, the eyebrow stud gleamed as the gents' room lights caught the metal and glinted.

He stood still while his thoughts collected, then splashed some water on his face to hasten refreshment. When his breathing normalised, he produced his phone and found his father's number. With his thumb poised above the 'call' icon, he tried to think of a coherent way to inform the old man he'd discovered Elizabeth.

But more sensible thoughts struck him once his fervour had waned a bit. He knew the medics wouldn't have been in collusion with a journalist, though goodness knew how Buckland had managed the coup.

But why did his father think she needed sectioning? And how had she ended up in that chalk stream? His handle on the story was incomplete and he couldn't involve Swann until he knew the full details. And besides, what could the professor do from so far away? Hugo could hardly ring him to claim he'd found Elizabeth only to say he'd immediately sent her packing to some undisclosed location in Kent.

No, a phone call now was not the answer, so he pulled his thumb away from the 'call' icon and put his device away.

'Is everything okay?' Elizabeth asked when he returned.

'I just felt sick all of a sudden. I'm feeling better now, though.' He noticed she'd emptied her plate in his absence. 'How was the food?'

'Put it this way: I'm no longer feeling hungry.'

'I'm glad you enjoyed the meal,' he said. 'But now you'll want to be getting back home. If I'm not mistaken, I promised I'd pay for your ticket.'

Her smile was one of gratitude. 'I really can't thank you enough,' she gushed. 'All I want now is a shower and my own bed to sleep in. From the bottom of my heart, thank you.'

'Don't worry,' grinned Hugo. 'You'll have plenty of time to thank me.'

'How so?'

'Because I'm coming with you to Kent.'

## CHAPTER 26

It was late afternoon when they arrived at Tunbridge Wells station. Hugo had been reluctant to spend any more student finances on a taxi, so they'd spent more than two hours walking to Elizabeth's abode.

Conditions had changed on the walk. The clouds had lifted to reveal the starry heavens in all their naked splendour, and a torch-like full moon shone down as if suspended on an invisible cosmic thread, just out of arm's reach. The cottage was a welcome sight as a silent frost descended on the landscape.

Elizabeth reached for her house key but was met with an empty pocket. She'd forgotten she'd left her home unlocked and hoped to God that no one had ransacked the place. They hadn't. The cottage's seclusion had protected it from burglars and squatters in the time she'd spent in hospital.

She opened the door to see a great pile of posts lying on the mat. Turning on the lights and stepping inside, she saw her key lying precisely where she'd left it. Suddenly, an overwhelming sense of gratitude flooded her. It was the same feeling she'd experienced in St-Martin-in-the-Fields.

They stepped through the door and closed it behind them. Elizabeth turned on the heating while Hugo walked through and stood at the living room window.

Elizabeth drew up next to him. 'It's a beautiful view across the Weald,' she said. 'But you'll have to wait until morning to see it properly.'

He squinted, but could only make out a few moonlit silhouettes in the blackness beyond the glass. *Roll on morning in that case.*

Hugo turned and surveyed the living room. It looked tired and dated. The furniture hadn't been replaced in years. There was an old two-seater sofa with a thin-legged, glass-topped coffee table in front of it. Adjacent, a brown leather armchair had seen better days, and the old-fashioned carpet was incongruous rather than quaint. But worst of all was an out of character 1970s fireplace. At least the room was clean and tidy.

'Have you always lived here?' he asked.

'No. I moved with my parents as a teenager and inherited the cottage when they died.'

He immediately felt awkward, and Elizabeth sensed it. 'Let's grab a seat on the sofa,' she said.

The furniture groaned as they sat down. The fabric was stone cold having spent weeks in an unheated room. Neither of them removed their coat as Elizabeth elucidated the details concerning her parents' deaths. 'They both went within a year of each other. Dad first with prostate cancer. He'd been ill for some time, so it wasn't unexpected. But when mum had a massive stroke just eleven months later, it was an enormous shock.'

Her tale resonated with Hugo's own experience, and he listened sympathetically. 'I'm so sorry to hear that,' he said. 'I lost my mother recently. My father's still not over it. I doubt he ever will be, fully.'

Elizabeth felt his sorrow. 'What does your father do?' she asked.

'He's a...'

That was a close call. He'd very nearly said 'psychiatrist'. For a moment, he'd forgotten the connection between his father and Elizabeth. A slip of the tongue there could have been disastrous. 'He's an NHS worker,' Hugo told her before quickly steering the conversation away from Swann. 'Your parents couldn't have been that old?'

'Actually, they were in their forties when they had me,' she said, taking off her gloves and placing them on the coffee table. She did the same with her beanie and ran her fingers through her hair. 'They were only in their sixties when they died. I was their only child.'

Hugo nodded but said nothing. The atmosphere had become melancholy.

'So,' said Elizabeth, slapping her thighs to change the subject. 'How about a glass of wine?'

The suggestion recalibrated things, and Hugo smiled approvingly.

'There's always alcohol in the house,' she said. 'Wait here. I'll be right back.'

She returned with a bottle of white wine and two glasses. The glug of pouring liquid helped restore a natural equilibrium, and Hugo leant back after taking his first sip. 'Okay,' he began, 'what is it you actually…do?'

'You mean for a job?'

'Yeah.'

'These days not a great deal,' she answered, taking a mouthful and leaning back herself. 'I used to work in a nursery looking after the children but gave that up after my parents died. There's no mortgage on the cottage, and I inherited a reasonable sum from the will.' She rotated her glass in her hand a couple of times. 'Now I just do a bit of seasonal fruit picking.'

'Fruit picking?'

'Helping out with the Poles and Romanians. Surely you know Kent is the Garden of England, Hugo?' She tittered, and Hugo twinkled back at her. 'The work keeps me occupied and provides some extra income.'

'What about when you're not working?' he pried. 'What do you like doing the rest of the time?'

She put her wine on the coffee table and looked straight at him. 'You really have to ask me that question?' she said, feigning incredulity.

'Of course!' Hugo slapped his forehead. 'Your *artwork!*'

'It's my only real hobby,' she said.

He thought back to the meadow he'd seen on the news app. If that was the result of twenty minutes at the hospital, he was fascinated to know what her proper paintings were like. 'May I see your work?' he asked.

She hesitated. 'Really? You want to see them?'

Hugo nodded. 'I'd love to,' he assured her. 'I've already told you how much I love art. Remind me where I was going when I bumped into you...'

'The National Gallery,' she remembered. His genuine interest delighted her. 'Wait here,' she said. 'I have a couple upstairs.'

She returned and placed two canvasses face down on the floor. She'd only been gone for a moment, and the paintings weren't the only things she'd brought back down with her. Hugo winced when she deposited the other items on the coffee table.

'You don't partake?' she asked, sensing his reluctance. 'I thought you were a student.'

'I partook once,' he admitted. 'Quite recently at a party. It didn't have a happy ending.'

She guffawed at his inexperience. 'Consider this an opportunity for redemption,' she joked.

'Go on then. Skin up.'

Hugo was a displeased spectator as her fingers assembled a neat little spliff. The casual way she approached recreational drug use worried him. At her age, she was hardly an experimenting fresher, and he wondered how habitual her consumption was given the drug's deleterious effects on mental health.

She sparked up and drew deeply before turning the first of her canvases over to reveal a Kentish oasthouse. The second was an autumn orchard at harvest time.

'These are brilliant,' he marvelled, taking the spliff when she offered it. 'Do you make any money from them?'

'I paint for pleasure rather than profit,' she said. 'But a few of the local cafés and shops have bought from me.'

'You're a professional artist, then.' It was a compliment rather than hyperbole.

'No,' she replied bashfully. 'But I'd love to open my own gallery or studio one day.'

'I think you should. You could start your own little business.'

He took his first drag without coughing, and his high came on a zephyr of delight. After another toke, he passed it back, keen to avoid collapsing in a stupor and disgracing himself for a second time.

Soon their sobriety buckled under the pressure of wine and weed. They continued talking, but sleep began to beckon as the fog of intoxication grew thick. Elizabeth flagged first, her ordeal on London's streets catching up with her. Hugo, too, was ready before long.

The cottage had two bedrooms, and Hugo was shown to the second. Elizabeth found him some fresh bedding, then retired to her own chamber for a night's rest.

Elizabeth lay still on her back, body exhausted, thoughts electric. In October, she'd tried to escape the prison of her past, that lesser hell on earth. She'd been unsuccessful, and the chain of events that followed was brought to an end by the young man in the room opposite. He'd been her salvation. She knew so little about him, but his presence in her thoughts was exquisite as she descended into unconsciousness.

Meanwhile, Hugo pondered his surroundings in the spare room. It would have been Elizabeth's own before she'd moved into the bigger master once her parents had died. He'd only known her a day, but already it felt like a lifetime. He was under her spell, and her magic delighted him: each time he closed his eyes, he saw the brilliant blue flash of her own.
He fell asleep, bewitched.

*The property had been refurbished throughout and the roof was fixed following the fire. Perhaps a year had passed since Jim's tragic death, and the girl looked distinctly older now. Hugo tasted her pain as he hovered unseen in the living room – the house seemed so much bigger with one person fewer.*

*Yet amidst this black despair, a ray of hope was forming. Sandra and the girl were huddled over a computer screen, and the mouse clicked audibly as the woman completed the booking. Hugo peered past them and saw the payment screen of a holiday website.*

*'There,' said Sandra. 'All booked. In the summer we'll be in Mallorca. All three of us.'*

'I can't wait,' replied the girl, her exuberance delighting Hugo. At last, they had something to look forward to. Something real – not just a quixotic pipedream.

But one thing puzzled him. What did Sandra mean when she said 'all three of us'? Surely she hadn't remarried or begun a relationship so soon after her husband's passing? And clearly, she wasn't referring to Hugo, who remained as shadowed as ever.

He received his answer immediately.

'Shall we phone your uncle and tell him?' asked Sandra, waving the landline handset in the air. Her daughter grabbed it eagerly.

Hugo listened as the ring tone sounded; before long, a man's voice answered.

'Uncle Pete!' chirped the effervescent girl. 'It's all sorted – we're off to Mallorca in the summer. Are you as excited as we are?'

Her uncle said that he was. 'Remember to pack your sun cream,' Hugo heard him tell her.

The conversation continued briskly, and Sandra's daughter had become so hyper that she struggled to regain the phone from her. When she finally clawed it back, she told Pete how much she was looking forward to seeing him, and how she hoped the holiday would provide some relief following his recent divorce.

She also told her brother to transfer half of the costs by the end of the day. Hugo couldn't help but laugh at that. He could almost feel the sun on his cheeks already.

The morning sunshine woke him and streamed through the window as though it were a summer's day. One glass of wine too many, and he'd forgotten to close the curtains last night. He opened his eyes and squinted at the brightness.

As he came to, the dream remained vivid – as if he'd lived every instance for real. But the terror of his earlier experiences was gone. All he felt now was contentment and hope. He rubbed his eyes and looked through the window. The sky was clear, and ground frost glittered like the Milky Way. His first view across the Weald was breathtaking.

A knock at the door startled him. 'Just a second,' he said, fumbling for his T-shirt. 'Okay, I'm ready.'

Elizabeth walked in wearing a dressing gown. 'Sleep well?'

'Very well,' he said. 'It's certainly a comfy mattress.'

She glanced out of the window and gestured through it. 'I told you it was a beautiful sight in the mornings.'

'A delight to wake up to,' he concurred.

She spent a moment gazing across the rolling fields, then placed her hands on her hips and turned her blue eyes on his. 'Come with me into my room,' she said. 'I want to show you a view that's even better.'

Hugo's pulse quickened, and he began to panic. It was too early in the morning to be propositioned like this! He couldn't help but notice how short her dressing gown was as she turned and exited his room. Nervously, he followed her across the landing.

'Now that *is* a view,' he remarked in relief as Elizabeth's meaning transpired.

Above her bed, resplendent in a timber frame, was a painting. He recognised the meadow immediately. It was painted from the same angle he'd seen on the news app. But this was no twenty-minute sketch. This was a masterpiece – bursting with effulgent colour and brimming with lifelike tones and contours.

'My place of solace,' she said. 'You can almost see it from the room you slept in. It took me weeks to complete it.'

'It's stunning,' he marvelled. 'Simply stunning.'

'Thank you,' said Elizabeth. 'After breakfast, I'll take you there.'

• CHAPTER 27 •

University students are not known for making early starts, especially on Saturday mornings. But the Radcliffe Science Library, on South Parks Road, Oxford, was already quite busy when Alice and Owen arrived having made the short walk up from Wadham. By mid-morning, the early frost had lifted, but the weight of an impending deadline still clung as they wrestled with an assignment on the psychology of dreams.

Both tapped away at their laptops as they worked in the bowels of the building, which forms part of Oxford University's Bodleian Libraries. On the table in front of them were several print resources on oneirology – the scientific study of dreams – sourced from the Psychology section of the library.

'I think I've distilled the main points,' said Owen, looking up from one of the books. 'But it would help if they used plain English.' He caught her gaze and smiled playfully. 'These texts are so unnecessarily sesquipedalian.'

Alice rolled her eyes. 'I can't believe you just used that word,' she groaned. *'Unnecessarily,'* she added with a joke of her own. She giggled and shook her head at him.

'"Unnecessarily" is a perfectly ordinary word,' he teased her.

'Oh my God, you're so unfunny, Owen! You know I meant sesquipedalian.'

'It's an ironic word, though, don't you think? When you realise what it means.'

''Spose so,' she said. 'But let's not get side-tracked. Tell me what you've found out so far.'

Owen turned his attention back to the matter at hand. 'I've got a bit of background info,' he began. 'Apparently, Eugene Aserinsky discovered REM in the 1950s...'

He broke off as a different snippet caught his eye. 'But how about this for an interesting aside? It says here that the average person will spend around six years of their life dreaming.' He looked up at her. *'Six years,* Alice.'

'Get back to the salient points, will you!'

'Sorry. Where was I? Ah yes. Most dreams last between five and twenty minutes. During REM, a condition called REM atonia occurs.'

'Meaning?'

'That certain motor neurons are stopped from working when the condition is active, which prevents people from acting out their dreams with dangerous body movements while they're sleeping.' Owen grinned at her. 'Well, I guess you wouldn't want to be next to someone who's dreaming they're in a boxing match.' He waited for a giggle, but none was forthcoming.

Alice was already familiar with REM, or rapid eye movement, and knew it was the period in sleep when dreaming takes place. Only that morning she'd woken to see Owen's eyes fluttering speedily beneath their lids. She remembered wondering what he'd been dreaming about. Had *she* been the subject of his slumbering visions?

As her daydream deepened, she thought of Hugo. She'd observed the same thing with him – eyes fluttering under closed lids while she cogitated on his possible visions. The thought made her pensive, and she wondered what he was doing right now. *Probably still in bed at Oriel.*

She made a mental note to WhatsApp him. It had been a couple of days since their split, and she wanted to make sure he was okay. Hopefully, he'd been granted some respite from the bad dreams he'd been having.

She paused and cast her mind back to his very first nightmare. It had been at Professor Swann's that time she and Hugo had visited him in Ealing. She recalled how serene he'd looked in the depths of his dream, how still he'd been before he'd started to wake in terror. No doubt REM atonia was responsible for that, but she distinctly remembered the stillness extending to his eyes. They had not been fluttering in a tell-tale sign of dreaming. Instead, they'd been as still as stones beneath their fleshy lids.

'Are you still with us?' mocked Owen, clicking his fingers to snap her out of her reverie.

She blinked herself back into the here and now, then looked across at him. 'Is it possible to experience a dream outside of REM?' she asked, giving nothing away of her real thoughts.

'Apparently so.' He glanced again at the text. 'But unless you're woken during REM, you're very unlikely to remember anything.'

*Then how come Hugo remembers everything perfectly?*

She grabbed the book and looked for herself. It confirmed that while most dreams occur during REM, they can take place in other stages in the sleep cycle. Such dreams, however, always lack the intensity of those experienced in REM.

*That doesn't apply to Hugo either – his dreams are always intense.*

Those two things cemented it for Alice: something strange was going on. The intensity of Hugo's dreams had been a key feature, and so was the way they stayed with him after he'd woken. Were they even dreams at all? Could there be another explanation? *When the dust has settled on the break-up, I should give him a call rather than WhatsApp him.*

Knowing the assignment was due soon, Alice put her thoughts of Hugo to one side and concentrated. She opened another tab on her laptop and began making fastidious notes from an online article.

'Any good nuggets?' enquired Owen.

'There's a section here called Dreaming Disorders.'

Owen nearly joked that 'Dreaming Disorders' was a good name for a band, but he refrained from doing so. 'What does it say?' he asked instead.

'Apparently, not all dreams are created equal,' replied Alice. 'There are, in fact, different types.'

'Go on.'

'Well, there's something called authentic dreaming, when the sleeping person's memories and experiences are brought to bear in the dream.'

'I've just read about that in *my* book,' he said. 'What else have you got?'

'Illusory dreaming,' she replied. 'Come across anything on that yet?'

'Nope. Enlighten me,'

'It's when bizarre episodes play out as old memories experience an accumulation of errors. Here's the interesting bit, though…'

He nodded for her to continue.

'It seems there's a parallel between the qualities of illusory dreaming and the symptoms suffered by those with certain mental disorders.'

'Such as?'

'The delusions of schizophrenics.'

'And there's your dissertation title right there.'

Owen meant it as a joke, but Alice didn't discount the idea. Keeping her thoughts on track, she made a note of the article and bookmarked it.

• CHAPTER 28 •

Sunlight streamed through the trees as they trudged. As they walked the narrow path towards the meadow, remnant frost was melting on the branches. Thick drops of water fell from above, striking the ground and their skin as they paced. The vegetation that lined the route was dying back, and moisture from half-rotted nettles and grasses dampened their trousers, chilling their shins with every step. Two abreast travel was impossible, so Hugo followed single file.

They ducked a low branch and advanced a few more paces before the vista widened. Elizabeth stopped and waited for him.

'This is gorgeous,' said Hugo, drawing level with her.

'You should see it in early summer,' she replied. 'Come on. Let's go for a wander.'

They ambled across the undulating landscape, the summer wildflowers a distant memory now. Instead, a million seed heads popped periscope-like from the grassy banks, their presence a guarantee of next year's blooms. Hugo heard a blackbird call and saw it swoop from a dense thicket to his left. Elizabeth was right; this place was paradise.

She led him deeper into the meadow, past her favourite oak tree and down to the little chalk stream, its waters glinting in the low autumn sunshine. A heron stood motionless on the opposite bank, body primed and ready to strike as it looked for movement beneath the shallow glides.

They'd walked a few yards downstream when Elizabeth suddenly halted and looked out across the water. 'Here we are,' she said. 'This is the spot.'

Her voice was grave, and Hugo understood immediately. 'So *this* is where you fell in,' he said.

The water ran clear and shallow. To Hugo, it seemed serene, and Elizabeth sensed his dubiety. 'It didn't look like this in October,' she assured him. 'It had swollen up after a full day's rain.'

'I remember that storm,' he said. *Poor Alice got soaked when she rushed from my room to her tutorial.* 'You had it worse down this way, though. Why on earth were you here in conditions like that?'

She considered his question and mulled it over. 'Let's take a wander down to those willows,' she eventually decided. 'We'll be able to sit down and have a proper chat there.'

Three mature willows protruded from the bank a little farther downstream, their curved trunks jutting flat across the water before rising sharply into the air. They sat down on one of the trunks, so close to each other their clothing touched.

Elizabeth sighed. 'I fell in while drunk,' she admitted, her eyes glued to the water. 'That was how I ended up in the stream.'

'It was an accident then?'

'Yes and no. I'd been waiting for a break in the weather and had consumed a lot of vodka.' Wishing to confide, she turned and met his eye. 'I came back with a couple of packs of pills to take over there by that oak tree.' She gestured to it, and Hugo's eyes followed. 'But before I could take them I'd slipped and toppled in.'

Hugo was stunned. *No wonder Dad thought she was a danger to herself.* 'But why?' he asked, choosing his words with sensitivity. 'Why attempt suicide?'

Disclosing the attempt was one thing; expounding the reasons was quite another, so she hooked her eyes to the far bank and shut up shop. 'Just "things", Hugo. Things from my past.'

'I understand,' he said, placing a reassuring hand on her shoulder. 'There's no need to rush. You can tell me when you feel ready.'

His caring presence soothed her like a silken blanket. When she turned to engage him again, her blue eyes harmonised with the sky above. They were so close they could feel each other's hot breath – like miniature oven doors opened wide in the cool meadow air. At first, their lips met tentatively, then with increasing confidence and vigour as their passions began to stir.

As they kissed, Hugo placed his hand against her cheek. Elizabeth responded by wrapping her arms around his neck and back, shuffling along the trunk so their bodies were even closer.

He removed his hand and slid it towards her hip, feathering the side of her body on the way down. Fire now roared as he kissed Elizabeth's neck. She shuddered, and Hugo's flames were stoked, his passions rising to bursting point. Again, his hand went roving – this time beneath her clothes. Elizabeth moaned when it made contact with her breast and squeezed it.

She slid from the trunk and positioned herself in front of him. Hugo tilted his head to the sky and watched a magpie traverse his vision. When it disappeared from view, he closed his eyes and gripped the trunk as Elizabeth kissed him passionately.

Their desires were unstoppable as they grabbed each other's clothes and tore them. Hugo heard the fabric rip as Elizabeth's leggings were hoisted south. She bent forward, draping herself over the trunk as Hugo moved behind her. When their bodies united in blissful lovemaking, Elizabeth moaned in rapture.

Buckled up, they perched on the trunk in silence, each trying to make sense of the erotic connection they felt for one another. Before long, Elizabeth stifled a giggle.

'What is it?' he asked.

'Don't worry,' Elizabeth said. 'I was just thinking that your tour of the meadow ended with a bit more than you bargained for.'

Hugo tittered. 'I do love a free gift when I make a purchase.' Both of them chortled for a moment.

They got up and kissed again before moving off. Hand in hand, they departed the meadow.

'Sorry about the tear in your trousers,' he said as they wandered back to Elizabeth's cottage.

Hugo sat on her sofa and waited. When Elizabeth returned from the kitchen, she had a cup of coffee in each hand. She smiled as she came back through, then set them down on the coffee table. 'You'll need the caffeine for the journey,' she said, plonking herself beside him. 'Oxford or London?'

It was afternoon now, and his impromptu visit to Kent had stolen nearly half the weekend. If he wasn't in Ealing by evening, there'd be little point in going at all.

'London,' he replied.

Hugo sounded ruminative. Things were playing on his mind. He'd see his father later that evening, but after what he and Elizabeth had shared at the meadow, he somehow felt duplicitous — was withholding the truth the same thing as lying? His conscience prompted him, and he had to level with her.

'Is something the matter?' she asked, seeing how pensive he was.

'Elizabeth,' he began, too ashamed to meet her gaze. 'You opened your heart to me at the meadow. It must have taken great courage to confide in someone you'd only just met.'

She shrugged.

'Well,' he continued. 'Now I'm the one with a confession to make.' He took a deep breath and blew, then forced himself to look at her. 'This…is a little awkward,' he said.

She looked worried. 'You're in a relationship?'

'Nooooo,' he confirmed. 'Goodness, no. I was, but I'm not anymore. It's over. Definitely over. Quite recently, but it's finished.' He'd started to procrastinate. 'Sorry,' he said. 'I'm just jabbering now.'

'Tell me what's going on, Hugo.'

Her stare exacerbated his discomfiture, and he coughed to clear his throat. 'Meeting you on the steps of the National Gallery was a one-in-a-million chance,' he explained. 'Would you agree with that?'

'Yes,' she nodded. 'But something tells me that isn't your point.'

'It isn't. There's something else, you're right. You see, one in a million became one in a billion after what you said to me in that pub.' He linked his fingers together and began twiddling his thumbs. Elizabeth saw that his knee had started to bounce up and down with the nerves. 'Remind me of the doctors' names,' he said. 'The ones who'd been treating you.'

'Nina Patel and Rupert Swann.' She folded her arms in protest. 'Where's this going, Hugo?'

Sweat began to accumulate on his palms and under his arms. He coughed again to steady his voice, which he knew had started to shake. 'Elizabeth,' he said timorously. 'Rupert Swann is my father.'

His eyes had closed as those words came out. When he opened them, Elizabeth's face was expressionless. 'Please say something,' he implored her.

Still no words. Just a stern look in those blue eyes of hers.

'Why would you say something like that?' she eventually muttered, thinking his admission was a poor attempt at humour.

'Elizabeth, please.' He sounded jaded now. 'My name is Hugo Swann.'

He reached into his pocket, fished out his wallet and fumbled for his university card. Elizabeth snatched it and looked. A passport-sized photograph of Hugo on the right was accompanied by text on the left that read:

**UNIVERSITY OF OXFORD**
**Hugo Swann**
**Undergraduate reading for BA English**
**English Faculty**
**Oriel College**

She was dumbstruck, scarcely able to believe it. 'You *bastard!*' she spat, throwing the card back at him. 'You *EVIL BASTARD!*'

'Elizabeth...'

'This is a cruel trick, isn't it!' There were tears in her eyes, and the pitch of her voice had risen. She was becoming hysterical. 'Swann knew where I was all along, didn't he! *DIDN'T HE, HUGO?* He sent you along to befriend me! You knew I was in Trafalgar Square!'

He raised his hands to calm her down. 'Please, Elizabeth, it's not like that.'

'*Liar!*' she screamed.

Hugo started to panic and regretted speaking up. It was too late to take things back now, though. 'It was all a coincidence,' he tried to assure her. 'I promise it was. An extraordinary coincidence.'

'That's *bullshit!*' She stood from the sofa and turned her back on him. Hugo watched from behind as she raised her right hand to her mouth 'I'd even started to trust you,' she sobbed. Her emotions were uncontrollable and her speech had started to stutter. 'How could you be so uncaring?' she wailed. 'You're nothing but a...*heartless bastard!*'

Hugo felt terrible. He got up and moved towards her, ready to place his hands on her shoulders. She heard him coming and turned around. '*Don't* come near me!' she ordered him. 'Your plan worked out just perfectly, didn't it!'

'There wasn't a plan,' he insisted.

'Swann's going to know my address. You going to tell him it, aren't you? How long before he's down here with a team of quacks?'

Hugo tried to approach her again. 'He doesn't even know we've met.' He kept his voice as gentle as possible.

'*GET OUT!*' she screamed, raising her hands to stop his advance. 'Get out of my house, Hugo. *Get out – and don't EVER come back here. YOU'RE A TOTAL FUCKING BASTARD!*'

Hugo departed her house in silence.

• CHAPTER 29 •

Darkness hung in Hugo's heart as he travelled up to London that afternoon. He hadn't betrayed Elizabeth, but he felt duplicitous anyway. He should never have revealed the truth. The woman was ill – so unwell that his father had wanted to section her. Of course, she wouldn't be thinking rationally. *Stupid, stupid idiot! If only I had my time again!*

The guilt was overpowering. She'd trusted him enough to disclose a suicide attempt, and they had shared intimate relations moments later. Now she thought he'd betrayed her, and heaven only knew what might happen next. *Please, God, don't let her do anything fatalistic.*

He couldn't even text her – she'd expelled him before they'd had a chance to swap numbers. His powerlessness was torture; all he could do was try to expunge her from his thoughts. It would be easier said than done, though.

By the time he arrived in Ealing, it was long since dark. He'd messaged his father while still on the train, and the old man opened the door with a tut.

'That stud will leave a scar,' said Swann.

'No problem,' replied Hugo. 'I intend to leave it in.'

He entered the house and took off his shoes in the hallway.

Swann's face was full of derision, and he stood with his arms folded. 'You'll have to take it out to appear credible in the courtroom,' he said.

'In the classroom,' Hugo corrected him. 'But that's a long way off yet.'

Swann sighed contemptuously. 'You've clearly still got some maturing to do, Hugo. Still some...*fads*...to get over.'

'And three full years to do so.' Hugo's surliness was unusual, and Swann shook his head reproachfully.

Hugo wandered through to the living room and sat on the sofa. His father followed and reclined in his armchair, the remnants of a whisky on the table next to him.

'So what brings you back then, Son? Cabin fever in Oxford, is it?'

So much had happened in the last couple of days that Hugo's reason for coming back seemed inconsequential. It also felt like half a lifetime ago.

'Alice and I have split up,' he said. 'I thought a change of scene would help me get my head together.'

'Oh, dear. Got bored of you already, has she?' Swann meant it as a joke to lighten the atmosphere but Hugo wasn't surprised at his lack of empathy. He avoided tutting by looking at the patterns cast by the light fitting. They succeeded in softening his mood.

'She's a lovely girl, but we just weren't right for each other.'

Swann picked up his glass and downed the dregs of his whisky. 'Well,' he began, 'there are twenty-four-thousand students at Oxford, and more than half of them are women. You'll be all right, Son.' It was a genuine attempt at sympathy, and Hugo smiled at its failure.

The old man crossed his legs and pointed at his empty glass. 'Can I offer you a whisky to help drown your sorrows?'

'Thanks, Dad. But I have an essay to write. If I'm not careful, Chaucer's going to be overdue.' He felt foolish having brought nothing with him. 'Can I use your laptop?' he asked sheepishly.

Swann rolled his eyes. 'Sure,' he said. 'But make sure you come prepared next time. I didn't buy you that MacBook to use as a paperweight.'

Hugo squirrelled himself away in the box room where there were fewer distractions. Still, it was hard to concentrate. Elizabeth preoccupied his thoughts, and Chaucer played second fiddle in his mind. By bedtime, he had precious little to show for his efforts and certainly nothing he could hand to his tutor without considerable embarrassment.

In the end, he gave up and retired to bed. Still ravaged with guilt after what had happened in Kent, he drifted into a disconsolate slumber.

*The hotel pool was busy. Sunshine shone, and palm trees swayed lethargically, their feathered branches rustling like shredded paper on a zephyr. Children's squeals filled the air as exuberant families played in the depths, inflatables bobbing on the surface like flotsam in the ocean. The Spanish glare was fierce, and sunlight reflected in the waves, wobbling the pool into a giant plasma ball as bodies splashed within and feet pitter-pattered on the tiled deck above.*

*It was the first full day in Mallorca, and the family were full of zest as they joined the morning throng. Sandra and the girl entered at the shallow end, but Pete lay on a lounger and slapped some sun cream on.*

*Sheltered in the background, a sense of déjà-vu struck Hugo. Watching the girl frolic transported him back to the suburban garden and that time by the paddling pool. Its juxtaposition with the present moment delivered a symmetry that vexed him. Back then, her joy was followed by the subsequent death of her father. He recalled the sudden fear he'd felt on that summer's day by the paddling pool. Now it was a swimming pool he beheld her in, and the feeling of dread was back. Was history about to repeat itself in some way?*

*Perhaps two years had passed since that first encounter, and the girl had changed physically. In the garden, she'd been about ten; now, she was twelve or thirteen. Taller and fuller in the face, she was growing up fast.*

*Sandra waded half the width of the shallow end, then sat on the bottom and leaned her back against the wall. Water lapped her chin as she tilted her head and relaxed, her hair gently* swaying as it floated and fanned from her scalp. In contrast, her daughter was a bundle of energy and splish-splashed her way to the deep end like a puppy in a puddle. Hugo watched from the poolside as she swam off by herself.

'Mum,' she squawked across the water. 'Do you think I can do a whole length without coming up?'

Sandra observed the distance between them and looked doubtful. 'Underwater? Not a chance!'

'You'll see,' her daughter boasted. 'Just you watch me!'

Full of confidence, the girl kicked off, keen to display her prowess. Barely half a length later, she surfaced for air, proud as punch 'til she saw how little she'd accomplished. Her change of expression was a comedic treasure when she realised how short she'd come up.

'Never mind!' laughed Sandra. 'Why don't you have another go?'

Hugo smiled too. The girl definitely needed practice.

Her pride wounded, she flipped around and headed back for a second attempt. She took a deep breath and was off again, arms pulling, legs kicking, determined to make a better fist of it. Sandra submerged her head as her daughter travelled towards her, closing her eyes and stealing a moment's peace at the shallow end. They resurfaced simultaneously and the result was clear to see. Two-thirds of a length this time – failed again.

Red-faced and gasping, the girl began to splutter. Sandra tried to calm things down. 'Be careful,' she said reprovingly. 'Catch your breath properly first.'

'I'm okay,' her daughter insisted, taking her mother's words with a pinch of salt. 'I just want one last go.'

In a flash, she was back at the deep end and ready for a final attempt. She gulped some air, then kicked off hard, gliding towards her mother like a living submarine. Again, Sandra submerged her head and waited.

At the poolside Hugo was rooting for her. She was under for longer this time, and for a moment, he thought she'd make it. Kicking and pulling, she cut through the water until forced up for oxygen. When her head broke the surface, she spluttered and gasped, eyes screwed shut and stinging with chlorine. She stood on the bottom, rubbed her eyes and blinked them open to see how near she'd come.

So close! Sandra was just ten feet away, but her head remained underwater. The girl blinked again to focus.

Something was wrong. Very wrong.

Hugo sensed it too and tried to shout for help. He bellowed hard, but no sound came out, his ethereal presence stifling his voice. All he could do was watch as Sandra kicked her legs and waved her arms in panic. She was trying to surface but had become stuck underwater.

The girl waded towards her, water resistance slowing her progress frustratingly. 'Mum,' she called, taking hold of a kicking leg and dragging herself those last few feet. 'What's the matter with you?'

When she looked through the water, her mother's features were terror-stricken and pleading for salvation. The girl froze for a moment, then screamed in horror.

'HELP!' she shrieked. 'Someone, please help!' Her cries filled the air, and people turned and looked. 'It's my mum!' she yelped. 'Her head's got stuck!'

Beneath the surface, Sandra was running out of air. Desperate to breathe, panic set in, and her struggling became more frantic. The girl grabbed her head and wrenched. It barely moved at all.

Assistance arrived and congregated at the scene. Those in the pool swam over, including a strong-looking man with a shaven head. Others traversed the pool deck and stood above the woman. Uncle Pete was roused from his sunbed and dashed over quickly. He knelt on the tiles and looked down at his sister, whose face was contorted in agony as she suppressed her breathing reflex. The strong-looking man grabbed her head and yanked as hard as he could. Again, it failed to move, his efforts only adding to the submerged woman's distress.

'My God!' cried Pete when he realised what was wrong. 'Her hair's wrapped round the return jet! That's why her head won't budge!'

A few of the guests turned in horror. For Hugo, the dread was unbearable.

'Does anyone have anything sharp?' yelled Pete. 'A knife? A pair of scissors? Anything?' Some people shook their heads and murmured; others stared blankly.

'Try Reception,' someone shouted, their position lost in the anarchy.

As Pete dashed off, more people wrenched at the poor woman's head, but try as they might, they could not dislodge it – her hair was tangled too tightly. Time was running out, and Sandra screwed her eyes shut as she fought the need to breathe.

The strong-looking man took a deep breath, plunged his head beneath the surface and pressed his lips to hers. The meagre supply of air wasn't enough, and she convulsed in agony. The man took another breath and dived back down to repeat his endeavour.

And then disaster struck.

Desperate for oxygen, Sandra inhaled before their mouths were fully secured. Instead of life-giving air, her lungs were invaded with thick, chlorinated liquid. She spluttered underwater, covering her mouth to suppress her reflex. It didn't work, and another heavy lungful rushed in. Her chest went into spasm, and her body began jerking from a mix of pain and panic.

Hugo could barely watch as streams of bubbles emanated from her crippled lungs and escaped through her nose and mouth. To his left, the sound of rushing feet grew louder. He turned to see Uncle Pete brandishing a knife in one hand and a pair of scissors in the other. Two hotel workers followed as he scampered across the pool deck and jumped straight in, barging a young woman out of the way. There was no time for an apology, and Pete began cutting furiously. 'Come on!' he shouted, as the scissors failed to work. They were too blunt for the job and her hair wouldn't cut. He cast them away in frustration, and Hugo watched them sink to the bottom. Precious seconds were wasted.

The knife was the final hope, and Pete began hacking in a frenzy. One or two people cheered as the first few clumps tore *loose. But her hair was wound so tight it was hard to cut cleanly, and the water turned red as the blade nicked her scalp and neck. A deeper gash near her ear began to ooze profusely.*

*Sandra's world was blackening now. Her violent jerks had become mere twitches, and her eyes had opened to a vacant stare. Hugo felt a dread like never before as the bubbles stopped streaming from her mouth and nose.*

*Pete severed the last few strands and pulled his sister's head clear. Above him, the two hotel workers hauled her onto the pool deck. 'She's not breathing!' cried Pete as he clambered out of the water. He crouched at her side and slapped her cheek a few times. 'Wake up,' he begged her. 'Please wake up! Oh God – I don't know what to do!'*

*One of the hotel workers urged him aside and allowed the other to take his place. 'My colleague's a first aider,' she explained in excellent English. 'I've called an ambulance and it's on its way.'*

*The first aider checked Sandra's pulse and airways, then asked the crowd to step back a bit. Pete went white when she started chest compressions, and Hugo, too, felt sick. Real CPR was nothing like what he'd seen in the movies, and some of the guests turned in shock as her ribs began to crack.*

*A few rounds later, Hugo expected Sandra to jerk and cough up water. After all, that was what always happened on TV. But this was for real. There was no film script here – no cinematic effects. The rounds of compressions came and went, yet Sandra remained unresponsive.*

*Distant sirens grew louder the closer they got. An external road ran along the length of the facility, separated from the pool by a thick, evergreen hedge. One of the hotel workers opened a gate at the back, and two paramedics bustled in and took over. They loaded Sandra onto a stretcher and exited the gate, bundling her into the waiting ambulance. Uncle Pete and the girl got in after her.*

*Hugo began to ascend from the nightmare. His dream was shallowing now, but as the ambulance screeched off, there was time for one last scene to play out.*

*He found himself in a Spanish hospital as a white-coated medic spoke to Pete. He was too far away to hear what was said but the body language gave things away. The girl flung her arms around her uncle, turning her head to one side and burying her cheek in his chest. Her deep sobs were uncontrollable.*

*Hugo's heart was crushed at the news of Sandra's drowning. Resuscitation had been impossible – her brain was too starved and her lungs too saturated. The girl to whom he felt so attached had now become an orphan. He thought back to the paddling pool and the subsequent death of Jim. History had indeed repeated itself.*

Hugo awoke and pulled himself clear of the dream. His sheets were so sweat-drenched he could have been lying in the swimming pool himself. He blinked and rubbed his eyes – what he'd seen remained vivid, as though he'd lived the episode for

# DREAMS

real. He didn't feel refreshed, but Sunday morning had arrived, so he tossed his sheets aside and rose to face the day.

• CHAPTER 30 •

Alice had always been a bright girl. As a child, her parents had marvelled at her curiosity, which went beyond the natural inquisitiveness innate in most children. As she'd developed from a child into a teen, this curiosity focused on academic discipline and a genuine desire to find things out. Once bitten by a topic, she would immerse herself in intellectual delight and become lost in the subject matter.

She had been a pupil at her local girls' grammar school in Lincolnshire, and Oxford had been her goal for as long as she could remember. Deep intelligence underpinned her success, and a strong work-ethic added power to her punch. Study was to Alice what hobbies are to other people. At school, her friends would take pleasure in music or sport; for Alice, it was study that gave her those butterflies. Her greedy mind demanded constant intellectual nourishment, and winning a place at Wadham to study Experimental Psychology seemed like the fulfilment of a destiny.

She had completed her assignment on oneirology late the previous evening and had submitted it online to her tutor. Owen was still working on his and had remained in his room to continue through the night.

After the luxury of a single bed to herself, Alice woke refreshed and raring that Sunday, eager to quench her cerebral thirst with a bit of morning study. She cleared a space at her desk, opened her laptop and returned to the article she'd bookmarked in the Radcliffe Science Library. She located the pertinent section on illusory dreaming and adjusted her glasses. Tucking into a couple of slices of toast, she began reading, brushing her curly hair aside as she ate.

The article explored an array of personality disorders, with schizophrenia chief among them. Alice devoured the text like a rabid animal, tearing through the paragraphs and digesting every word. Schizophrenics, she read, often believe their thoughts are controlled by external agencies like aliens or demons, whilst some believe their thoughts are deleted by such beings. The section concluded with the striking assertion that notions of thought insertion and removal were the likely origins of belief in telepathy.

Alice sometimes wished she was telepathic. Life would be so much simpler if she had access to other people's thoughts. *What a shame it's only science fiction.*

Refocusing on the topic, she opened another tab and typed 'illusory dreams schizophrenia psychological' into Google, hoping to find some additional links.

Coincidentally, an article in the search results was actually titled 'Telepathy'. Intrigued, she cast her eyes over the preview, and two of her search terms – 'psychological' and 'schizophrenia' – appeared in bold. The text of the preview read:

<u>Telepathy</u>
...similarities have been noted between telepathy and two **psychological** concepts: delusions of thought insertion/removal and **psychological** symbiosis...thought insertion/removal of the kind experienced by sufferers of **schizophrenia**...Melanie Klein was an early proponent of **psychological**...

Alice clicked on the link to examine the other concept mentioned: psychological symbiosis. It was a phenomenon she hadn't heard of before and, according to the article, was not well established in academic circles. It theorised that infant children could not distinguish between their own reality and the experience they have of their mothers. Whilst this psychological symbiosis ends as the child develops, the article said it might be possible to detect elements of it into adulthood.

She made some notes, pleased that her dissertation ideas were beginning to take shape. Nevertheless, her mind began to wander. The pages she'd read on personality disorders and her recent work on dreams returned her thinking to Hugo. She'd promised herself she'd call him, so she found her phone and opened FaceTime.

Hugo answered the call with an awkward greeting.

Alice saw his face and stared. 'Blimey!' she exclaimed. 'What's that above your eye?'

He blushed and touched the stud. 'Oh…' he said, 'I've just had it done.' At least his hair was flat that morning – not gelled into a quiff like Owen's.

'That doesn't look like Oriel in the background.'

'No,' he confirmed. 'I'm back in London for the weekend.'

Hugo was sat at the kitchen table eating breakfast. The room was small but tremendously elegant. Alice remembered it perfectly. Chrome downlights illuminated the expensive-looking floor tiles, and neat black handles adorned the off-white cupboards and drawers. Behind Hugo, the pine worktops and Belfast sink reminded her of when he'd fled up the stairs on the morning after his first dream. She thought back to the moment longingly.

'Just fancied a change of scene?' she asked.

'Pretty much.'

It was a basic answer, and Alice could tell he wasn't going to elaborate further.

'How are the essays going?' she asked. 'Got any on the go at the moment?'

'Chaucer,' he replied, reaching for a banana. 'And it's progressing very slowly.' He removed the skin and stuck half the fruit in his mouth. 'How about you,' he asked.

'I've just submitted one.'

'On what?'

'Dreams.'

Both of them smiled at the irony. 'The technical term is oneirology,' she explained. 'And working on it made me think of you. It was my reason for calling, actually. I know you've been having some nightmares recently, and I wanted to make sure you're okay.'

She removed her oversized glasses and wiped the lenses with her cuff. 'Like I said the other day, I really hope we can stay friends. We might have broken up, but I still care for you.'

'That's very sweet,' he said, finishing his banana and wiping his hand on his jeans. 'And what you said is right – of course, we should stay friends. I'm sorry I hung up on you so abruptly.'

'It was perfectly understandable given the circumstances.'

Repairing their friendship was cathartic for both of them, and Alice pressed on with her reason for ringing. 'So from one friend to another,' she said, 'how are things with the dreams? Any respite?'

Hugo's face grew grave. 'They're getting worse, Alice. I had a terrible one last night.'

Reading those articles made her wonder about the origin of his troubles, and she looked at him sympathetically. 'Why don't you have a word with your dad?' she suggested.

'About what?'

'The cause of your dreams. Maybe there's a medical explanation. You said yourself how strange they are compared to normal ones.'

Hugo hadn't thought of that. 'You think there might be a physiological cause?'

'Possibly. Or a psychological one.'

His shoulders sagged, and he cocked his head in disapproval. 'Alice,' he chided her. 'I'm not going crazy if that's what you think!'

'No, no, that's not what I mean at all!' She tried to row back from the suggestion. Perhaps dangling the carrot of illusory dreams and schizophrenic tendencies wasn't such a good idea over FaceTime. 'I don't think you're going crazy,' she said. 'I just wondered if things were stress-related, that's all.'

'I'm perfectly well, Alice.'

'Of course, you are,' she agreed, looking to dig herself out of the hole she'd created.

There was a clunking noise off camera – someone had opened the kitchen door and walked in.

'It's not like I'm comparing you to that woman in Kent,' continued Alice. 'You know, the one they found on that riverbank – Elizabeth, was it?'

Hugo went ashen-faced at the comment. 'What did you mention her for?' He'd almost forgotten it was Alice who'd first shown him the article in his room at Oriel.

'To distinguish her case from yours. She really *was* crazy, whereas all you need is—'

'And what makes you the great expert?' interjected a deep and dominant voice. It was Swann himself who'd entered the kitchen. Now he'd hijacked the conversation, too.

'Oh, Professor...' Alice looked like a rabbit in headlights.

'I hear my son's no longer good enough for you.' He leaned over Hugo and looked straight at the camera.

'We…we've split up,' she confirmed. 'But we've decided to stay friends. I was calling to see how he was. He's been having some bad dreams—'

'That's hardly a surprise given your treatment of him!'

Poor Hugo was caught in the middle. It was time to wind things up, so he tilted his phone away from his father. 'Alice,' he said, 'it's been lovely talking to you, and I'm glad we can still remain friends. But I'm fine, honestly. There's nothing for you to worry about.'

'Okay,' she nodded, as keen to get off the phone as he was. 'Just do me a favour and have a think about what I said?'

'I will,' he promised before the screen went black.

Hugo sat quietly at the table while his father helped himself to a cup of coffee and a bowl of cereal. Swann sat down opposite Hugo and looked at him. 'You're still on speaking terms, I see.'

'She's a really nice girl. Things just weren't meant to be between us.'

Swann consumed some cereal and then took a healthy swig of his coffee. Hugo could sense that further words were imminent.

'I'm sorry if I came across brusque,' began Swann. 'It was just a little frustrating to hear her mention the woman from Kent like that. You both saw it on the news, too, I take it?'

'Read about it, actually.' Hugo's cheeks were like chalk. He knew so much more than his father could possibly imagine.

'Well, she was my patient, Hugo. Can you believe that? My bloody patient.'

*I know! She told me so herself!*

He tried to feign surprise. 'Your patient?' he repeated. 'That's incredible, Dad!'

'She was undergoing assessment at the hospital,' said Swann. 'Mike Buckland was there and overheard a conversation I was having with a junior colleague. He ambushed her as soon as I'd left.'

'What on earth was Buckland doing at the hospital?'

'Having his arm seen to.'

'Ah yes,' nodded Hugo. 'The England captain's security man. I hear Buckland's suing for assault.'

'He's a slippery one,' said Swann, taking a sip of his coffee and replacing it on the table with a thud. 'He duped my colleague into letting him take a photo of her meadow picture.'

'That's terrible,' said Hugo.

'The Press Complaints Commission is looking into it,' affirmed Swann. 'The courts are interested, too. Buckland might be pressing charges over his arm, but he's going to be in some hot legal water himself after what he did back there.'

Hugo thought back to the Ship and Shovell, and the moment he'd nearly called his father. Here was his chance to find out what really happened. 'So what's the story, Dad? What happened at the hospital?'

Swann sat back and crossed his legs. 'Buckland said he could help us identify Elizabeth. My colleague hoped a member of the public would get in touch, so she let him take a photo.'

'Of her face?' asked Hugo, dumbfounded.

'Of the picture,' said Swann firmly. 'But she was naïve enough to allow him along the corridor to *look* at her face.'

'And without her noticing, he took the photo,' Hugo deduced. 'No wonder he's being investigated.'

Swann's features unhardened. 'Nina Patel is young and inexperienced,' he said. 'She was trying to help but was deceived by Buckland. He's a wily old fox, and the fault lies squarely with him. I was furious when I saw the initial report but managed to stop any further developments by pulling a few levers with some lawyers I know.'

*So I was right in the Ship and Shovell. You did stop things from going any further.*

'Your colleague must have felt terrible,' said Hugo.

'She did,' replied Swann. 'And so did I. You see, I'm not entirely innocent myself.'

'What do you mean?' Hugo grabbed an apple from the well-stocked fruit bowl on the table. Too nervous to bite, he began rotating it in his hand like a cricket ball.

'Elizabeth was extremely vulnerable and needed to be sectioned for her own safety. Stop doing that, Hugo!'

He put the apple back in the bowl.

'A meeting was arranged, but I jumped the gun and paid her an unofficial visit. After I left, she discharged herself. She must have intuited what was going on.'

*Yep. That's exactly what she told me.*

'How's Dr Patel now?' asked Hugo.

'All the better for being loved up with a young Polish guy. Or so she said on the phone yesterday evening. I was ringing to pass on some news I had.'

'What kind of news?'

Swann took another swig of his coffee and replaced it more gently this time. He uncrossed his legs and leaned in. 'We may have a lead concerning her whereabouts,' he said. 'It's important we follow things up as we still have a duty of care.'

Hugo's trepidation rose and his legs started to shake under the table. Elizabeth would certainly blame him if a group of professionals arrived at her home. *Team of quacks* was the term she'd used.

'What sort of a lead?'

'A member of the public has been in touch...'

Hugo mopped his brow.

'Are you all right, Son?'

'I'm fine,' he lied. 'Who's this member of the public?'

'Says he wants to remain anonymous. But he's given us what he says is her address. If he's telling the truth, we'll be able to finish what we started and offer her the necessary support.'

Hugo nearly descended into a blind panic. He knew precisely how vulnerable Elizabeth was. If they got to her before he did, the consequences didn't bear thinking about. He had to warn her, but there was no way of getting in contact without a phone number. There was only one thing for it – a return to Kent in person.

• CHAPTER 31 •

Hugo left London at dusk, having spent the remaining daylight finishing his Chaucer essay. He'd submitted it online before heading to the station and hoped the tutorial he'd miss on Monday wouldn't be noticed too badly. The journey south was another expense for the impoverished undergraduate, but at least his father had given him twenty pounds to cover the cost of what Hugo had told him was a ticket back to Oxford.

Elizabeth's cottage was hard to find on his own. The last time he'd walked from Tunbridge Wells in the dark, the Kent woman had been at his side. But on this occasion, her sweet voice was a mere echo in his memory, and he took several wrong turns on the way.

He felt vulnerable. Every sound was unsettling in the whispering blackness. A hawthorn shivered and rattled as a startled deer brushed past it, the sound of escaping hooves dissolving into the vast blanket of the night like a fading record. Worst of all were the foxes with their bloodcurdling cries in the distance – he almost jumped out of his skin when one shrieked like the devil from just a few yards away.

It was a relief when he finally stumbled upon the little path that led to her cottage.

*Sanctuary.*

But as he approached, his nerves increased. What sort of welcome would he receive given the manner of Saturday's departure? A light still burned in one of the downstairs rooms, so with butterflies in his belly, he knocked on the door and waited.

Silence – the velvet cloak of night pierced only by the hoot of a tawny owl.

'Elizabeth!' he called, knocking on the door for a second time. 'Elizabeth, it's me, Hugo. Please open up. There's something I need to talk to you about. Something important.'

Feet scurried in the hall and a jingle of keys followed. Hugo's heart thumped as he watched the door swing open. Elizabeth stood before him in a dressing gown, her hair still wet from a shower.

The sight of her face almost shredded his nerves and words got stuck in his larynx. 'I...couldn't...couldn't contact you...' was all he managed to stammer. 'Came on the train to see you...couldn't call.'

He cleared his throat to regain his composure. 'Let me start again,' he begged, 'and please don't close the door on me.' His voice trembled with fear, but at least his words were lucid. 'Not having your number meant I had to come all this way in person,' he explained.

Elizabeth's face remained expressionless, but Hugo persisted anyway. 'In Ealing last night, my father told me something. That's why I came back here. To warn you. All I ask is that you hear me out.'

The silence was transitory but seemed to last an age. 'You'd better come in,' she said cordially. 'You must be freezing out there.'

He breathed a sigh of relief, then followed her in and through to the living room. His glasses steamed up from the instant warmth, and he wiped them clear with his shirt tails. Elizabeth stayed on her feet as Hugo sat on the sofa. 'Glass of wine?' she offered him.

'Thank you.'

'I'm afraid it's only the cheap stuff.'

She returned with two glasses of white, which she placed on the coffee table before sitting adjacent to him. He grabbed one and took a quick glug. Immediately, his stiffness left him.

'As I said,' he began, 'please hear me out before deciding what to do. I'll explain everything in a moment, but first I want you to know something. You see, I really was heading up to the National Gallery when we met. It was a total fluke, I promise. I had no idea—'

'I know,' she interjected, failing to heed his request for a full hearing. Hugo didn't care – he hadn't anticipated this first hurdle being cleared quite so easily.

'You do?'

Elizabeth nodded. 'I owe you an apology,' she said remorsefully. 'Kicking you out the way I did was ridiculous. Once I'd calmed down, I realised how stupid it was.' She gulped some wine and drained nearly half the glass before speaking again. 'I left the hospital without telling anyone where I was going. Even *I* didn't know I'd end up in Trafalgar Square. Of course, it was a coincidence. A one in a million chance, you called it.'

*Or maybe just destiny.*

It certainly felt like fate. Hugo's feelings were far more intense than they were for Alice. The connection he and Elizabeth shared seemed other-worldly – perhaps the gods had ordained their encounter?

'Will you forgive me?' Elizabeth asked quietly.

'There's nothing to forgive,' he said, hoisting his arms aloft to invite a redemptive hug.

She shifted along the sofa and into his soft embrace. Their broken bonds repaired the moment they entwined. It was a restorative moment that went far beyond the tentative truce that might be expected.

'I hope this means we're friends again,' quipped Hugo.

Elizabeth smiled. 'How about we swap numbers?'

'Before you throw me out again?'

They laughed and exchanged their details there and then. Elizabeth put her feet up and rested her head on his shoulder. 'I'm so glad you came back,' she said as she snuggled against his body. 'Sending you off like that was idiotic. I thought I'd blown it completely. The truth is, I've been pining ever since you left.'

'So have I,' he admitted. 'On the train to London. All last night at Dad's. I just couldn't get you out of my head.'

She took hold of his arm and draped it over her shoulder. 'And now we've been given a second chance. Let's not waste it, Hugo.'

'Amen to that,' he said.

Again they hugged, shutting their eyes and pulling each other close in a moment of quiet restitution. When Elizabeth was ready she untangled herself and withdrew to her end of the sofa. 'So,' she said in a business-like tone. 'What's this news you've come with? It must be pretty important to have travelled all this way.'

Hugo's pulse quickened and he sat bolt upright, his nerves returning with a vengeance. He reached for his glass and drank some wine, but the jitters failed to dissipate. 'I was speaking with my father at breakfast,' he informed her. 'We were talking about your case—'

'He knows we've met?'

His discomfort spiked at the question, so he stole another quick sip of wine. 'Goodness, no,' he reassured her. 'We were just talking in the context of the news story.' He thought it best to omit Alice's part in the tale.

Her vexation receded when Hugo told her what he'd discovered about Buckland's craftiness, and how his father had indeed prevented the initial story from going any further. Elizabeth nodded as she took it all in.

But Hugo's apprehension remained and an accumulation of sweat now glistened on his top lip. 'That first report went far and wide,' he continued. 'And that's why I had to come back here. Dad said someone's been in touch with him. Someone who saw it on TV.'

A concerned look now haunted her eyes. Hugo swallowed hard and coughed. 'This member of the public says they know you. I'm afraid they've given...'

His hesitation frustrated her. 'Given what?' she demanded.

'They've given him your address.'

Crestfallen, Elizabeth raised her hand to her mouth. 'Shit,' she said, dropping her head at the news. She got up slowly and wandered to the window. All that gazed back was the infinite black of a melancholy autumn evening.

Her hands were clasped behind her back, and Hugo noticed the middle and index fingers of her right hand wagging back and forth in agitation. 'Elizabeth, please, I'm telling you the truth. My father has your address, but I'm not the source.'

'Don't worry,' she muttered. 'I know exactly who the source is. It's *him*.'

Hugo was thankful to avoid a second dismissal, but her reaction disturbed him nonetheless. 'So there's substance to this claim? You actually know this person?'

Elizabeth sighed audibly. 'This *person*,' she began, her voice strained with emotion, 'is the reason I ended up in hospital.'

She turned around, and Hugo noticed her cheeks were streaked with tears. She wiped them away with her dressing gown sleeve. 'He's the reason I tried to kill myself,' she said.

'Jesus,' said Hugo. 'Who is this man?'

Elizabeth took a deep breath. 'Do you remember back at the meadow? We had a heart-to-heart about why I was there in such atrocious conditions.' Her voice was quavering badly. 'I told you about my suicide plans but didn't go into detail. Do you recall what you said in response?'

Hugo nodded gravely. 'I do,' he said. 'I told you there was no need to rush – that you could tell me whenever you were ready.'

'Well, I'm ready now,' she said before giving her cheeks another wipe. 'Those "things" I told you about – those things from my past – they were all *his* fault.'

Hugo listened on tenterhooks, and the sweat spread across his body. 'What on earth did he do?'

She stalled for a moment, then made the pronouncement.

'He raped me,' she sobbed, jerking uncontrollably as her diaphragm went into spasm.

Hugo didn't know where to look or what to say, but by the time she spoke again, her equanimity had returned. 'Over and over, he raped me,' she continued, her tone more measured now that the initial disclosure had passed. 'I was only a child, yet it went on for months and months. Do you know what effect that has, Hugo? On a little girl!'

He shook his head sheepishly. Words seemed improper in the context of what Elizabeth had just confided. More tears threatened, but another quick wipe stymied the flow.

'Something like that never leaves you,' she said. 'You try to move on with your life, but the memories are always present. It's like you're stuck on a hamster wheel. You run faster and faster to try and escape, but the memories always keep pace.' She took a huge breath and exhaled loudly. Hugo was shocked by how matter-of-fact she'd become. 'When things happen at such a young age, the imprint left is indelible. Think back to your own early teenage years. They weren't so long ago for you – think of the music, the hobbies, the sights and the sounds, the memories of home and school. Are those memories golden for you, Hugo?'

'They are,' he lied. But protestations over his social anxiety and the fraught relationship with his father seemed churlish to point out in the circumstances.

'And we carry those memories with us, don't we?' There was anger in her voice now. Hugo could tell it was pent-up vitriol. 'In essence, those memories *are* us. Well, for me, those memories are of rape. My days are spent trying to forget them, but even the night doesn't bring solace. Sometimes I dream about what happened, and then when I wake…'

She paused and shook her head. 'It might as well have been yesterday,' she lamented. 'The result is depression, Hugo. I drink, and I smoke weed – you might have noticed that – I do it to blot out the past. To escape my memories. But any relief is temporary. Long term, there *is* no escape.' She looked away and snorted before engaging his eyes again. 'And *that's* why I was at the meadow last month.'

'Elizabeth,' he stuttered, still sweating and winded by the gravity of her declaration. 'That's so utterly tragic for you. I don't know what to say.'

'You don't need to say anything,' she assured him. 'I had my counselling in the early years, not that it did much good. Thankfully my parents were a great source of strength. But now they're gone it's just me on my own. It was exactly like I told you – cancer with my dad and a stroke with my mum.'

Hugo felt a tidal wave of empathy. He got up and walked over, his silence conveying more meaning than his words ever could. When they hugged, the front of his shirt moistened as Elizabeth's tears began to stream again.

'I'm so terribly sorry,' he offered, his own eyes dampening as well. 'I can't begin to imagine your suffering.'

'And now he's back,' she sobbed, the sound muffling against his chest. 'Why can't he just leave me alone?'

'You're certain he's the one who got in touch?'

'Who else could it be? And besides, he's done it before.'

Hugo drew away perplexed. 'What do you mean, he's done it before?'

She took a step back, looked him in the eye and told him what had happened. 'After serving his jail term, he tracked me down to this house. I think he used his various contacts and possibly a private investigator.'

Hugo couldn't believe what he was hearing. 'That's just awful!'

'He waited until he knew I was on my own, then knocked on the door and asked to see me. He'd come to beg my forgiveness. Said he'd mended his ways, changed his character. I was all alone in the house – can you imagine how terrified I was?'

He shook his head, shocked. 'What did you do?' he asked incredulously.

'I called the police straight away. They returned him to jail for breach of his parole conditions.'

'No wonder he wants to remain anonymous this time.'

'No wonder.' She headed back in for another hug. It was her way of curtailing any further discussion.

'I understand,' he said, realising how exhausted she was. He knew that further probing would be inappropriate in the present moment, so he rounded things off with a final comment. 'When we spoke at the meadow, I had no idea you were hiding things *this* awful. Thank you for sharing the details.

## CHAPTER 32

In bed next to Elizabeth, Hugo felt like a repugnant parasite. Ordinarily, he was relaxed around her. But not tonight. Not after what she'd disclosed downstairs. His propinquity seemed like a violation – as though he were besmirching her sanctity with his presence in her room. The resultant awkwardness was almost overpowering.

Nakedness would be an affront to decency, so he left his T-shirt and boxers on in a chagrined show of self-flagellation. He lay still on his back, his body stiff and frozen.

'What's the matter?' she complained, disappointed at the lack of affection. 'You seem very distant. Why don't you come and give me a cuddle?'

'I'm sorry,' he replied. 'It just feels a bit…you know…'

'What?'

'Kind of…wrong. In the circumstances.'

She rolled her eyes more in pity than derision. 'Come here and kiss me before we go to sleep,' she demanded.

She gave him a yank and pulled him close. Hugo brushed her hair aside and tucked it behind her ear before kissing her briefly on the lips.

'That's better,' she said. 'You can turn over and go to sleep now.'

Elizabeth also rolled over, and Hugo let his mind unwind as he slid softly into unconsciousness.

*He found himself in the familiar setting of a suburban home, but this abode was different from the one he had seen half destroyed by fire. It was late evening, and although the lights were on, a timid dusk struggled to dislodge the stubborn light of day. It was midsummer, and a dozen months had passed since that ill-fated trip to Mallorca.*

*Pete sat on the sofa with his feet up, the remote control in one hand and a beer in the other. He was watching the cricket highlights on TV following the first day's play of the Second Test. Meanwhile, the girl was curled up on an adjacent armchair, flicking through a book and bored by the cricket.*

*The house belonged to Uncle Pete – the girl had moved in following the terrible loss of her second parent. Her sole surviving relative, the burden of responsibility was on him now. He looked pretty much as Hugo remembered: light brown hair, a medium build and blue-grey eyes. But the indefatigable march of time had worked its magic on the girl. At thirteen, she was becoming a young woman now.*

*The last few years were tragic, but at least she could depend on Pete. The familial support of a cherished uncle could not replace the love of her parents, but it was a better option than foster care. Hugo admired the man for stepping up to the plate.*

*Yet as bedtime approached, her features transmogrified from dead vacancy into base fear – like that of a creature alert to predation. Ready for bed, she prepared to leave, but Pete raised his arm to prevent her.*

*'Give me a kiss goodnight before you go,' said Pete. 'Just a little peck on the cheek.' He displayed the target by pointing to the spot with his index finger.*

*She planted her lips against his cheek and flinched at what happened next. Pete's right hand moved through the air and...*

*Hugo couldn't believe what he saw. It was sexual assault he was witnessing!*

*The girl's face contorted, and she tried to retreat, drawing away with her head bowed. She left the room without saying a word.*

*'I'll be up and with you shortly,' Pete called after her.*

*Hugo's jaw dropped in horror. He looked askance at Pete, who relaxed and finished his beer as if nothing had happened. When he finally rose to head up the stairs, an anxious Hugo followed him.*

*The girl was already in bed. She'd pulled the covers up, and her face was illuminated by the dim light of a lava lamp. Hugo looked into her eyes and saw a frightened animal caught in a trap.*

*Uncle Pete perched on the edge of the bed and attempted to open the cocoon she had fashioned. The dead-eyed girl resisted, a muted 'Noooooo' expressing her disgust.*

*But Pete was not to be thwarted.*

*This was a script the child knew well, having suffered the same fate on previous occasions. She screwed her eyes in abhorrence.*

*Hugo stood enraged at the side. He could barely believe what he was witnessing. His blood boiled, and he stared at Pete in revulsion. He wanted to lash out and strike the abuser, but trapped in his dream, he could neither move nor speak. All he could do was watch as her childhood innocence was violated.*

He sprang bolt upright – as if someone had injected him with a stimulant. His head ached, and his heart raced. The pulse in his neck was throbbing like the pistons of an engine. Instantly alert, he sat rigidly. Moments ago, Uncle Pete had raped his niece in a sickening act of forced incest. Shocked, his thoughts went haywire.

His dream was still vivid. The boundary between this world and the other seemed indistinct – had he even woken at all? Perhaps he was still asleep and trapped in the next scene?

A silvery light provided a hint of illumination and answered things definitively. At first, he thought it was the girl's lava lamp, but all became clear once he'd rubbed his eyes and blinked a few times. Outside the window, a full moon penetrated and sprinkled the room with a soft pewter glow. It was still the early hours. Daybreak was some way off.

He turned and saw Elizabeth sleeping next to him, her face half-lit, half-shadowed in the moonlight. His awakening hadn't stirred her, so quiet as a barn owl, he slid out of bed and tiptoed across the room. She wasn't disturbed by the creaking door, and he breathed a sigh of relief as he snuck through and scurried to the bathroom.

He switched on the light, went to the sink and splashed some water on his face. Next, he looked in the mirror. He didn't bother trying to mould his hair back into a quiff; it was a useless exercise without gel. 'Okay,' he whispered, feeling the weight of his eyebrow stud. 'What the hell is going on here?'

This dream had been different. Until now, they had seemed so independent, so unconnected to his own experiences – as though he were watching a film or a documentary about other people's lives. Yet last night, just before bed, Elizabeth had disclosed her childhood rape, and moments later, he'd dreamt of the girl's molestation.

It couldn't be a coincidence. Elizabeth's revelation had surely left its mark and affected his slumbering visions. It seemed his thoughts, memories, and emotions *were* impacting his night time encounters. Were they ordinary dreams after all?

He dried his face and glanced at the mirror again. Those thoughts of rape haunted him – both Elizabeth's and the one he'd seen in his sleep. A strange thought struck him while he gazed at his reflection. Could the two attacks be linked? Did his dream echo what Elizabeth experienced all those summers ago? Perhaps her memories had somehow channelled their way into his consciousness...

'Don't be ridiculous,' he murmured out loud. 'Elizabeth grew up with her parents right here in this very cottage.'

He shook his head as the thoughts pulsated. *The girl lives in suburbia, and her parents died when she was young – I saw it happen in the dreams. But who is she, and why am I dreaming about her?*

Then he remembered what Alice had said over FaceTime. Perhaps she was right in suggesting a medical cause for his nocturnal torments. It certainly sounded rational. He didn't feel ill, but the lines between his waking reality and his night-time dread were becoming increasingly blurred. He was struggling to determine his real experiences from his imagined ones. Maybe Alice was right – perhaps he was losing his mind.

When he returned from the bathroom, Elizabeth was wide awake and sitting up in bed. 'I was wondering where you'd gone,' she said, glancing his way with a troubled look in her eyes.

'Sorry, I didn't mean to wake you. I just needed to pop to the loo.' He got back into bed, but Elizabeth remained bolt upright.

'You didn't wake me,' she clarified. 'I was having a bit of a nightmare and woke up naturally.'

'Snap,' he said, lying himself flat. 'Tell me what yours was about.'

With a melancholy air, she stared straight ahead and announced it vacantly. 'My attack. The one I told you about last night.'

The coincidence staggered Hugo. He tried to speak but couldn't assemble his thoughts into coherent sentences.

Elizabeth filled the void for him. 'It must have been talking to you that brought it all back,' she continued. 'I told you I sometimes dream of it. Well, last night, I did so again.'

He sat up, motioned towards her and placed his arm on her shoulder. 'I think I dreamt it too,' he said.

With sceptical features, Elizabeth turned to regard him. 'Dreamt what?' It was almost an accusation.

Hugo blurted his answer without really thinking. 'The rape,' he said before regretting his indiscretion. 'I mean...not yours...not specifically...' He winced and fumbled for an outlet. 'I've been having these dreams, you see. There's a little girl in them, and last night she was molested...it was horrible.'

Elizabeth could scarcely believe his insensitivity. Her eyes widened with incredulity, and Hugo realised how fatuous his comments must have sounded. He was about to apologise, but Elizabeth spoke first.

'What happened to me was *real*,' she said. 'It wasn't some stupid dream. And once more, it's as fresh as yesterday.'

Hugo felt terrible. 'I'm so sorry,' he mumbled. 'I wasn't thinking...'

'Let's get back to sleep,' she said, lying back down and turning her face away from him.

'Good idea,' he concurred before prostrating himself next to her. 'I think I should have a chat with my dad at some point this week. I really don't think I'm well.'

Sleep did not return easily that night. Hugo closed his eyes, but his mind raced too fast for his consciousness to give way. Instead, Alice's words rang loudly in his ears. *A physiological cause,* he'd assumed when she'd mooted a medical explanation for his dreams.

*Or a psychological one,* she'd replied.

A psychological one. The thought terrified him.

• CHAPTER 33 •

Monday morning and the clock on the bedside table showed 8.15 AM. Terry still felt groggy but dragged himself out of bed and freshened up in the bathroom. A quick cup of coffee and he was back to his usual self – bright and alert and ready for the day's rigours.

He downed the last of his coffee on an old grey sofa in the living room. His south London flat was small and pokey, its décor scarred by years of neglect. Nicotine from countless previous tenants stained the peeling wallpaper, and a naked lightbulb provided the only illumination.

A small kitchenette at one end, with dilapidated units and ugly lino flooring, completed the grim feel, whilst mould and crumbling plaster signified the building's problem with damp. Terry glanced to his right. Across the road were other flats in

'60s blocks like his. It was a depressing, brutalist vista, but at least his rent was cheap.

It would be 10 AM before his shift began at the supermarket. He'd been there over a year now, working mostly on the checkouts. It was mind-numbing work and certainly didn't return the sort of pay estate agency once had, but that was hardly the point. In truth, Terry was grateful to have paid employment at all.

Each day, he got up and arrived before his shift began. He was a model employee, diligent in the discharge of his duties and unfailingly polite and helpful with the customers. Nevertheless, he chose to keep his colleagues at a distance. He was always civil, sometimes cordial, but wanted them to remain at arm's length. They knew he was part of the company's charity partnership that offered employment to ex-offenders, but they didn't know the precise nature of his crime.

Nor would they: for Terry wished to confine that side of his character to history. He was a reformed man these days, his moral compass intact. He knew he'd committed some terrible sins, but he couldn't change that now.

But he *could* control the future, and one opportunity came out of the blue while he watching the news last week. If seeing Elizabeth's face on TV had astonished him, the accompanying story had shocked him to the core. Once he'd processed things, the shame set in – shame at what he'd done, but also at the consequences for her subsequent life. Filled with bitter regret, he'd ached with remorse at Buckland's words.

Still, the chance for recompense had prompted Terry to make that call to the hospital. He'd deliberated at first, remembering what had happened the last time he'd tried to make amends. But this time, he could remain anonymous, so he'd picked up the phone and disclosed her address from the safety of his flat.

It could never put things right, but he'd had to do something. Her misfortunes were all his fault, and Terry wouldn't countenance sitting idly by. Those years had taken their toll on both of them – if only he had his time again! He'd made a mistake, that was all; an error of judgement. He'd never *intended* any hurt. Was falling in love such a crime? Elizabeth was beautiful, radiant, and captivating; she was...thirteen years old at the time. It was most certainly a crime and one he'd spent thirteen years in prison for. *Thirteen years.* There was a poetic symmetry about that number, and Terry felt sick with guilt.

But those years had given him time to reflect and ponder, and words now could barely express his sorrow. Nibbled by remorse, he'd contemplated suicide but never had the guts to go through with it. Instead, his depression had led to other, more humiliating acts. Thinking back, he shuddered.

It was a spell of particularly low mood just after his release from prison that weighed so heavily on his mind. What the hell had he been thinking turning up like that! Was he expecting her to welcome him with open arms and say all was forgiven? *Stupid, stupid fool!* That little episode had cost him another four years in the slammer.

All he'd wanted to do was say how sorry he was, how regretful. Could she not see that? Her response on opening the door still haunted him: her moment's hesitation had turned to fear and shock – as if he'd violated her all over again. If only she could have listened instead of slamming the door in his face and screaming.

*Elizabeth, please, I don't want to hurt you,* he remembered calling through the letterbox. *I just want to tell you how sorry I am. How truly sorry. I never meant to harm you. I did it because I loved you. But I realise now how wrong it was. How much hurt I caused you. I'm so very sorry, Elizabeth. Please open the door...I just want to apologise properly.*

Those were his words, his idiotic words. Why didn't she want to hear them? It was only later, when back in his right mind, that he realised what a fool he'd been. The police had arrived just ten minutes later. She must have called them while cowering inside and ignoring his pleas through her letterbox.

*Oh, the sheer ignominy!*

Outside his tiny first-floor flat, the night-time shadows had retreated entirely. The sky was bluing with every passing minute, and the sun was rising like a waking lion. Terry peered through the cheap aluminium blind and looked out of the window. He glanced at his watch and was surprised when he saw how many minutes his reverie had stolen. If he wasn't careful, he'd be late for work, and he was too punctilious to let that happen.

His surplus of time had eroded completely, so Terry rose from his seat and banished his historical distractions. With a final shake of his bald head, he let out a sigh and prepared to leave for the supermarket.

• CHAPTER 34 •

'I really ought to think about leaving,' said Hugo, finishing a boiled egg and wiping his mouth. Although breakfast was delicious, time was of the essence at nearly 10 AM. Monday's tutorial was about to start, and he pictured a lonely academic waiting for a student who would never arrive.

He should have left already, but they'd overslept following last night's disturbed slumber. Late to rise, he was grateful suburban visions hadn't returned to darken his thoughts, but a leisurely journey back was out of the question now. He had every intention of making his afternoon class, but if he wasn't careful, he'd miss it – getting to and from Kent was a bugger when relying on public transport. *If only I had a car.*

Elizabeth got up and walked to the kitchen with their plates. 'Have you got enough money to get back?' she shouted through, her words just audible over the sound of crashing crockery.

'I'll hammer the credit card again,' he replied, getting up off the living room sofa and preparing to head to the bathroom. 'Can I borrow your toothpaste?'

'Sure.'

He ran up the stairs, closed the door and turned on the taps. Brushing vigorously, vibrations reverberated through his head, and the noise of cascading water filled the air. The cacophony muffled all external sounds, but unless he was mistaken…

He stopped what he was doing and listened.

Was that a knock at the front door, or was he hearing things? He turned off the taps and listened again.

The *tap-tap-tap* of a second knock confirmed his suspicions. *Someone's at the door!*

Footsteps scurried up the stairs and the bathroom door swung open. Elizabeth walked through and joined him inside. 'Shit, Hugo! No one ever comes to the door.'

'Do you think it's them?' he whispered back.

'The authorities? Who else could it be?'

He spat some toothpaste out and rinsed his mouth. 'But I thought it would take weeks!' He dried his lips and looked square at her. 'There's normally a *huge* backlog of cases. Apparently, social workers—'

*TAP-TAP-TAP-TAP-TAP-TAP-TAP-TAP.* Longer, louder, more peremptory, the third knock cut him off. They exchanged befuddled glances and shrugged at what to do next.

'Why don't *you* answer it?' Elizabeth suggested. 'Just tell them I'm not in or something.'

Hugo nodded, then trotted down a couple of stairs. When a thought hit him, he stopped and turned his head. 'Wait,' he said. 'Why don't I say this is *my* house?'

She looked at him quizzically.

'I could say their information was false,' he continued. 'Tell them I've never heard of you and send them on their way.'

'They'll never believe someone so young owns a house like this.'

The fourth knock was accompanied by a woman's voice through the letterbox. 'Hello Elizabeth,' said the caller. 'This is Lynn from social services. We've come to make sure you're okay and to see if there's anything we can do to help you. Why don't you come to the door and let us in?'

Hugo gesticulated urgently. 'Have you got any better ideas?' he implored, knowing they couldn't stall any longer.

Elizabeth shook her head. 'It's the only idea we've got,' she said. 'We might as well give it a try.' With that, she hid in her bedroom, and Hugo was left to defend the line alone.

He descended the stairs and opened the door. Blinded by the light of a low sun directly behind the visitors, all he could make out were two silhouettes as the door creaked open. He squinted, then raised a horizontal hand to make a peak above his eyes. Ever so slowly, the visitors' images sharpened.

The woman was short and rotund, with a dark bob and thick black glasses. She was about to speak, but the man at her side broke the silence first. Middle-aged, with thinning hair and a muscular build, his more delicate spectacles gave him an intellectual appearance. When he spoke, his voice was deep and authoritative.

'My *GOD!*' the old man boomed.

'Dad...'

• CHAPTER 35 •

Terry was on the tills today. There was nothing unusual in that: he was often deployed as a checkout worker, but sometimes he stacked the shelves instead.

If only he were doing that now! Time went so much quicker when he wasn't on the checkouts.

He was feeling so restless. His body was pumped with adrenaline, and sitting still was torture. How he yearned for the gift of movement!

Instead, he found himself on checkout number seven, scanning the barcodes and trying to ignore the monotonous beeps of the till. A bag of apples; a box of chocolates; a pint of semi-skimmed milk…

*I need to get out of this seat.*

Fat chance – his first break was ages away. For now, he'd have to remain static and do his best to ignore the thoughts that seethed in his head like a boiling kettle.

Those roiling thoughts of Elizabeth: his mind remained fixated on what he'd seen on the news. He tried to maintain his focus by greeting each shopper and engaging them in small talk. At least his bosses would be pleased – checkout employees were encouraged to chat with the customers. But some accomplished it better than others, and Terry wasn't a natural. Normally he endured the policy; today, he found it a godsend.

Despite his restlessness, Terry's mood was buoyant. His mind was flying high with ideas and possibilities, his thoughts in overdrive at the turn of recent events. It was his usual reaction when memories of Elizabeth returned to his reckoning. Nevertheless, it was an ominous sign: he knew from experience that crashes invariably followed these highs. The pattern was set, and he knew it inside out.

When it would strike, he couldn't be sure, but a different state of mind was in the post – a *darker* state of mind. Soon, Terry would return to those despairing times he knew so well. He was so unpredictable when they hit.

While Terry waited for the present customer to pay, he noticed his hands had started to shake. When the shopper departed, he bid him farewell and prepared for the next person.

'Good morning,' said Terry, as the woman waited expectantly.

She smiled back, then bagged her first scanned item – a large, family pack of cereal. 'How are you this morning?' he asked, setting things up for the small talk.

It was still a couple of hours 'til his break.

• CHAPTER 36 •

Hugo looked like a startled deer. Never in his wildest dreams had he expected his father to turn up in person. For his part, the professor looked like his head might explode.

Lynn, the poor woman from social services, didn't know what to think and regarded the pair as they eyed each other in shell-shocked contemplation.

'What the devil's going on?' demanded Swann.

Hugo stammered. 'I…I…'

'I'M WAITING, HUGO!'

'I don't know,' he fumbled, his plan to claim residency kyboshed by his father's presence. He thought on his feet. 'My friend lives here,' he announced, clutching at straws and struggling to elaborate. 'We came down last night, but we're heading to Oxford later.' He knew he was rambling so gave a staccato nod to affirm his ludicrous claims.

Swann's eyes narrowed suspiciously, but the shock of seeing his son left him lost for words.

As the Swann men froze, Lynn filled the void. 'We're looking for Elizabeth,' she explained. 'She requires professional support and we're here to check on her welfare. This is the address we were given. Are you saying she doesn't live here?'

Swann interjected before Hugo could answer. 'Tell me what's going on,' he blurted. 'Who's this so-called friend of yours?'

Hugo felt dizzy. 'A guy called Tom…' He did his best to concoct a tale but winced at how pathetic it sounded.

The elder Swann looked unimpressed. 'And where, precisely, is this Tom character now?'

'…At the shops…?' replied Hugo. It was more of a question than an affirmation. Placed on the spot, he spoke like a schoolboy denying a misdemeanour when caught in the act. 'He'll probably be quite a while,' he continued piteously. 'I shouldn't think we'll head back 'til this evening.'

Swann shifted on his feet. 'A friend called Tom…' he scoffed. He could barely have sounded more derogatory. Hugo thought he was going to barge right in, so he threw out an arm and grabbed the door jamb.

The psychiatrist saw right through his defences. 'I think you'd better tell me what's going on right now,' he demanded. 'What have you got yourself involved in, young man?'

'Well…I…'

'*Hugo...!*'

'This is cringe-worthy,' came a voice from inside the cottage. Hugo turned to see Elizabeth coming down the stairs. 'I don't think either of us expected you to arrive quite so soon,' she said. 'And certainly not the professor himself.'

Swann peered past his son and looked at the woman behind him. 'Elizabeth...' he murmured before shooting confused glances at Hugo and Lynn.

'No doubt you'll want an explanation,' Elizabeth added. 'So why don't you both come in for a cup of tea?'

Three souls sat in the living room while Elizabeth made the tea. Swann had already helped himself to the brown leather armchair, so Hugo retrieved a wooden seat from the kitchen and placed it down for Lynn. When Elizabeth returned, she set down the cups and sat next to Hugo on the sofa.

Hugo squirmed as Elizabeth expounded the details of Friday's chance encounter in Trafalgar Square. He was so embarrassed he wanted the sofa to swallow him whole as she told them about their visit to the pub, their shared interest in art and the thoughtful way he'd helped her get home. He gulped his tea through nerves more than thirst.

Bemused, Swann struggled to fathom it. 'So between that chance meeting and this present moment, he managed to squeeze in a visit to Ealing?' He turned and glared at Hugo. 'A shame my son didn't use the opportunity to inform me of your acquaintance.'

Hugo stared at his empty cup.

'Anyway,' said Swann, 'why's he here now?'

'We didn't part on the best of terms on Saturday,' replied Elizabeth. 'When I discovered the two of you were related, I threw him out.'

'Hold on!' Swann exclaimed, grabbing the sides of his armchair and throwing his weight to the edge of the seat. 'You mean Hugo *came back with you?*'

'What did you think I meant?'

'That he paid for your ticket and sent you on your way. Not that he accompanied you back here *physically*.'

Again, he scrutinised his son. 'Rather a busy weekend, Hugo – back in London on Saturday night and down here again on Sunday. You told me you were going straight back to Oxford. I distinctly remember giving you twenty pounds to fund the journey!'

Hugo's toes curled with embarrassment. He needed to speak before things became humiliating. 'I had to make sure she got back safely,' he said, still staring at the floor and avoiding eye contact. 'That's why I accompanied her from Trafalgar Square. Then, on Sunday, I came back down because I knew you had her address. I had to warn her.'

He could tell his father was about to interrupt, so he progressed to the crux without drawing breath. 'She thought you and I were in collusion,' he explained. 'That we were working with the press to identify her.'

Finally, he looked Swann in the eye. 'So, I came and explained that the initial report had nothing to do with you and that you were the one who stopped the story from going any further. She didn't believe you when you told her that at the hospital.'

'It's true,' Elizabeth confirmed. 'Thanks to Hugo, I know you're not the bad guy.'

'And so, you see,' Hugo concluded. 'I came back here to clear your name. To clear *our* names.'

Swann averted his gaze to digest things.

'Returning to the matter at hand,' said Lynn, sensing an opportunity and speaking for the first time since entering the cottage, 'we're here to conduct a needs assessment for Elizabeth. You were very insistent, Professor, that this meeting took place as soon as possible.'

Everyone looked at Swann, whose mood changed instantly from the pressure to explain his decision. He flicked his eyes to Elizabeth. 'You left the hospital so abruptly,' he said. 'We were hugely concerned for your welfare, and the manner of your departure caught us off guard. Given what you said to me at the hospital...'

'I told your dad about the suicide attempt,' she interjected.

'...And that's why we wanted to reach you,' Swann explained with a methodical nod. 'To provide you with the appropriate care and support.'

Elizabeth looked away and smirked. 'You haven't got a clue, Professor. Do you honestly think I didn't know what you were up to when you paid me that visit in the hospital?'

Swann furrowed his brow and waited.

'You were trying to section me!'

Swann raised his eyebrows. The accentuated wrinkles on his forehead made him look haggard for a moment. 'I needed to assess your risk factors,' he explained, keeping his voice measured and professional. 'I had to build a picture of what we were dealing with to make sure any treatment you received was appropriate.'

'Did building your picture involve listening to what I was actually saying?'

Swann let her speak without trying to justify himself.

'When you asked why I started talking after such a long silence, I told you it was because there were people out there who knew about my past. People who would come looking for me if that news report went public.'

Hugo sensed what was coming next. 'Elizabeth,' he cautioned her. 'You don't have to do this. You don't have to say anything you don't want to.'

'I *do* want to,' she said, grabbing her dark blonde hair and making a ponytail with her fists. 'You see, Professor, the member of the public who gave you my address...' she let go of her hair and allowed it to cascade back over her shoulders, '...is the man who raped me when I was a child.'

Swann swallowed hard and crossed his legs. Meanwhile, Lynn's features became intent. She pushed her thick black glasses up the bridge of her nose and began making fastidious notes.

Elizabeth kept the details scant but explained how things had come to a head in October. Depressed and despairing, she'd tried to end her life at the meadow. Then, having woken in the hospital, she knew she had to escape before the authorities sectioned her. Lonely and frightened, she'd discharged herself onto the mean streets of London. It had all seemed so hopeless – but a young man who shared her passion for art had saved her. Like her, he knew the pain of losing a parent, and they'd bonded almost immediately.

The mention of Hugo's mother was a bolt from the blue for Swann. For the first time that morning, he looked vulnerable.

When Elizabeth finished, Lynn put her pen down. 'These are some very significant life events,' she said, taking a swig of her tea. 'Can we move on to discuss the support mechanisms you have in place?'

'No!' Elizabeth slapped her knees with her hands. 'I don't want to answer any more of your questions. I've explained my situation, and I'm in a much better place than I was. I don't need counselling or a prescription for anti-depressants. I'm no longer a risk to myself – or anyone else, for that matter. I'm of perfectly sound mind, and I most definitely don't need sectioning. Now, with respect, I'd like you to go and leave me in peace.'

Her rant was over.

Swann looked at Lynn, his moment of fluster behind him. 'What's your assessment, Lynn? From a medical perspective, I think we're done. The patient clearly doesn't want any therapeutic interventions and seems quite capable of making that judgement herself. No one needs sectioning today.'

'I agree,' said Lynn, who turned to address Elizabeth. 'Your answers suggest that you don't meet the criteria for social services intervention either. I think we can leave you in peace. However, I'd like to make you aware of a few charities before we depart, especially those specialising in helping the survivors of rape and sexual assault. I'd recommend you seek their support.'

It was a sensible suggestion and only took a few minutes to disseminate. When Swann and Lynn rose to depart, Hugo stood up too. He knew what his father expected of him.

'Make sure you've got everything,' Swann instructed him. 'Looks like my drive to London will include a detour to Oxford.'

Hugo had to play along. Any hint that he'd rather stay in Kent would signify the relationship had run much deeper than that of a concerned stranger. He glanced towards Elizabeth, who nodded to show her understanding.

As␣Lynn departed, Hugo bumbled for his shoes in the hallway. Once he'd slipped them on, he and his father exited the front door and headed off down the path. Swann's Jaguar was waiting around the corner, but Elizabeth hollered before they reached it.

'Professor…'

Swann turned his head and waited.

'When you're in the car, try talking to your son. He's the one who needs your expertise, not me.'

Swann looked perplexed. 'What do you mean by that?'

'Find out about the dreams he's been having. Try opening your eyes to *his* tribulations.'

She left it at that and closed the door on them.

• CHAPTER 37 •

The slow journey up the A21 was made insufferable by the near silence in which it passed. Hugo attempted small talk, but Swann's terse responses rendered more elaborate discourse difficult.

Devoid of conversation, Hugo pulled down the sun visor and reclined in the Jaguar's passenger seat. With a tilt of his head, he stared at the Kent countryside as it rewound past the window. He started to feel morose.

Things sped up on the M25, which was mercifully clear save for the section near Heathrow, where frustrating start-stop jams mirrored the earlier attempts at conversation. Still, the atmosphere was awkward rather than frosty, and neither man was unduly concerned at the lack of tete-a-tete. But his father's refusal to drive above seventy miles an hour irritated Hugo: all it did was accentuate the vehicle's silence.

But as they left the London orbital to head northwest on the M40, Swann's tongue loosened from the roof of his mouth. When they joined the main carriageway, he began to probe immediately.

'You shouldn't have gone to Kent,' he said, laying his opinion bare. 'There was no reason for you to become so deeply involved.'

Hugo would have preferred the awkward silence, but without a means to escape the four-wheeled prison, he knew he had to engage. Before answering, he watched the lorry they were overtaking recede from view. 'I've already told you. I couldn't just let her go off on her own. I knew she was vulnerable and had to make sure she got home safely.'

'Vulnerable, yes. But she needed professional care, not a kind heart. You should have called me instead.'

*You've no idea how close I came in the Ship and Shovell!*

Hugo stared through the passenger side window. This time it was one of the Oxford-bound coach services they were overtaking.

'You stayed there overnight,' said Swann disapprovingly.

'In the spare room,' Hugo pointed out. 'By the time we'd arrived, it was far too late for me to head back to London.'

'She's in her thirties, Hugo.'

'And?'

Swann glared at him. It was only a fleeting glance but long enough for Hugo to see the reproof his father intended.

'She's too old for a start. There are plenty of girls your age in Oxford.'

'We were talking about art, Dad! And besides, when I found out her parents had died, it seemed good to share my memories of Mum. You always say yourself how important it is to talk about these things.'

Swann kept his eyes on the road and ignored what Hugo told him. 'Her emotional state was tremendously volatile. You should have remained dispassionate.'

'Dispassionate?' he expostulated. 'With an intriguing case like hers? I was fascinated enough having read it in the news, but to have *bumped into her* in London…I mean, what are the chances! How could I possibly have remained dispassionate? You'd have done the same if you were in my shoes.'

Silence descended on the car once more. Hugo wasn't sure if his father was done, but he wished the Buckinghamshire Chilterns would roll past a little quicker.

After several minutes of ruminating, Swann spoke again, and when he did, he was no less reproving. 'Engaging with her is one thing,' he conceded, gripping the wheel with both hands and staring intently ahead. 'But following her to Kent and staying the night is quite another.'

Hugo shrugged, but Swann pressed him further. 'Did anything physical happen between you?'

'Of course not!' It was a vehement denial, but Hugo's cheeks flushed a livid pink. He hoped to conceal his embarrassment by turning his head and looking out of the window. To his left, the blue county sign of Oxfordshire flashed past and glinted in the autumn sunshine. *At least we're on the final stretch.*

Swann continued his cross-examination. 'Nothing at all?' he asked. 'Not even a kiss?'

'No!'

Passing through the Stokenchurch Gap, the chalk cliffs appeared like giant yellowing teeth as they drove along the tarmac tongue between them. High above the hills, he spotted a soaring red kite and envied its freedom.

His father's interrogation was remorseless. 'You've become emotionally involved at the very least.'

'No, I haven't,' he lied.

'All those visits? Of course you have!' Swann was becoming supercilious in his reproach. 'No doubt it's detracting from your studies, too. Was there a tutorial today?'

'No.' Another lie.

The next pause was shorter, and Hugo knew the climax was coming.

'I don't want you seeing her again,' said Swann. It was an authoritarian command, not an expression of opinion. 'Do you understand me, Hugo? She's entirely unsuitable. You'll only end up getting hurt. Not to mention the effect it'll have on your degree.'

Hugo tried to protest. 'Dad, I promise nothing happened...'

'ENOUGH NOW!' boomed Swann. 'There'll be no further discussion of the matter.'

Hugo shrugged again. 'Fine.'

He made it sound blasé but inside, his blood was boiling. How dare his father command whom he may or may not see! The injustice was contemptible, but he kept his anguish hidden.

Any bubbling to the surface would confirm Swann's suspicions, so he sat there quietly as they drove deeper into Oxfordshire.

They were nearly at the outskirts of the city when Swann broke the hush. 'So what are these dreams you've been having?' he asked, all empathy and compassion now. 'Alice mentioned them yesterday on FaceTime, then Elizabeth did so this morning. Is everything all right, Son?'

It was as if a switch had flicked in Swann, and Hugo could scarcely believe how oblivious he was to the damage he'd just caused. Nevertheless, the chance to explore his issues with a medical expert was difficult to turn down.

He shifted his weight and angled his body towards his father. 'I don't know what's going on, Dad. These dreams are crazy. When I wake, they don't fade like normal ones do. They stay with me. They're more like memories than dreams.'

Swann chewed it over. 'Bizarre episodes?'

'Not really. As I say, they're most un-dreamlike. There's none of the weirdness you get with normal dreams.'

Struggling to articulate, he scratched his scalp with his ring finger. 'They all revolve around this suburban family,' he explained. 'There's a girl, and terrible things keep happening to her. Things that *I* keep seeing.'

'Such as?'

'Her parents died for a start. They died in separate incidents – one in a house fire and the other in a swimming pool. Then, in last night's dream, the girl was raped by her uncle. It's like I'm ploughing through a DVD box set, each episode building on the last.'

Swann stroked his chin thoughtfully. 'And this happens every time you go to sleep?'

'No, it's more haphazard than that.' Hugo spoke calmly, but the agitation was growing inside him. 'I have normal dreams most nights where bits of 'me' are reflected. They're all perfectly ordinary, and they fade as soon as I wake. These others are totally different, though – there's nothing whatsoever of my own experiences. It's like I'm living a different life. When I wake, I'm more exhausted than ever.'

Swann gave a pondering 'Hmm' and followed it with a long, slow nod.

'Any ideas, Dad?'

Swann eased off the accelerator and the car slowed by ten miles an hour. He kept his concentration on the road but glanced intermittently at his son. 'It's probably nothing to worry about, but the symptoms you describe are consistent with certain forms of psychosis.'

Hugo's face went white.

Swann continued. 'Sometimes the dream state and waking realities become confused and blurred—'

'You mean like schizophrenia?' blurted Hugo.

Swann perceived his distress and slowed the car still further. 'Not necessarily,' he reassured him. 'I know the word sounds scary but it's not as bad as it sounds. There are many forms of psychosis.'

When the road ahead was clear, Swann looked to his left for longer. Hugo's cheeks were ashen. 'You're probably fine, Son.

# DREAMS

But it's worth having an assessment when you're back for the Christmas holidays.'

Hugo nodded meekly. 'The Christmas holidays – they're not that far away now. Just a few short weeks.'

'In the meantime,' said Swann, turning his head to the front and speeding the car back up, 'try not to exacerbate the symptoms. It would be good to avoid alcohol. And make sure you're getting enough sleep. I know that probably sounds ironic.'

'Thanks, Dad. I'll do my best.'

'And whatever you do, don't smoke cannabis.'

Hugo smiled wryly. 'You certainly don't have to worry about that, Dad.'

• CHAPTER 38 •

Oxford returned to an air of normality after the craziest weekend of Hugo's life. Not only were the events extraordinary, but they also seemed to last an eternity. Was Friday's haircut and piercing really so recent? Could he even recall what life was like before he'd met Elizabeth? So much had happened since his split with Alice! Even so, he was glad to be back at university and able to pause for breath.

He told Elizabeth what his father had said in the car. Indignant at the professor's instruction, he'd called her after his class on Monday and swore he had no intention of complying with the old man's wishes. Nevertheless, there was the insoluble problem of distance. Kent was miles from Oxford, so snatching an afternoon drink or popping round on the hoof for an evening movie was totally out of the question.

Things would be tricky from now on. Neither could drive, and Hugo's student loan wouldn't stretch to making frequent trips to the Weald. And besides, he had a degree to study for.

Neither could Elizabeth visit him without considerable difficulty. Even if she were prepared to use public transport, he could hardly sneak her in and out of Oriel without awkward questions being asked. And Oxford hotel rooms were expensive.

Physical meetings would be few and far between and, with Christmas impending, they might only see each other once or twice more before Hugo broke up. At least they had the wonders of modern technology with which to keep in touch. They were no substitute for the bliss of real encounters but would have to do in the circumstances. How had they fallen so far and so fast in one weekend?

And that was why the L-word sounded so foolish at first. Surely a single weekend was too soon to profess it, but 'love' was what they'd declared during Hugo's next call. They did so tentatively at first but with increasing confidence as each became sure of the other's sincerity.

They had to wait a fortnight before seeing one another in person, and Hugo travelled to Kent for a weekend that seemed so brief in comparison to the one in which they'd met. They spent the time lost in each other's worlds, walking through the countryside and enjoying their evenings curled up on the sofa with a bottle of wine.

But all too soon, it was over, and Hugo returned to Oxford, knowing they wouldn't meet again until the new year. It seemed so far away, but Christmas was coming, and he'd be trapped with his father in Ealing.

One Wednesday afternoon in early December, Hugo was finishing a beer with some friends in the King's Arms pub on Holywell Street, close to the Bodleian Library. They'd been doing some work over the road and had agreed on a well-earned drink once their academic obligations were done and dusted.

Having finished their beers, the group was losing patience with the slow-drinking Hugo, who still had half a pint left. The beer ran from the corners of his mouth as each delicate sip made little impact on the remaining volume. Eager to go, his friends were becoming exasperated, and the consumption process was painstaking.

Sensing their disdain, he doubled down on his efforts and began to gulp. But before he could finish, he lost interest. Two distracting figures had entered the pub and were making their way to the bar. To reach it, they'd need to pass his table, and the pair were approaching it rapidly.

He fixed his stare on the new arrivals, oblivious to the eye-rolling of his discontented friends. The two new entrants were almost upon him, the woman slightly ahead of her male companion. Mixed race, with curly hair and massive-lensed glasses, Alice saw him and smiled.

'Hi, Hugo!' She sounded genuinely pleased to see him. 'I haven't seen you for ages. I take it you've been in the Bodleian?'

Hugo responded bashfully. 'Been doing a bit of work with these guys,' he said, gesturing to his friends. 'We just popped in for a quick beer before going back.'

One of those friends had clearly had enough. 'We're heading off, Hugo. If you want to come with us, you'll have to leave your drink.'

'I'll catch you up in a bit,' he replied dismissively, waving his hand and shooing them away.

When he turned back round, Alice's companion had drawn level with her. Embarrassingly for Hugo, the Wales rugby top he saw was the one he'd vomited on at the house party a few weeks before. 'Hi Owen,' he cringed.

Owen mumbled a response, and Hugo felt suddenly isolated now that his friends had left him. Self-conscious and mildly tipsy after his beer, he clumsily attempted small talk. 'So, what brings you two here?' he asked, trying to sink more liquid into his already bloated stomach.

Alice smiled condescendingly. 'This is our local,' she reminded him. 'Wadham is right next door.'

'The college owns this pub,' added Owen.

'Of course,' Hugo said, taking another sip of his remnant pint. It did nothing to quell his unease.

Whilst Hugo had spoken to Alice via text and a couple of times on FaceTime, this was the first occasion all three had met in person since *that* house party, and the awkwardness was not his to monopolise.

Perceptively, Alice sensed an opportunity to clear the air and banish any hard feelings between the two young men. 'We're just going to get a couple of drinks from the bar,' she said. 'Do you mind if we join you after we've got them?'

'No problem,' said Hugo, trying to mask his alarm at the idea. Owen's contorted features suggested he was just as unsure.

Alice's face lit up. 'Great. Wait here while we go and get them. It looks like you'll be a while yet with that pint.'

She meant it harmlessly, but Owen smirked as she led him to the bar.

Hugo awaited their return by playing with his eyebrow stud and sipping his warm lager. The young couple returned a few minutes later and placed their drinks on the table opposite him.

Sitting herself down, Alice noticed the top of his head for the first time. 'You've changed your hairstyle,' she observed.

Hugo blushed. 'Oh...yeah...' he stammered, fighting the urge to touch his quiff. 'I had it done a while back. Same time as this.' He pointed to the stud above his eye.

Alice had seen the piercing when they'd spoken on FaceTime, but his hair had been flat that morning in Ealing.

'It kind of suits you,' lied Owen. He tried to sound sincere, but feigning compliments wasn't his forte.

Hugo looked at Owen, whose brown eyes shone in the soft pub lighting. Devilishly handsome, his high cheekbones and smooth dark skin contrasted mockingly with his own pink features. The new look was a failed attempt at aping Owen; all three knew it, and Hugo's cheeks burned as they rouged ever deeper.

Alice gave it a moment, then spoke. 'Did you chat with your dad in the end?' She picked up her glass and took a sip of wine.

Hugo darted his eyes to Owen and immediately back to Alice.

'She told me about the dreams,' Owen confirmed.

'I hope you don't mind,' said Alice, replacing her glass of white. 'I thought it would make sense to explain what happened at the party. The dreams, and all that.'

Hugo removed his spectacles and cleaned them on his shirt tails. He'd started to sweat, and moisture now glistened on his forehead from the embarrassment of having his dream issue made public. 'It's fine,' he said, replacing his glasses and pushing them up the bridge of his aquiline nose. 'I'm going for some tests over Christmas.'

Alice smiled warmly. 'I hope you get the answers you're looking for,' she said.

'Me too. But it's been a couple of weeks since I dreamt anything out of the ordinary. Perhaps they've stopped altogether.'

'Either way, it's worth getting the test done. I know how debilitating things have been for you.' She stole a sip of wine and suddenly rose from her seat. 'Will you two wait for me here? I'm just gonna nip to the loo.' She pushed her chair under the table and headed off to the toilet.

The two young men were left on their own, and each imbibed some beer in painful acknowledgement of the awkwardness thrust upon them. Owen, the more socially agile of the pair, spoke first. 'Look, man,' he said in his rich Welsh accent. 'I hope there are no hard feelings between us.' Another glug of his dark brown ale followed.

'None whatsoever.' Hugo mirrored Owen by drinking his lager, which went down far less smoothly.

'It can't have been easy finding out Alice and I are together. I've been through breakups myself, and they're not nice.' Owen had begun rotating his beer glass round and round on a soggy coaster. He may have looked and sounded cool, but Hugo perceived how embarrassed he was.

'It's perfectly all right,' said Hugo. 'Alice is great, but she and I were never right for each other. Good luck to you both. I'm sure you'll be fantastic together.'

Owen smiled at his magnanimity. 'She adores you as a friend, you know.'

'I do know,' he replied solemnly. 'And I value her friendship.'

He looked beyond Owen and saw a mass of curly hair coming back from the toilet. When Alice sat back down, Hugo drained the final dregs of his drink and stood up himself.

'Leaving so soon?' asked a disappointed Alice.

'I'd better be off,' he said. 'Can't have the guys think I'm still nursing that pint!'

The lovebirds chuckled at his humour.

'But before I go, I need the loo myself.' Hugo gestured at some items on the table. 'Will you look after my phone and keys 'til I'm back?'

'No problem,' said Alice.

Once Hugo had disappeared, the couple were left alone. Owen said something amusing, and Alice chortled dutifully. Then, when a barmaid collected the empties, Hugo's phone began to vibrate.

The Wadham pair looked at each other before turning their heads to the phone. Alice flipped it over and read the name on the screen.

'Who is it?' asked Owen.

'FaceTime call. Someone called Elizabeth.'

'Do you know her?'

'No.'

The ringtone continued.

Alice dithered, then prompted Owen. 'What do you think?' she asked urgently. 'Should I answer it?'

'What if it's Hugo's new girlfriend?' quipped Owen.

Still, the tone continued.

'Don't be silly,' she rebuked him. 'Quickly, yes or no?'

'Go for it,' he said, reclining back in his wooden chair. 'You never know – it might be important.'

Alice grabbed the device and pressed the green button. 'Hi, this is Hugo's phone.'

The caller was caught off guard. 'Oh…hello,' she said uncertainly. 'I was expecting…to speak to Hugo…'

Alice tilted the phone, so the caller could see her and Owen in the frame. She was certain the woman looked familiar. 'We're friends of his,' she explained. 'He's just gone to the toilet. We're in the pub right now.'

'Oh…okay…'

The woman looked unsure.

'We thought we'd better answer in case it was important,' added Owen. 'Do you want us to pass on a message?'

The woman collected her thoughts and shook her head. 'It's fine,' she uttered. 'I was only ringing for a chat. Just say Elizabeth called and tell him I'll ring back later.'

'Sure,' said Alice, 'we'll let him know.'

They hung up, and the screen went dark.

Alice replaced the phone, and Owen noticed how pensive she looked. 'What's wrong?' he asked her.

'Just that woman,' she murmured. 'Somehow she seemed...familiar...'

Owen humoured her. 'She certainly had very blue eyes.'

Alice's own eyes bulged at the comment. The penny had dropped, and she sat bolt upright. 'Fuck me!' she exclaimed, turning to Owen and grabbing his arm with both hands. 'It's that woman from the news article!'

Owen looked underwhelmed. 'News article? What on earth are you talking about?'

Alice tightened her grip. 'They pulled her from a swollen river in Kent. Don't you remember?'

Owen shook his head. 'Not really.'

'She drew a picture!' squealed Alice. 'She signed it "Elizabeth Ritchie." She couldn't speak or anything!'

Slowly, something stirred in Owen, and he nodded in vague acknowledgement. 'Now you mention it, I think I do remember...'

'I should have connected the dots as soon as I saw her. Those blue eyes! They're her dominant feature.'

Suddenly Hugo's phone pinged loudly on the table. It was the sound of an incoming text. Alice seized the device and read the preview on the screen:

**Elizabeth:**

Just tried to FaceTime. Call me when you get the chance.

Love you xxx

Alice repeated the message out loud. 'It *is* Hugo's new girlfriend!' She put the phone on the table and grabbed his arm again.

Owen looked unconvinced. 'Are you sure it's the same woman?'

'I'm positive,' she affirmed. 'How the hell does he know her?'

'You can ask him that yourself,' he said, peering beyond her shoulder. 'He's on his way back, look.'

She let go of his arm and stole a quick glance; then, turning back, she shot him an instructive stare. Owen interpreted it for the signal it was – his presence wasn't required for this conversation, so he downed his pint and stood up. 'I'll see you back at Wadham,' he said before grabbing his coat and leaving.

Oblivious to what had transpired, Hugo returned and reached for his coat. 'Thanks for watching my keys and phone,' he said. 'Why did Owen rush off so—'

'Hugo...' Alice cut him off sternly. 'Please sit down for a moment.'

He could tell something had happened, so he resumed his seat and listened. Suddenly he felt the glare of the spotlight, his cheeks reddening to beetroot as Alice explained the FaceTime conversation.

'So what's going on?' She was smiling inquisitively, her tone suggesting intrigue rather than interrogation. 'How do you know her, Hugo?'

Like a defendant in the dock, he fumbled for a reply. It certainly felt like an interrogation! 'It began with a chance encounter,' he said. 'I'll spare you the details, though. Suffice it to say that we bumped into each other in London. That same weekend you and I FaceTimed.'

'You *bumped into her*?' she parroted. 'In *London*. By *chance*?'

'Honestly!' He tried to sound nonchalant, but underneath the table, his knee was bouncing up and down with the nerves. 'It happened in Trafalgar Square when I was on my way up to the National Gallery.'

Furrowing her brow, Alice showed her scepticism. 'So you bumped into her – and immediately gave her your phone number?'

'I recognised her straightaway,' said Hugo, his heart thumping like mad. 'We ended up talking about—'

'Talking? I thought she couldn't speak.'

He swallowed hard and paused. *Where the hell do I begin with this?*

'She started talking in the hospital,' he told her. 'It's a long story, but if you really want to know...'

He cherry-picked some details and expounded them for Alice – the encounter in Trafalgar Square; the meal in the Ship and Shovell; his promise to help her get home. He left out the romantic elements and painted a picture of platonic acquaintance.

Alice listened deadpan. 'Take a look at your phone,' she urged him.

Hugo's heart hammered when he saw the preview of the text. He unlocked his device and read the entire message, then slipped the phone away again.

'No more obfuscation, Hugo. Just tell me what's going on.'

Caught in the glare of an intensified spotlight, Hugo felt like a cowering animal. 'Alice,' he mumbled guiltily. 'What can I say? It just felt...right...'

Alice scowled like a headmistress. 'Oh Hugo,' she lamented. 'The woman's mentally ill!'

He shook his head defensively. 'She isn't,' he protested. 'Not like that, anyway. Things have simply...happened to her.'

'What on earth did your father say?'

'This is where things get...complicated.'

'Complicated?' she repeated. 'What do you mean they get complicated?'

'My dad doesn't know we're together. He has his suspicions, and he knows we've met, but...'

She craned her neck at his pause. 'Come on, Hugo, spit it out.'

'...The thing is,' he continued. 'Elizabeth was Dad's patient.'

Alice's jaw dropped. 'Oh, Hugo! I see what you mean by "complicated."'

'I only found out once we'd talked for a bit,' he said, raising his hands in a defensive gesture. 'Dad thinks I should stop seeing her.'

'Maybe he has a point. She's in her thirties, for goodness sake.'

Hugo scowled. 'That's exactly what my father said when he began sniffing around my personal life.'

'I just don't want to see you get hurt,' she said, her big brown eyes exuding concern. 'Maybe you should wait a while before getting involved with someone new.'

'Wait 'til when?'

'Until you've had your tests. You might be unwell yourself, remember.'

Desiring to keep things civil, he fought the urge to protest. 'Thank you for your concern,' he said, standing tall and picking up his coat. 'But my private life is my own. I'm not a child, Alice.'

She could see she'd annoyed him, so Alice finished her wine in silence. As Hugo buttoned up his jacket, his next words rose like a tide in his throat. 'You ought to know it's serious,' he said. 'We're very much in love, she and I.'

And with that, he returned to Oriel.

• CHAPTER 39 •

Like a snowball hurtling down a mountain slope, Hugo's first term seemed to gather pace as the Christmas break drew closer.

The Michaelmas Term expired in mid-December, and those caught in its clutch were allowed their brief opportunity to pause. In the blink of an eye, the students packed their belongings, said their goodbyes, and headed back to their homes for the near six-week Christmas holidays.

Hugo was one of those students, and he returned to Ealing in the passenger seat of his father's Jaguar, boxes containing his possessions packed in the boot like sardines. London would dominate his life until at least the middle of January when the Hilary Term would dawn and the days, ever so slowly, would begin to lengthen once more.

He had few friends in London, but his online life sustained him. Most treasured of all were the private moments he shared with Elizabeth, now more clandestine than ever given his father's proximity. Physical meetings seemed so far away, but as each day passed, their return grew closer.

It was early January, once Christmas and New Year were out of the way, that Hugo went for his tests, his father having recommended he undergo a sleep study – known medically as a polysomnography.

'What the hell does that involve?' Hugo asked when Swann first mooted the idea.

'It's nothing to worry about,' his father reassured him. 'You simply stay overnight and sleep in a lab. You'll be having an electroencephalogram.'

'A what?'

'You've probably heard it referred to as an EEG. They'll hook you up to some small sensors and monitor your brain activity while you're asleep. It'll help them determine whether you're suffering from a sleep disorder. Among other things.'

He arrived at the lab two hours before his usual bedtime. Hooked up to the instruments, he felt he probably looked rather foolish. The wires were uncomfortable, but he soon got used to them and submitted to their intrusion like a pet being manhandled.

He was told it didn't matter if he couldn't get to sleep right away. Even a few short hours would yield plenty of valuable data. When the lights finally dimmed, he was surprised by just how dark it was. And oh, the screaming silence!

He lay flat on his back, eyes open, pupils dilated. He rolled onto his left, then over to his right – but despite the dearth of external stimulation, his mind remained electric, like a TV left on standby. Imprisoned in the boundless black cloak of a silent tomb, it was a couple of hours before his consciousness gave way.

*A scream. Faint at first but growing louder. Outside, the night was black, but glaring lights inside burned bright. Where was he? Not in softly furnished suburbia, that was for sure. He was somewhere different, somewhere more…institutional.*

*Another scream, but not a piercing shriek of terror. Deep and resonant, it was the sound of…*

*Agony.*

*Slowly, the dream took shape, and Hugo realised where he was – a hospital ward!*

*The room was sparse but strangely comforting, with instrumentation humming in the background. The patient screamed again – whatever was wrong, it sounded serious.*

*Heavy, rasping breathing followed. He looked towards the bed, but three bustling bodies obscured the patient's features. All he could see, raised in the air, was a pair of parted legs.*

*And that was when things became clear. The splayed legs; the deep, sustained screams…*

*The three attendees weren't doctors or nurses – they were midwives. He was on a maternity ward!*

*Nervously, Hugo edged closer. It was obvious who the patient was, but he peered past the midwives anyway.*

*Lying on the bed, the girl's body heaved, features contorting, skin glistening in the brightness of the lights. Lank hair fanned from her scalp, and the pillow was drenched with sweat. Little remained of the child he'd met in the paddling pool; she was fourteen now, and nine months had passed since he'd witnessed the rape.*

*Another contraction, another scream.*

*The whitened knuckles of her left hand were grasping the edge of the bed, while her right hand was held by a midwife, whose encouragements to push were met with a string of pain-induced expletives.*

*Yet another contraction, and Hugo's eyes roved south to see a grey head protruding from her abdomen, birth fluids leaking around it like river water breaching lock gates. He felt queasy, but the midwives weren't concerned; it was all in a day's work for them.*

*A few more heaves and the baby was born, its body pulled clear by the professionals' skilful manoeuvres. In a trice, the pain was over, and the girl relaxed, exhausted. A new life had entered the world.*

*The midwife who'd held her hand was the one who cut the cord. She smiled, then mopped the teenager's brow. As Hugo watched things unfold, his thoughts turned away from this miracle of life and towards the absent father.*

*Uncle Pete…*

*The monster who'd molested his niece.*

## DREAMS

*Just what had become of that beast?*

*The sights and sounds of the ward grew faint as a new scene materialised. His dream was transporting him elsewhere – a different type of institution: smaller, sparser and entirely bereft of hope.*

*A prison cell – claustrophobic and filled with despair and loneliness.*

*Before him, a convict sat perched on the edge of a single bed. His head was in his hands, and his elbows were on his knees. All Hugo could see was a thick mass of light brown hair, but there was no doubting who this person was. When the man looked up, his suspicions were confirmed. He was staring straight into the eyes of a haunted Uncle Pete.*

He woke with a start and struggled for breath. *Where the hell am I?*

The sensors strapped to his head reminded him, and he tore them away in distress.

A light came on and a doctor rushed in. 'Mr Swann...'

'What time is it?' choked Hugo.

The medic told him it was half-past-three. 'Please, Mr Swann. You mustn't tear the equipment like that...'

'But it's the dream!' he yelled. 'It's back again! I've seen the next instalment!'

The medic blinked in confusion. 'I don't understand. We've been monitoring your brain waves and sleep cycles—'

'She's given birth! I saw it happen!'

The doctor frowned and shook his head. 'That's impossible,' he explained, urging Hugo to calm himself. 'When you woke, you weren't experiencing REM. You were in a totally different stage of the sleep cycle.'

'What do you mean?' implored Hugo.

'Mr Swann,' the doctor said calmly. 'According to our instrumentation and data, you haven't been dreaming at all.'

• CHAPTER 40 •

It was Saturday morning in Ealing. At the kitchen table, Hugo sat with his head in his hands, his world crashing around him, sickness burning in the pit of his stomach. 'Why does it have to be so drastic?' he asked, neither raising his head nor making eye contact with his father.

Swann gave him short shrift. 'I know it's difficult, but it's for your own good,' he said, grabbing a banana from the fruit bowl and peeling it.

It was ten days since his tests, and Hugo was facing the prospect of not returning to Oxford for the Hilary Term.

His diagnosis had shocked him.

Psychosis…

The word had conjured fearful connotations. The fact the precise form remained unknown frightened him further, hardly helped by his father's refusal to rule out schizophrenia.

All sorts of dark thoughts had descended when he'd first heard the news – images of nineteenth-century lunatic asylums, and the infamous serial killers of yesteryear. The concept of serious mental illness was something he just couldn't reconcile with the cause of his nocturnal torments.

'It's not just the degree,' Hugo protested, his voice meek and pleading. 'It's the social side as well. After everything that happened at school...I've got friends at university. I actually fit in there.'

Swann bit into the banana and chewed it. 'Your friends will still be there when you return,' he said. 'Try to see the bigger picture, Hugo.'

Finally, Hugo looked up. 'Things will have moved on by then, and you know it.'

They would have. And Swann *did* know it. But that wasn't the point. Hugo's health was paramount, and the suspension of his studies was a price worth paying if it meant a full recovery. Doubtless, he'd need to repeat the year, so he wouldn't be back 'til the autumn. It was a bitter pill to swallow.

Unmoved by his protestations, Swann continued. 'It's about managing the condition,' he insisted, finishing the banana and speaking with his mouth full. 'We need to get you on the right medication and at the right dosage. Doing so will take time.'

But Hugo wasn't ready to acquiesce just yet. 'I feel fine, Dad. The only symptom is the dreaming.'

'Which is getting progressively worse, as you yourself have admitted.' Swann crossed his legs and let that sink in for a moment. 'And how long before things progress? How long before these visions occupy your waking moments as well as your sleeping ones?'

'Surely that's what the medication's for.'

Swann shot him a disdainful look before softening his demeanour. 'Sorting the right medication at the correct dose isn't a quick fix,' he explained, walking his banana peel to the bin and throwing it away. 'Meanwhile, there are the potential side effects to consider. I don't suppose you've thought about those, have you? But you might have done if you weren't so insistent on being such a bloody know-all.' He washed his hands at the sink, then returned to the table and sat back down.

'What kind of side effects?' asked Hugo.

'Different people are affected differently. You might not experience any at all. But if you do, we could be talking about things like impaired concentration or increased lethargy.' He leant in and offered a fleeting glimpse of compassion. 'Suicidal thoughts aren't uncommon either.'

Hugo gulped.

'None of which are conducive to being away from home and in the pressured environment of Oxford.'

Deep down, Hugo knew his father was right. The University of Oxford had been around for nearly a thousand years; it would still be there in October. Nevertheless, it seemed like such a waste. The others in his cohort would forget all about him. Socially and intellectually, he'd have to start afresh in the autumn.

Mid-January seemed especially gloomy this year. A new term was about to commence that Hugo would play no part in. He'd told his friends of the tests via WhatsApp. The diagnosis had staggered them, and they'd sympathised greatly on learning, offering their support and promising to remain in touch. He knew they wouldn't.

He went to Oxford the next day for a final visit. A low-key farewell had been arranged, and he'd promised the old man he'd abstain from alcohol. What he didn't do was disclose his other plan — a trip to Kent the following morning for a reunion with Elizabeth. It had been so long since they'd met in person. He'd explained the situation during one of their secret FaceTime calls, and she'd been as scared as him on hearing the word 'psychosis'. But when he'd mentioned suspending his studies, her mind went sick with worry.

He said his goodbyes in Oxford, then set off for Kent in the morning, his spirits cheered at the thought of seeing Elizabeth again. But at the back of his mind, something vexed him. Maybe he was just being paranoid — an early side effect of his medication, perhaps?

He didn't think he'd imagined it, though. She'd definitely seemed more distant of late. Their recent FaceTime calls had been cagey. He pondered the reason with dread — was the word 'psychosis' troubling her? He'd done his best to say he was fine, but still, her calls seemed cold.

But *what* she'd said had worried him most. *Let's wait 'til we meet in person*, she'd told him. *I don't want to discuss it over FaceTime.*

What could it possibly be? Was she planning on ending things? If so, it would be far more devastating than his split with Alice had been.

Hugo's trepidation grew as his train rolled past the chalk escarpments of the North Downs and deeper into Kent. It was cold that January morning, with the temperature still below freezing. Silver hilltops glittered in the distance, and naked trees flashed by like sentinels guarding the landscape.

It was gone midday when Hugo arrived at the cottage. Pockets of frost remained on the path, and lengthy shadows lined the approach as he walked along it. A solitary crow heralded his arrival with loud caws, and he glanced at the bird on a branch to his right.

He was still on the path when the door swung open – Elizabeth must have seen him coming. She stood in the doorway, shielding her eyes from the sun, her features veiled by a concealing shadow.

Hugo's pulse quickened. He looked at the crow, still cawing and strutting on the branch to his right.

Nervously, he entered the cottage.

• CHAPTER 41 •

Terry's head was all over the place. He'd been feeling like shit for days now. Or was it weeks? Probably weeks by this stage.

It was early afternoon in south London, and Terry was sitting in his flat, his evening shift still hours away. He wished his work would come sooner.

His thoughts were bleak as he sat on his own; even the bright sunshine outside didn't help. He scratched his bald head, got up from his seat and wandered to the window. Narrowing his eyes, he peered through the aluminium blind. The brutalist vista, grim and foreboding, did nothing to correct his mood.

He sat back down. It was a tired old sofa, uncomfortable at the best of times; right now, it felt even worse.

Terry's mind was hyperactive. He stood straight up, then sank back down, incapable of remaining still. *This is useless.* He tapped his fingers against the adjacent cushion in frustration. Shaking his head decidedly, he stood up one last time. *I need to get some fresh air.*

He grabbed his keys and departed his first floor flat, locking the door behind him. The communal stairs, freezing cold and scarred with graffiti, reeked with the pungent stink of piss. Terry held his nose and hurried down, only breathing again when he reached the bottom. With a sharp intake of breath, he stepped into the crisp January air outside.

Squinting in the sunlight, he started walking. A biting northerly licked his cheeks and caused his eyes to water; that was a good thing, though. Perhaps the cold would cleanse his mind and leave him feeling refreshed.

He hadn't put his coat on. His jeans and light sweater offered scant protection against the elements, but Terry still felt glad: a chill to the bone might numb his mood and mitigate the darkness that hung in his heart.

He wandered aimlessly, his pace less brisk than normal in these blistering atmospherics. Round the block, he trudged – listlessly shuffling past the concrete blocks and iron palisades that adorned his local streets. Around him, grim grey flats rose like a towering concrete forest, while the pavements below were scattered with pedestrians, bustling to and fro like ants on the forest floor.

A red shape pulled up to his right – a London bus – the sharp shrill of its air brakes piercing the cold when it stopped. Some people disembarked, and Terry veered left to avoid them. Skirting around the bus stop, he glanced at the row of shops he passed: two pawnbrokers, a minimart and a boarded-up dry cleaners. This part of London lacked soul. Just like he did.

The bus heaved off, and Terry watched it proceed down the long, straight road to God-knows-where. When the noise of its engine faded to nothing, London's silence ached in his ears. He'd been walking for twenty minutes, but he remained in torment still.

It was time to head for home.

He completed his loop, returned to the flat and stepped through the front door. His hands were like blocks of ice from the cold, so he sat on the sofa, put his feet up, and lay on his palms to warm them. Terry thought hard, then closed his eyes with a sigh. *Get out of my mind, Elizabeth!*

He was in that spell of depression.

It was the news broadcast that had brought it back. Now his wounds were open again and they oozed with guilt and regret. Still, he was right to have called the authorities. He was confident of that, at least.

Thoughts of his crimes were bad enough, but not having updates hurt him most. He'd checked the news almost every day but the story seemed to be cold. Had the authorities paid her their visit? Had she worked out who'd contacted them? Was she safe and well? These were questions he just couldn't answer. *Elizabeth, my sweet – what on earth's become of you?*

Imprisoned in his ignorance, Terry felt isolated – like an exile cast adrift. He poured a drink to steady himself: a small brandy – just enough to take the edge of things and warm him after his walk.

He'd tasted depression before, of course. Sometimes his bouts would go on for weeks; more often, they'd last for months. Those dark, despairing winters-of-the-mind – he could be so erratic when they struck! Once, he'd even turned up at Elizabeth's house…

*No! Don't you think about it!*

There was no need to dwell on that stupid, stupid moment. Four extra years it had cost him, but that was nothing compared to the humiliation it had caused. He wouldn't be repeating that little exercise any time soon.

But then again, what if he just…

*Really, Terry? Are we really going to entertain these crazy notions? Snap out of it, man!* He fought to reason with himself, but it was a losing fight in the grips of depression. He didn't have the strength of will to resist.

He *needed* news of Elizabeth. All he wanted was to glimpse her. It was hardly the same as banging on her door and frightening the life out of her. He could go along in his little car and remain inside it. He could park on the road and stay unnoticed. She wouldn't even know he was there.

'Yes,' he murmured, his spirits lifting at the thought. *She doesn't know what car I drive. I can do it inconspicuously.*

A quick look at her face, and he'd be on his way. Just a peek as she popped to the shops or returned from a walk – that was all he'd need to rid himself of these intrusive thoughts and get on with his life in peace.

Today was out of the question; he had a shift at the supermarket later.

*Tomorrow, then.*

He'd have a good night's sleep and drive to her village tomorrow. It was an excellent plan; he was sure of that. He poured himself another brandy, an even smaller one this time. Terry felt better already.

*Tomorrow,* he resolved.

• CHAPTER 42 •

They said hello and hugged, but Hugo's mind was troubled. He'd been nervous and worried all journey. What did she want to talk to him about? They'd barely sat down before he enquired.

'Not now,' Elizabeth said, reclining back on the living room sofa. 'Let's enjoy the day together first.'

Her brush-off was unsatisfactory. She'd seemed so distant lately, and Hugo's concerns were far from assuaged. 'Will this be the last time we see each other?' he asked pathetically.

She smiled apologetically, distressed she'd conveyed that impression. Her feelings, she promised, were just as strong as ever; she had no intention of ending things.

But that was where she left it. There were no further disclosures, and serious discussion could wait until tomorrow. Why cloud such a beautiful day when it had been so long since they'd seen each other?

Hugo knew better than to persist. He'd have to wait until morning.

The afternoon stayed cold and crisp. Frost clung to the ground as blinding low sunshine pierced the firmament, its timid rays no match for the winking galaxy below. Wrapped up warm, they went for a walk, the four o'clock January sunset making their jaunt at the meadow a brief one.

At dusk, they headed up to the village, past the frozen pond and into the local pub. The building was old and rustic, a former coaching inn on the road to Tunbridge Wells. Inside, thick, bare-brick walls were decorated with sketches of Kent's agricultural heritage. In the lounge, an open fire roared, with antique horse tack proudly displayed around it. Red-cheeked and streaming-nosed, they sat themselves down to thaw.

The scene was reminiscent of the Ship and Shovell, and a meal and drinks were ordered. Wisely, Hugo stuck to cola, his father's caution against excessive alcohol still ringing in his ears.

Elizabeth also abstained. 'An act of solidarity,' she told him.

But Hugo still felt puzzled by her choice to stick to orange juice. *It's not like her to avoid a drink.*

Back at the cottage, they sat on the sofa. 'I guess skinning up isn't a good idea,' Elizabeth jested.

'Better not,' he agreed. 'I might turn into a monster.'

In mocking satire, he bulged his eyes and raised his hands to her neck like a crazed strangler, then dropped them and laughed hysterically. Elizabeth dug him in the ribs and chuckled – his diagnosis was terrible, but at least they saw the funny side.

Before long it was time for bed. They freshened up and clambered in next to one another. When Hugo moved in for a cuddle, his companion reciprocated eagerly.

They kissed, and Hugo's roving hand explored the length of her body before coming to rest against the soft comfort of her breast.

Elizabeth grabbed his wrist and stopped him. 'No,' she said with gentle firmness. 'Not tonight.'

Hugo's excitement waned. 'What's the matter?' he asked, perplexed.

'Nothing's the matter,' she said, touching him sweetly on the shoulder. 'I'm just not in the mood this evening.' She buried herself in the sheets and spooned her body away from him.

'Okay,' he replied, rolling onto his back and staring at the ceiling. 'I guess we can leave it tonight.'

'I love you,' Elizabeth said quietly, turning over and kissing him on the cheek.

'I love you too,' he replied tremulously.

Befuddled, he lay there motionless. Why didn't she want him? Had he done something wrong? As he drifted into unconsciousness, he thought of the crow he'd seen in the tree. A darker omen he couldn't imagine.

*The setting was unfamiliar. Where was he? What was happening? And why on earth did he find himself...*

*Sitting in the back of a car?*

*The vehicle was stationary, and a woman was in the driver's seat. Sat directly behind her, Hugo could see a mass of curly dark hair protruding above the headrest. It was only when he glanced in the rear-view mirror that he saw a pair of hazel eyes reflecting. Warm and friendly, he watched their gaze. He didn't know who she was, but the woman looked...*

*Strangely familiar.*

*He cocked his head and peered through the window. They were in a school car park. It was home time, and streams of children were walking through the gates, the slam of car doors echoing like a drum solo as parents picked up their offspring.*

*It was the middle of April – the first day back after the Easter holidays. Daffodils shone in splendid yellow, and beech and birch were bursting into leaf. White clouds were high in the sky, and now and then, the sun poked through.*

*Yet still, the world seemed grey...*

*The local comprehensive was housed in a '60s concrete eyesore, a giant grey cube that looked like a Soviet housing block. A breeze block wall skirted the perimeter, and potholed tarmac stretched across the site.*

*Hugo cast his eyes towards the crumbling main school building. At that moment, he spotted her. She looked different in her uniform – a neat navy blazer, white shirt, and smart, knee-length skirt – but the girl was unmistakable, even amidst the* mass of identically dressed children who thronged towards the exit gates.

The girl opened the door and got into the passenger side front seat.

'How was your first day?' asked the curly-haired driver. She seemed a little anxious, but the girl looked over and beamed.

'It was great!' she replied with bristling enthusiasm. 'I think I'll like it here. They buddied me up with a really nice girl. I'll probably make some friends.'

The woman's anxiety lifted and she smiled. 'I was worried you'd hate it. It's a funny time of year to be starting a brand new school. I thought you'd be overwhelmed. Especially after everything that's happened.'

'Are you kidding?' the girl breezed back. 'I feel like a normal teenager again. It's great to be back at a school.'

Hugo admired her fortitude. By the tender age of fourteen, she had witnessed the deaths of both her parents, had suffered repeated rapes by her uncle and had given birth to his child. Yet all she asked was to live like a normal teenager.

The woman started the engine and trundled towards the gates. 'That reminds me,' she said, looking across at the youngster. 'Normality is coming in other ways, too.'

The girl looked pleased but strangely pained. 'Really?' she said with a sense of trepidation. She knew what the woman was talking about.

'I had a call this morning,' the woman informed her. 'The necessary papers have all gone through. Next weekend...'

He woke to the sound of retching in the bathroom. Unused to being roused externally, he lay there dazed and startled. What had just happened? One moment he was in the back of a car; the next, he'd woken in Elizabeth's bed.

Another dream had struck. A *psychotic* dream, as he now knew them to be. Despite the medication, they were still plaguing him. *I wish they'd got the dosage right.* In his head, the dream was vivid: the girl; the car; the school. But something different nagged this time.

It was the woman.

Who was she? He recognised her, but that was all. Those hazel eyes – where had he seen them before? He racked his brains, but…

Nothing!

He looked at the clock on the bedside table – ten past six in the morning. It was still dark outside, but things were stirring in the January blackness.

Another heave next door and vomit slopped into the toilet bowl. The sound of flushing followed it.

Hugo sat himself up and turned the bedside lamp on. *Who was that woman?*

Normally his dreams would end naturally, but this one got interrupted before concluding. Intuition told him the night had unfinished business – he couldn't say when, but he knew he'd see the end of that car journey.

But that would happen when he slept. Right now, he was awake, and the noise next door concerned him. Stomping feet had arrived at the sink, and moments later, the taps turned on. Loud gargling followed. *Elizabeth's unwell.*

When she returned, Elizabeth looked at him guiltily. 'I'm sorry,' she said, 'I didn't mean to wake you.'

'It's fine,' he replied, scratching his head and regarding her. 'In fact, I should probably thank you. I was having another nightmare.'

She smiled sadly, then sat on the end of the bed and gazed into space.

'Are you unwell?' he sympathised, fearing she'd caught a winter bug. 'I heard you being sick in the toilet.'

Slowly, she turned her head and engaged him with a silent, haunted stare. 'This isn't how I wanted to do it,' she lamented. 'But are you ready to have that chat I promised you?'

Hugo gasped as the penny dropped.

The scales fell from his eyes like leaves on a breeze – he knew exactly what she was going to say.

Her pronouncement came with a whimper.

• CHAPTER 43 •

It was dark when Terry set off in his little green hatchback. It was still dark when he turned onto the A21 – the trunk road that connects London with the counties of Kent and Sussex.

But as he ventured south, daybreak stirred from the shadows. To the east, the dim glow of twilight appeared on the horizon. A new day was dawning and the promise of seeing Elizabeth warmed his heart like the first rays of sunshine. Even scraping the ice off his windscreen had been a semi-pleasurable experience.

Of course, it wasn't a promise; it was more of a hope than an expectation. But how he wanted to see her! It would be a bitter disappointment to come all this way only to miss out on clocking her. Still, it got him out of the flat and gave him a sense of purpose. The shortest encounter would do.

*All I need is a glimpse.*

The frigid blackness of night was still receding when Terry arrived in the village. Even at this hour, the first few commuters were well on their way, and he was slowed to a crawl as he motored past the pond.

At the T-junction, he turned left onto the quiet little lane that led out of the village. Intending to remain inconspicuous, he planned to park some distance from the cottage.

But Terry couldn't resist taking a closer look, so he killed his headlights and trundled up the potholed path to her house. He stopped the car and peered through the passenger side window. *She's only a few metres away. She's probably all tucked up in bed, safe and sound. Just as well she doesn't know I'm here.*

Remembering what had happened the last time he'd shown up, he jerked his head to the front and exhaled sharply. A sudden rush of guilt ran through him. What he'd done to Elizabeth was inexcusable.

Shamed by the memories, he turned the car around and drove back onto the public lane. When he found a suitable place, he parked and switched off the engine. Now it was simply a case of waiting.

• CHAPTER 44 •

*Morning sickness!*

*Hugo's mind pulsated as the thought struck home. No wonder she stuck to orange juice in the pub.*

Elizabeth confirmed it with a dispirited murmur. 'I'm pregnant,' she sighed, leaving the words to hang.

Still propped up in bed, his head dropped down with a jerk. He puffed his cheeks and blew.

'Say something,' she urged him.

For a moment, he stayed unresponsive. Then, ever so slowly, he raised his head and engaged her. 'Are you certain?' he asked clumsily.

'One hundred per cent.'

She'd known for just over a week, but her suspicions had grown much sooner. She'd missed a period, and what turned out to be morning sickness had begun about six weeks after they'd first had sex at the meadow. The test she'd bought at a local chemist confirmed her fears.

Hugo now understood why she'd been so distant; she couldn't possibly have told him something like this over FaceTime.

'Are you angry?' she asked, furrowing her brow with worry.

'Angry?' He shifted along the bed and sat next to her. 'Why would I be angry?' He grabbed her hand and squeezed it.

'Men can run away from these things,' she shrugged. 'They disappear off and leave the women to deal with them.'

He squeezed her hand more tightly. 'Do you honestly think I'd do that?'

'You're eighteen. You have your life ahead of you. This isn't a romantic drama, Hugo. This is real life.'

Elizabeth was right. Making a woman pregnant at his age was a seismic shift in perspective. How long would the knight in shining armour last once reality set in? His diagnosis added a complication. Could a psychotic adolescent be a father to a child? Suddenly, he felt like a lost little boy. 'What are we going to do?' he asked like a serf seeking counsel from his lady.

She looked away, then shook her head before resting it on his shoulder. 'I don't know. But whatever we do we should decide it together.'

They didn't go back to sleep. Instead, they sat in the living room and watched as the morning encroached. It was sunny again, and ground frost glittered outside like a carpet of winking granite. At the rear of Elizabeth's cottage, three silver birches sprang like ghosts and froze in winter's breath. Silent, inanimate, dormant – Hugo almost wished he was one of them.

They'd been discussing what to do for hours. Hugo never used the words 'abortion' or 'termination' – whenever he tried to steer things in that direction, Elizabeth slapped him down. Soon, her implicit message became apparent: she wanted to have this baby.

'But I thought we were deciding together,' he pointed out.

'We are,' she nodded. 'But let me be clear about what we're deciding.'

Hugo narrowed his eyes in caution.

'I'm going to have this baby,' Elizabeth continued. 'Make no mistake – I will be a mother. The thing we're deciding together concerns the role you're going to play in the baby's life. The question is: will it be my child or our child.'

She said it sensitively; it was an invitation rather than an ultimatum. Nevertheless, Hugo knew precisely where he stood. For a moment, he sat there terrified.

'Take your time,' she reassured him. 'Whatever you choose it needs to be final.'

Hugo knew what she meant. The child needed stability, not a capricious eighteen-year-old playing the role of a semi-absentee father. If he decided to walk away and reduce Elizabeth to single motherhood, then so be it; it would be better than creating a bond between father and baby, only to break it when the realities of parenthood became too great for him to bear.

On the other hand, he could show some maturity and step up to his adult responsibilities like the man he almost was. But if he chose that path, there could be no going back. It wouldn't be fair on Elizabeth or the child to backtrack.

Thank goodness he had time to decide. *But what will I tell my father?*

He began to reflect immediately. The child's financial needs would require attention right away. His Oxford studies would be left in tatters, his dreams of becoming a teacher kyboshed by the imminent need to support his family.

The permutations hurt his head, and he needed fresh air to calm it. Stepping through the front door, he entered the shivering blueness of the Kent outdoors. Bare trees and naked hedging lined the path that led to the lane. As he walked along it, the sound of his footfalls were amplified on the frozen ground beneath him. A few moments later, he turned right at the intersection and headed towards the village. A gentle stroll and a few minutes at the pond would do him the world of good.

He'd walked a couple of hundred yards before coming to the little row of houses that lined the route. Centuries-old, the tiny cottages were packed together in neat little terraces, with minute front gardens that remained pretty in the depths of winter. In the absence of driveways, the residents' cars were parked parallel to the front of their properties.

At first, Hugo paid scant attention to the stationary vehicles. But as he drew closer, something stirred in the little green hatchback at the front of the line. For no apparent reason, a lone figure was sitting in the car. Hugo was about to walk past but another sudden movement drew his eye.

He turned and looked inside the hatchback.

When he saw the occupant's face he let out a yelp and stopped dead in his tracks. His heart nearly burst through his ribcage and he staggered backwards, thrusting out a hand to grab hold of a wall or hedge – anything to steady himself and avoid toppling over in shock.

The occupant saw what was happening and wound down the window. Are you all right?' he hollered.

Hugo stared straight at him. The face was older – perhaps twenty years older. The mop of light brown hair had long since gone, but the bald head was no disguise for the features he knew so well. The man was about sixty, but Hugo remembered a more youthful form – he'd seen him before in his dreams.

'My God,' he gasped. 'It's you! You're...you're'...he struggled to get the words out. 'You're Uncle Pete!'

He didn't wait for a response. With scrambled senses, all Hugo could think was to run. He turned and started sprinting back from whence he came. When he arrived at the cottage, he burst through the door, legs trembling, heart palpitating.

'Elizabeth!'

His panic made her spring from the sofa. By the time he reached the living room, she was already on her feet.

'Elizabeth,' he repeated, bounding towards her like a dog being summoned. 'Something's just happened.' He grabbed her arms and stared into her eyes. 'Something outside. On the road. Please, take a seat. I don't think you're going to believe it.'

### CHAPTER 45

Hugo sat on the sofa, hands shaking, face whitened to chalk. Elizabeth perched next to him and used her palm to stroke his back in soothing, circular motions.

'Take your time,' she consoled him. 'Is it the illness? Do you need to take your medication?'

He didn't answer, but looked at her with a shell-shocked, frightened stare. When she saw his eyes she recoiled in alarm. 'Jesus, Hugo! You look like you've seen a ghost!'

'Perhaps I have,' he trembled. His body was in the room, but his mind was stuck outside.

Elizabeth was stunned at the change. He'd been fine a few moments ago; it had to be the psychosis. She'd never witnessed an episode, and seeing one happen was frightening for her.

When he'd calmed down sufficiently, she went to put the kettle on. Alone in the living room, he could collect his thoughts in peace. It was a chance for her to do likewise.

The taste of tea helped quiet him. He took a big swig from his plain white cup before attempting an explanation. 'Where to begin?' he thought out loud. His mind was less ordered than an assorted box of jigsaw pieces.

'Begin at the beginning,' she encouraged him. 'It's always the best place to start.'

'Sage advice,' he acknowledged with the faintest of nods. 'Okay then; here goes...'

He cleared his throat and started his tale. 'It's my dreams,' he began. 'Not the ordinary ones, but the...*other*...ones.'

*The psychotic ones* thought Elizabeth. 'Go on,' she urged him.

Hugo did just that. 'Have I ever discussed their content with you?'

Elizabeth shook her head. 'Not really. I know there's a little girl, but that's about it. You said she was raped in one of them – you told me that on the evening I mentioned my own attack – but apart from that, nothing.'

He took another mouthful of tea. 'The dreams began in the autumn,' he explained. 'Not long after I started at Oxford. The little girl was about ten back then. She lived with her mother and father...'

Hugo froze.

'What's wrong?' Elizabeth asked.

'Maybe the beginning isn't the best place to start after all.'

He stood up as an idea electrified his brain like a lightning bolt. 'Perhaps it's easier if I just show you!'

Now her alarm increased. 'Show me? Show me what? I don't understand what you're talking about.'

Hugo tried to slow his whirring mind. 'This is crazy,' he said, slapping his thighs with a thud. 'But I need you to come with me.'

Unmoved, Elizabeth remained seated. 'Where?' she queried.

'Outside for a moment.'

'Hugo, it's freezing cold.'

'Just trust me.'

He thrust out an arm and yanked her to her feet. Now Elizabeth was the one with the racing thoughts. Without medical training, she didn't know how to react. Should she humour him and follow in the hope the episode would pass, or was it safer to keep him indoors?

Hugo took the decision out of her hands by dragging her to the front door. There was little point in arguing, so she followed him dutifully.

'We're not going far,' he said. 'Just a couple of hundred metres up the road.'

She just had time to grab her coat before he bundled her into the frigid winter air. Seizing her hand, he sped her up the path like an excited puppy tugging on the lead. Elizabeth could barely keep pace as clouds of ghost-white breath grew thick with every exhalation.

Everything about him was animated. 'I need to tell you,' he yelled, 'if my theory's right, then what you're about to see will be tremendously upsetting for you.'

'Hugo, what the hell is going on?'

'Trust me!' he repeated.

At the end of the path, they wheeled right onto the lane that led to the T-junction. Hugo spun and looked at her. On either side, the usually green fields shivered in metallic shades of blue. 'We don't need to get too close,' he assured her, walking backwards and gesturing excitedly. 'You just need to see him!'

Elizabeth followed warily. 'Hugo, you're scaring me.'

'One look is all you'll need!'

They continued a few more metres before Hugo suddenly stopped. Ten yards behind him, Elizabeth did so too. 'It's the little green hatchback,' he said, his voice now soft and mellow. 'Take a look inside it.'

Elizabeth peered past him. 'What green hatchback?' she asked confusedly. 'There's a red saloon and a black SUV. Those are the neighbours' cars, Hugo. What am I meant to be looking at?'

He swivelled around and looked to the front. '*Shit!*' he exclaimed. He ran twenty yards forward, then turned again and thrust his arms to the side. 'He was here only minutes ago!'

'Hugo, there isn't a green hatchback in sight.'

'But there *was!*' he insisted.

He looked at her with pleading eyes, then spun around and sprinted to the line of cars. When he arrived, he started looking between them before crossing the road to search the scrubby hedgerow on the other side. It was as if he were looking for a child's lost toy.

Slowly, his energy faded, and his shoulders dropped. Elizabeth approached and calmed him with her presence. 'Hugo, there's nothing here. Let's go back to the cottage and sit down.'

Once again, he found himself being consoled on Elizabeth's sofa. 'I don't want to sound like your father,' she said, 'but have you taken your medication?'

'Yes,' he replied, running his fingers through his lank hair and scowling. 'The next dose is hours away.'

When he looked her in the eye, he noticed the corners of her mouth were slightly upturned. It was a display of sympathy.

'This is the first time I've seen it,' she said.

'Seen what?'

'The psychosis.' She touched him on the shoulder and stroked it. 'I thought it only struck while you slept. Is this the first time it's affected your daytime?'

Hugo struggled to hide his exasperation. 'That car was there,' he said. 'I promise it was. He must have just driven off.'

Elizabeth wasn't persuaded. 'Hallucinations are a symptom,' she said, still stroking his shoulder. 'And episodes of delirium, too. Come on, Hugo, you were looking for a car in a hedgerow.' She pursed her lips and looked right at him. 'Things seem to be getting worse for you, don't they? You should probably speak to your father again.'

'He was *there*, Elizabeth, I swear it.'

But *could* he swear it? The professional diagnosis had been 'psychosis'. Elizabeth was correct: hallucinations and delirium were symptoms all right. Pete's presence in that car had seemed so real, yet so were the scenes in his dreams. Maybe she was right: perhaps his illness was worsening and encroaching on his daylight hours too now. In horror, he started to doubt himself. Was what he saw outside a mere illusion? Was he creeping towards insanity after all?

He had one final card to play, one last empirical test to help determine things. His subject was sitting right next to him, and her responses would yield a definitive answer. It was time to tap into her memories.

'Elizabeth,' he began tentatively, knowing that broaching the echoes of her past would upset her. 'If you'll humour me and listen, then I might be able to explain things for you.'

He scratched his head and wondered where to start.

'Before I took you outside, I was going to ask you something. I wanted you to come with me to see the *evidence*, but since none was there, perhaps we can go back to the original question.'

'Okay,' she agreed, sensing a talk would be good for him. She stopped stroking his shoulder and moved along the sofa, adopting a more purposeful pose and inviting him to start. 'You were going to tell me about your dreams,' she said. 'The ones involving that little girl.'

'I was,' he affirmed, his discomfort all too palpable. 'And this is so terribly hard to say – but I think that little girl...'

He forced himself to utter it.

'...I think that little girl...could be *you*.'

His assertion was preposterous, but she wasn't surprised given the diagnosis. She listened sympathetically, but her sceptical eyes gave her true thoughts away. 'And what makes you say that?' she enquired patiently.

He expected her dubiety and progressed with his tale unabated. 'The things I've been dreaming,' he explained. 'When you put them together with what I saw in that car – with *who* I saw in that car – there's no doubt something strange is happening.'

She nodded and let him continue.

'Before I start, please know that this will be very upsetting for you.'

She folded her arms. 'You said something similar when you dragged me outside. Just talk to me, Hugo.'

'All right,' he said. 'But if you want me to stop, just tell me.'

He began with the dream in Ealing – the one involving the paddling pool in the garden, and how his initial joy had morphed into dread when the girl's parents went inside. 'It was most un-dream like,' he told her. 'There was no bizarreness and nothing from my own memories or experiences.'

Elizabeth listened, her arms still folded in front of her.

'Which is why I need to ask you,' continued Hugo, 'was your childhood spent in suburbia? Before you moved to the cottage, I mean.'

Almost imperceptibly, the fingertips of Elizabeth's right hand tightened their grip on her left elbow. 'Yes,' she replied. It felt like a game, but the concern was brewing inside her.

'And did your house have a garden?'

'Yes – I grew up in a three-bed semi in Bromley. It's a suburb in southeast London.' She smiled quizzically, but Hugo's next question changed the dynamic.

'And here's the crux,' he stated solemnly. 'Were your parents called Jim and Sandra?'

The smile faded and a grave stare replaced it. She struggled to absorb his question and looked at his face with suspicion. Now her fingertips tightened around her elbow like a vice. 'How could you possibly know that?'

Hugo removed his spectacles and massaged his forehead. 'Then it's true,' he murmured. 'All this time, and it was *your* life I was seeing.'

Elizabeth barely heard him. 'What else do you know about my parents?'

Hugo replaced his glasses. He knew his words would hurt, so he spoke in a sensitive voice. 'I know they both died when you were young,' he said. 'I saw the events occur – the fire first, and then the accident in the pool.'

She sprang into action at that. '*No!*' she screamed, jolting up from the sofa and clasping her hand to her mouth in disbelief. 'What game are you playing?' she yelled, moving to the window to put some distance between them. 'Tell me what's going on, Hugo! Who have you been speaking to? I demand to know! How do you know what happened to my parents?'

'Elizabeth, please,' he said, remembering what had happened the last time she became hysterical. Fearing another expulsion, he offered a calming hand gesture. 'Please,' he repeated. 'I need you to hear me out. It's important.'

He waited until a tear had rolled down her cheek, then patted the space she'd vacated on the sofa. 'Come and sit back down,' he implored. 'If you're prepared to listen, I can prove these things are true.'

'How?' she snapped without moving a muscle.

'I know things about those events that no one else could,' he explained delicately. 'No one except you, that is.'

She hesitated, but intrigue got the better of her. 'What kind of things?' she asked before sitting back down.

'Things like the Candlelight service you attended when your father died. You told your mother you could smell bonfires as you walked back home.'

Elizabeth listened, astonished.

'And in Mallorca, you tried three times to swim a length of the pool underwater. You never quite managed a full one.'

Her mouth opened wide and she stopped breathing for a moment. Hugo took hold of her hand and squeezed it. 'Elizabeth,' he offered. 'I'm so terribly sorry these things have happened to you.'

It was a while before she replied, but when she did, her words confirmed his theory. 'My God,' she uttered. 'You *have* been dreaming about me.'

They paused to let things sink in. This time it was Hugo who made the tea while Elizabeth sat on the sofa and waited. When he returned, she pressed him for additional details.

Hugo dredged the depths of his dreams. He wanted to avoid the more gruesome events of her parents' deaths, but Elizabeth insisted on hearing them. With a stir of his tea, he went through what he'd witnessed.

He chronicled how the firefighters held back Sandra when the roof collapsed in the blaze. He described what he'd seen on the stretcher when Jim's blackened body was carried to the waiting ambulance. He even told her about the moment Jim was pronounced dead, and the clock on the wall that read two-forty-five.

Next, Hugo spoke of Mallorca and the panic he'd seen in the pool. He explained the frenzied way that Pete had tried to sever his sister's hair, and the harrowing events of the CPR procedure.

Finally, he recalled the Spanish hospital and how she'd collapsed in her uncle's arms when Sandra's death was confirmed. Her sobs still hurt him now.

Elizabeth's mind was blown. 'Jesus,' she said, wiping the tears from her eyes. 'You remember it better than I do.'

'I guess it's just more recent for me.'

He took a deep breath before continuing. 'Elizabeth,' he murmured, 'I know what happened with your uncle.'

'Tell me everything you know,' she instructed him. 'Don't leave anything out.'

He nodded, then drank some tea from his cup. 'I dreamt it the night you told me about being attacked,' he began. 'At first, I thought my dream was different, but…'

He stopped mid-sentence as the realisation dawned. *'HANG ON!'* he exclaimed.

'What is it?'

She still hadn't joined the dots.

'Don't you remember!' he cried, rising up and placing his hands on top of his head. 'That night, I dreamt about the girl's molestation – I went to the bathroom to freshen up, and when I came back, you were already awake. You'd been dreaming about *your* attack as a child!'

Now those dots got joined. The significance hit her right away: 'My God,' she said for a second time. 'We must have been dreaming it simultaneously. We were seeing—'

'Exactly the same thing at exactly the same time,' confirmed Hugo, finishing the sentence for her.

He furnished her with the details of what he'd seen that night: her uncle's physical appearance; the televised cricket match; the book she'd been reading; the horror of the assault he'd witnessed. They matched her memories perfectly.

Then he recalled the deadness he'd seen in her eyes. Those *blue* eyes – they'd been hiding in plain sight all along. How had he not seen things sooner?

He'd considered the idea before – in the bathroom – immediately after the dream. *Don't be ridiculous,* he remembered telling himself. *Elizabeth grew up with her parents right here in this very cottage.*

Except they weren't her parents. Her birth mother and father had died in the fire and the pool. The ones who owned this cottage must have been her adoptive parents.

It was then that another thing struck him.

*That woman in the car.* Suddenly he knew where he'd seen her. The curly hair, the hazel eyes – she'd been one of the midwives he'd seen at the birth. The one who'd held her hand and cut the cord. Only, she wasn't a midwife; he'd simply *mistaken* her for one.

In fact, she was the girl's adoptive mother, the woman who'd picked her up from school. Now that dream made sense, or what he'd seen of it, at least. *What was it trying to tell me before it was interrupted?*

It was Elizabeth who returned him to the here and now. 'What made you think it was me?' she asked, trying to understand how he'd put two and two together.

The pair were still on their feet, their brains overwhelmed by the revelations. Hugo's hands were still on his head, but he dropped them to his sides with a slap. 'It was what I saw outside,' he explained. 'When I looked into that green hatchback...'

Elizabeth twitched her eyebrows. 'But I thought that was the psychosis,' she said. 'There wasn't anything out there when we looked.'

'Don't you see?' cried Hugo. 'There *is* no psychosis! That car was definitely there. But the car itself isn't important. It's the person *driving* it who matters.'

His urgency jolted her understanding. 'Who was it?' she asked, fearing she knew the answer.

Hugo looked at her gravely. 'It was your Uncle Pete,' he said.

## DREAMS

When the shock wore off, they sat back down on the sofa. Elizabeth was beside herself. Had Pete Terry not learned his lesson? The last time he'd appeared, he'd been returned to prison; now, he was turning up again.

They thought about calling the police but decided against it. As long as he left her alone, Pete could sit in his car as much as he liked. There were more important things to worry about – like what was going on with these dreams? Each asked the other what could be causing them. Neither had an explanation.

But there was one thing Hugo *could* say with conviction. 'I'm going to be a father to our baby,' he declared out of the blue. It seemed natural: right now, he felt closer to Elizabeth than ever.

Elizabeth scrutinised him. 'You're sure?' she probed, seeking to test his mettle. 'You remember what I said about sticking to decisions?'

'I remember. And I've never been more sure about anything. I'm going to be here for that baby.' He slid along the sofa and took hold of both her hands. 'And I'm going to be here for *you*,' he added. There's a special bond between us, and I know you feel it too.'

She nodded to show that she did.

'And these dreams,' he continued. 'I don't know what's going on, but they have to be connected somehow – it's like they're trying to tell me something. Whatever it is, you and I are meant to be together.'

Elizabeth became euphoric. 'I love you; I love you; I love you,' she announced, kissing him and pulling him close. Hugo reciprocated by hugging her tightly.

They were going to be a family. At last, after everything that had happened to her, she finally had a future to look forward to. 'You can't be a father from a distance,' she told him. 'Will you move in with me down here?'

Hugo's face looked eager. 'I'd love to,' he replied. 'But before that can happen, there's something we need to do. Will you come with me? I'm not sure I can do it on my own.'

She looked perplexed.

'We have to go to Ealing,' he explained. 'It's time we came clean to my father. About everything.'

• CHAPTER 46 •

When evening came, winter's grip grew stronger. Metallic objects were the first to bear the brunt as a glitter-like frost descended. As darkness fell, parked cars and manhole covers twinkled in the frigid streets of central Oxford.

By 7 PM, the city had been shrouded in blackness for nearly three hours. Dinner at Wadham College had finished fifteen minutes earlier, and it wouldn't be long before the manicured lawns of the Front and Back Quads would be transfigured from dormant green to a ghostly silver blue. Even the Cloister Garden wouldn't escape the unforgiving onslaught.

Out the front, the paving slabs and tarmac on Parks Road were already vanquished into a thousand silver sparkles, winking in surrender beneath silent streetlights and the candle-like vigil of a torpid half-moon.

But inside, things were different. The college bar fizzed with ideas and chat, and the lights in bedrooms burned as students laboured on their projects. Wadham was warm and alive — a veritable ants' nest of activity and a toasty shield against the freezing siege outside.

Snug in her bedroom, Alice sat alone at her desk after dinner. A few books and papers festooned her work surface and a lamp at the side blazed brilliantly. She focused her mind like a laser: a long night lay ahead if she was going to ameliorate things. The error she'd made was cataclysmic — Hugo had sought his father's medical expertise at *her* behest, which had resulted in the suspension of his studies.

She'd been racked with indomitable guilt ever since. A simple explanation and a straightforward course of treatment were what she'd expected: a little light therapy, or some exercises in stress reduction, perhaps. Whatever the interventions, they were supposed to relieve his symptoms and grant him the solace he needed to return refreshed and invigorated for the Hilary term.

Instead, he'd been diagnosed with psychosis and had dropped out of university altogether. If only she hadn't advised him on a subject she knew nothing about. If she'd kept her mouth shut, he would have arrived for the new term like everyone else. She felt like his unwitting assassin: culpable for his downfall, yet powerless to do anything about it. The situation seemed hopeless.

But that was before she stumbled upon a book yesterday morning in the library. The concept of dream telepathy, from the world of parapsychology, had sounded farfetched at first, but the more she'd read, the more she'd begun to wonder. A relatively short book, Alice had devoured it in a little over a day and had been inspired to extend her thinking with some additional research of her own. Thus, she sat at her desk and beavered urgently, the minutes melting away like butter on a baked potato.

Her concentration was so focused that she barely noticed the knock at her door or the intrusive entry that followed without an official invitation.

The deep voice made her jump. 'We need to have another word with the porter,' said Owen in his lilting Welsh accent. 'I thought they were going to do something about this incessant heat. I'm practically melting.'

Alice turned and addressed him. 'You could stick your head out the window,' she jested. 'You'd cool down pretty quick on a night like this.'

He simpered at her logic, then walked to the bed and sat on it. 'But seriously – how hard can it be to get the heating levels right? It's hardly rocket science.'

'It's true,' she conceded, suspecting there was a problem with the thermostat. 'I've got a bit of a sweat on myself.'

She stood up and removed her jumper before sitting back down at her desk. Owen encouraged her to join him on the bed. 'Haven't you done enough work for today? Why don't you come and give me a cuddle instead?'

His suggestion brought a coy smile to her face, but it didn't prevent a rebuffing. 'I'm afraid I'm going to be working for some time yet,' she said. 'Maybe you should get on with some of your own. Surely you have some reading to do?'

Owen wrinkled his nose in disappointment. 'I've finished all mine for today. What are you working on anyway?'

'The same thing as earlier.'

'Really?' he scoffed. 'Come on, Alice, you're wasting your time – it's pseudoscientific nonsense. A load of old bollocks.'

'And what makes you say that?' she protested.

'*Dream telepathy*? It's one step away from the occult, for Christ's sake! Even Freud had to admit defeat on that one.'

Owen was right. Freud had been one of the first to posit dream telepathy as a real phenomenon, yet despite his best efforts, he found no evidence to back it up. Neither did Jung, for that matter. Thus, in the absence of empirical verification, most scholars dismissed dream telepathy and ridiculed those who pursued it.

But neither Freud nor Jung were deterred by a mere lack of evidence; indeed, both had remained open to the possibility of dream telepathy throughout their careers. And, as Alice had discovered in her reading, subsequent researchers had been more successful in recording potential incidents.

In the 1960s, the psychoanalyst Montague Ullman conducted what became known as his 'picture experiments', where he woke sleeping subjects during REM and asked them whether they could identify a picture placed in another room.

The connection with Alice's oneirology assignment back in the Michaelmas Term wasn't lost on her. She remembered working on it with Owen in the Radcliffe Science Library and reading that Eugene Aserinsky had discovered REM in the 1950s. *Only a decade or so before Ullman's investigation*, she'd thought while studying the dream telepathy book. *No wonder Freud and Jung hadn't found any evidence – they were working before* Aserinsky, *so they weren't aware of the dream stages in the sleep cycle.*

Ullman, however, writing later, had used similar instrumentation to Asierinsky and had ensured his participants were woken at precisely the right moment during REM. This technology enabled him to collect the first empirical evidence of dream telepathy as a real phenomenon.

Alice had marvelled at what he'd discovered. For Ullman's initial research subject had been woken whilst dreaming about a chariot race, which had reminded her of a scene from the novel Ben Hur. It had recently been made into a film, and the participant remarked that she'd like to see it one day, given how much she'd enjoyed the book.

Yet in a room not far from where she'd been sleeping, an image from the movie Ben Hur had secretly lain sealed in an envelope – it was the picture Ullman had hoped she'd visualise in her sleep. He had discovered the very first evidence of dream telepathy and had succeeded where Freud and Jung had failed.

The next step was to replicate the results, but nothing definitive was forthcoming. While some experiments yielded partial success, others resulted in nothing whatsoever. Even with Aserinsky's instrumentation and the newfound knowledge of REM, nothing conclusive was ever found. It was back to square one and the days of Freud and Jung. Most experts were highly critical of Ullman's work, with many opting for outright ridicule.

The references to Aserinsky fired Alice's mind and she thought back to her oneirology assignment in the autumn. She hadn't realised how fateful those moments in the Radcliffe Science Library were when she'd read that article about dreaming disorders and the correlation between illusory dreaming and the clinical presentation of patients with certain mental disorders – *the delusions of schizophrenics*, she remembered telling Owen in a voice churlishly loud for a library.

That comment was the root of her mistake. She'd been too eager to make the link with Hugo's dream experiences, which were so out of the ordinary that they must have resulted from some medical abnormality of the sort she'd encountered in her reading.

Or so she'd presumed.

For just before dinner, she'd come across an interview with one of Ullman's collaborators that had taken her beyond what she'd encountered in the dream telepathy book; indeed, the thoughts of Professor Stanley Krippner had made her tremble at what she'd done to poor Hugo.

The guilt was almost too much to bear, and her nerves had begun to prickle. Whilst Krippner had accepted that the evidence for dream telepathy was patchy, he maintained that this should not detract from other important values that derived from his and his colleagues' work.

In particular, he pointed out that once the experimentation results had become widely known in psychiatric circles, professional attitudes towards those experiencing unusual dreams began to change. No longer were people who reported visions of distant events in the past or future considered automatic candidates for mental disorders. Similarly, those who encountered unfamiliar people and places were no longer assumed to be suffering schizophrenic delusions.

The early research participants in the dream telepathy experiments were not psychotic individuals; indeed, they weren't even borderline. They were ordinary people with stable personalities and good mental health.

Just like Hugo.

*Oh, Jesus Christ – just like Hugo!* The miscalculation had haunted her since the beginning of term. *Dear sweet Hugo.*

They may not have been compatible as a couple, but he remained a friend she cared deeply about and probably always would do. Feeling she owed him a debt, she was desperate to right the wrongs of her ill-advised suggestion and negate its deleterious effects. Somehow, she had to help him.

The present thought of Hugo increased her self-flagellation, and Owen's scepticism irked her. 'It's not dream telepathy as a theory,' Alice explained temperately. 'It's the associated issues that are important.'

Owen reclined on the bed and put his feet up. 'Such as?'

Alice prepared to admonish him. 'The connection between dreams and mental health for a start. And with everything that's happened to poor Hugo recently—'

'Not bloody Hugo again.' He put his head back and tutted.

Alice was incandescent. 'What?' she snapped, lurching forward to challenge him. 'Where's your compassion, Owen? You know what he's been going through with his dreams. They've cost him the rest of this year at university. Just you remember that.'

Owen rolled his eyes and stared dispassionately at the ceiling. 'Hugo's unwell,' he sighed. 'He's been professionally diagnosed with psychosis.'

'And what if the diagnosis is wrong?'

Owen couldn't believe what he was hearing. He sprang up, then swivelled to engage her. 'You're kidding me,' he protested, throwing his hands in the air before letting them slap back down on his thighs. 'I feel sorry for him; really, I do. But the answer to his problem lies with the professionals. You and I can't help him.'

'Are you jealous?'

'No.'

Alice's patience was wearing thin, and Owen's presence was irritating her. 'Just because he's my ex doesn't mean I've stopped caring for him.'

Owen was placed on the defensive. 'And I understand that. But come on, Alice, you've spent the day researching dream telepathy. You might as well go hunting for fairies at the bottom of the garden.'

She couldn't contain things at that. 'Look,' she spat, 'no one's forcing you to be here, Owen. If you're going to make snide remarks, you might as well sod off.' She pointed to the door in disgust.

Owen stood up, his pride wounded. 'Well, if that's your attitude, I'm off to the bar for a pint.' He jumped from the bed and headed for the exit. 'And for what it's worth, you should tell Hugo to take his medication properly. Doing so would help him an awful lot more than your fairy hunt.'

*Fuck off*, thought Alice, as she watched him leave the room.

Owen's insensitivity riled her. *How dare he be so cruel to Hugo.* She was almost moved to tears as she thought back to that morning in Ealing and the time she'd witnessed his struggles first-hand. He'd seemed so serene as she'd gazed upon his features, his face immobile and his eyes as still as stones beneath their lids. Little did she know the terror he was experiencing until he'd started to stir...

*OH. MY. GOD.* Alice rose to her feet in astonishment. The realisation hit her like an express train.

Hugo's eyes had been completely motionless that morning – they hadn't been fluttering at all while he slept. The explanation seemed simple: his dream must have been happening *outside* of REM. Was that even possible?

She remembered thinking such things in the Radcliffe Science Library when working on the oneirology assignment with Owen and had even asked him about the possibility. It had seemed an irrelevant curiosity at the time. But in the context of her dream telepathy research, it took on a new significance. If Hugo's affliction resulted from telepathic messages, then the mechanics of dream telepathy functioned on an entirely different level from the mechanics of ordinary dreaming.

*No wonder Ullman couldn't replicate his original data. He'd been using Aserinsky's instrumentation to wake people in the wrong stage of their sleep!* What had happened with his first participant must have been anomalous – either that or it involved some sort of carryover from the telepathic event into REM.

Quite by chance, Alice had made a discovery that had huge ramifications. With Hugo as a kind of quasi test subject, she had worked out that REM only governed the world of ordinary dreams; it was not responsible for the phenomena associated with dream telepathy. Hugo's experiences, with his eyes dead still, showed that telepathic dreams share no commonalities with the normal dreams of REM.

Alice started to shake. Not only had she, a first-year undergraduate, stumbled upon a connection that university professors had spent their entire careers failing to see, but she had also taken a first step towards solving the riddle of her ex-boyfriend's mysterious affliction.

Again, she thought back to that autumn morning at Swann's and her time in bed with Hugo. Everything she'd witnessed in Ealing, including what Hugo himself had reported, convinced her that dream telepathy was real. It was this phenomenon, not psychosis, that was responsible for his nocturnal experiences.

But her discovery only resulted in further questions: if Hugo really was receiving telepathic messages, then who was instigating them? And why?

And most perplexing of all, why did Hugo seem to be the only person affected when everyone else remained untouched? Hugo's dreams were complex, vivid and all-consuming – quite unlike those reported by Ullman's research participant.

Alice was a long way from the answers. Nevertheless, she wanted to speak to Hugo and inform him of what she'd discovered. Her conscience was heavy, and she felt she had a duty to tell him.

She whipped her phone from her pocket.

Typing a quick text message, she waited for what seemed an age. In truth, the response came in under a minute. When it did, the exchange read as follows:

**You free?**

Can be. Why?

**I have information. It's hard to explain. Can we FaceTime?**

Give me two minutes, then call me :)

Alice waited for two minutes and then called him on FaceTime. When the ringtone sounded, her heart began to pound. Eventually, the call connected.

### • CHAPTER 47 •

Hugo's voice pierced the quiet like sonar. Alice turned the volume down and squinted at her iPhone screen. She could barely see his face, so she got up from her desk and moved from the glare of the lamp.

Positioning herself on the bed, she lay flat to enjoy the cool of the mattress. She held the phone above her eyes and saw Hugo was standing outside, his features semi-veiled in the darkness. Only a dim silver splash from the moon lit his face.

'Hugo, where are you? I thought you'd be in your room at home.'

Hugo confirmed that he wasn't. 'I'm in Kent,' he said, walking a few yards up the path. Alice could see the cottage behind him slowly recede as he paced. 'I came straight down from Oxford,' he added. 'My dad thinks I'm still there.'

Alice changed the settings to speakerphone. 'What on earth are you doing in Kent?' she asked before remembering the King's Arms pub. 'Ah yes, the new girlfriend – *Elizabeth*.' She touched her cheeks with her palm.

'I stayed at hers last night,' he admitted. 'I'll be back in Ealing tomorrow, though. Christ, Alice, so much has happened over the last twenty-four hours. I wouldn't know where to begin.'

'Is this a good time to talk?' Alice asked stolidly.

'Yes,' he replied, sensing her news was important. 'I came outside specially to take this call. I wish I'd put my coat on, though – it's absolutely perishing down here.'

Alice smiled wryly. The contrast in temperature seemed a derisive metaphor – Hugo was out in the cold on so many different levels. 'I've something urgent to talk to you about,' she said. 'But just like you, I don't know where to begin.'

He took a few more paces up the path. 'Go ahead. But may I suggest you begin at the beginning? It's always the best place to start.'

Alice heard him chuckle but didn't know why it was funny.

She placed the phone on the mattress and tied her hair up. When she picked up the conversation, Hugo had reached the intersection with the lane that led to the village.

'I've made a terrible mistake,' she declared. 'And I owe you a massive apology.'

The culprit, she told him, was an online article about dreaming disorders. If only she hadn't paid attention to it.

Hugo assured her there was nothing to apologise for.

'You don't understand,' she insisted. 'I felt terrible when I heard you weren't coming back. I knew it was all my fault. I've never felt so guilty in all my life.'

He offered the faintest of nods.

'I had to make amends, so I started to do some research. Then, yesterday, I stumbled across a book.'

'What kind of a book?' His expressionless features were barely visible, but his voice offered a hint of intrigue.

Alice seized the moment. 'It's called *Dream Telepathy*. Don't laugh – it's not as crazy as it sounds.'

Hugo wasn't laughing; he was listening intently. After the madness of seeing Uncle Pete in his car, nothing seemed beyond the realms of possibility. He blew on his hands to warm them.

'I know it sounds farfetched,' continued Alice, 'but the things I've read over the last couple of days. The things I've seen. The things I've...*found out*. Oh, Hugo, I don't think you have psychosis at all. I think the doctors have made a mistake!'

Her words seemed prophetic, and he took a couple of steps down the lane before positioning himself in front of a hedge, the frozen grass crackling beneath his feet as he shuffled onto the verge. 'Alice,' he murmured, 'you won't believe the coincidence. Something happened today that made me reach the same conclusion. You're right about the psychosis – I'm no more ill than you are!'

She sat straight up at that.

'I'm going to need every detail of your research,' he said, 'but just wait 'til you hear about what happened earlier. Whatever's going on with these dreams, the explanation isn't medical.'

Alice lifted the pillow and propped her back against the wall. 'Tell me everything that happened,' she instructed him. 'Don't leave anything out.'

'Okay,' said Hugo. 'But you'd better hold on to your hat...'

He began by exploring the dreams: the paddling pool, the house fire, the drowning in Mallorca. Alice had known there was a girl involved but was shocked when she heard what had happened to her. He also mentioned the rape by Uncle Pete.

But what he said next astounded her. 'You see,' he disclosed, 'Elizabeth, too, was raped as a child. She told me the night I dreamt about the girl's molestation.'

Sensing a revelation was coming, Alice adjusted the brightness on her screen.

'After serving his sentence, the attacker came to her house – it was an egregious breach of his parole conditions and they returned him to prison for doing so. Then, on my walk this morning, you'll never guess what I saw.'

She thought she jolly well *could* guess.

'There he was in his car! Sat in the driver's seat. Just a few yards from where I'm standing now. It wasn't just a dream after all – it was a real event I'd seen.'

Informing her gave him a rush. 'I ran straight back to Elizabeth,' he told her breathlessly. 'We compared our stories, and they matched up perfectly. Uncle Pete was *Elizabeth's* uncle! And *she* was the girl he attacked!'

Alice absorbed things quietly. Hugo thought she'd be sceptical, dismissive even. Instead, she lay there silently, turning things in her mind like a maid tossing linen.

Her expression stayed blank; for a moment, he thought he'd lost her. 'Alice...'

'Oh my God,' she whispered. 'Elizabeth is the telepathist!'

'She's the what?'

Alice refocused. 'It goes back to what I was telling you about dream telepathy,' she said, bringing him up to date on the experiments of Ullman and Krippner.

Hugo couldn't believe what she had told him. Out of nowhere, the person controlling his dreams had been discovered, and the details were beyond his wildest imagination.

*Elizabeth* – the woman from the river. Together, they'd seen her blue-eyed gaze in the news article; now, she and Hugo had met and fallen in love. There had to be a reason for it.

Alice was lost in her thoughts. 'Let's go through what we've got so far,' she insisted. 'There's a puzzle to assemble, and we need to piece it together.'

Hugo agreed but was all at sea. 'Where do we begin?' he asked confusedly. 'I'm at a complete loss to explain things.'

'There must be something we're missing,' replied Alice. 'Think, Hugo – is there anything you haven't told me?'

He thought as hard as he could. 'Not really,' he said, shaking his head and sounding defeated. 'Although there is the...*bond*...we share.'

Alice's ears pricked up. Was this the link they were looking for? 'What do you mean by "bond"?' she asked.

'It's hard to explain but I felt it the moment I saw her in the article.' He checked himself before proceeding. 'Sorry — I know you and I were still together then.'

'It's fine. Just carry on.'

'It goes beyond the depth of ordinary romantic emotion.' He was glad it was dark so she couldn't see his cheeks had rouged. 'Elizabeth feels it too. It's like there's something strange at work. You could call it fate, I suppose. I don't know how else to describe it.'

Alice reflected and tried to comprehend things. 'So it began with the news article, and you met her in person very soon after. Trafalgar Square, if I remember correctly.'

'You see what I mean by fate? What were the chances of bumping into each other like that in central London?'

'Very slim indeed,' she concurred.

'Now factor in that my own father had been treating her.'

Alice had almost forgotten that. 'Two ludicrously improbable coincidences. You're right — there has to be a deeper meaning at play.'

But what could it possibly be? Frustration was beginning to boil and Alice was losing patience. 'Come on, Hugo, you need to think harder. There has to be something we're missing.'

Nothing was jumping out, but he searched his mind nonetheless. Then, jigging on the spot from the cold, something surfaced inside him. 'It's probably nothing,' he shrugged, 'but do you remember what I said about the rape dream? I had it the night Elizabeth told me *she'd* been attacked as a child.'

Alice nodded fervently. 'What's your point?'

He took her through what had happened – his trip to the bathroom and subsequent chat with Elizabeth. She, too, had dreamt of the attack – *her* attack.

'We'd assumed they were different events,' he said. 'It was only this morning that we put two and two together and realised we'd been seeing the same thing simultaneously.'

Alice's eyes flashed like torches. 'Simultaneous dreaming,' she mused, her voice a mere whisper in the shadows. 'Is this what happens with all of them? She dreams the events and live streams them while you're sleeping?'

Hugo wasn't sure. This morning's discovery had been serendipitous; he'd been so shocked he hadn't thought about the other dreams. 'I don't know,' he admitted. 'We didn't get that far. I'd need to go back and speak to her.'

'See what you can find out,' said Alice. 'If you *are* dreaming simultaneously, it could be very significant.'

She told him what she'd noticed in Ealing and how his dreams seemed to be happening *outside* of REM. Hugo was flabbergasted and thought back to his EEG.

*No wonder the doctors thought I wasn't dreaming.*

'I'll talk to her this evening,' he promised. 'Perhaps there's some kind of symbiotic relationship at play.'

Something stirred at the back of Alice's mind. *A symbiotic relationship.* She removed her glasses and wiped some sweat from her brow. 'What did you just say?' she asked methodically.

He repeated his words, but Alice stayed silent. Again, he thought he'd lost her. 'Alice...are you still there?'

'Still here,' she confirmed. 'And you've just reminded me of something I read in an article last term.'

'About symbiotic relationships?' It didn't sound too promising.

'Sort of. But I need to go back and revisit it.'

'Are you onto something?'

'Maybe. Give me some time to look into it. I'll call you back when I can.'

Hugo's glasses steamed up the second he re-entered the cottage. He was still wiping them clear as he walked into the living room, but Elizabeth's blurred image was unmistakable on the sofa.

'Everything all right?' she asked.

Hugo assured her it was. 'I just had a call from my ex,' he announced. 'We're still good friends as it happens.'

She looked a little worried, and Hugo understood her concern.

'We weren't together very long,' he said. 'You've spoken before, in fact – she answered my phone in the pub that time you called me.'

Her flickers of jealousy dampened.

Hugo put his glasses on and sat on the armchair opposite her. 'She's a Psychology student,' he explained. 'She knows about my dreams and is looking to find some answers.'

Elizabeth listened as he brought her up to speed. She was relaxed at first but grew more tense as he proceeded. Eventually, she was on tenterhooks.

The theory of dream telepathy was startling enough, but her mouth went wide when he mentioned simultaneous dreaming.

'So we need to find out,' said Hugo, leaning forward and resting his hands on his knees, 'are you dreaming these things when I do?'

She couldn't say for sure, but scratched her head and thought about it. 'I've already told you I dream about my past,' she offered. 'But there's no way I could give the specifics. I couldn't even say when they happen – they always seem to fade as soon as I wake.'

'That's natural. You have to be woken in REM to remember them vividly.'

Elizabeth looked at him sceptically. 'So how come you remember yours?'

Hugo sank back, closed his eyes and puffed his cheeks – not for the first time, he barely knew where to begin. When he flicked his eyes open, he saw she was staring expectantly. He had to provide an explanation. Delineating the events of the EEG was easy, but describing what Alice had seen in Ealing made his cheeks colour.

Elizabeth took it in her stride. 'How's that possible?' she asked. 'I've never seen that myself.'

'Exactly!' Hugo said. 'If we're dreaming simultaneously, then you'll *never* see an episode – you'll be dreaming yourself and sending me the telepathic messages!'

Elizabeth's eyes shone with comprehension. Finally, she understood what he meant.

'What we need,' pressed Hugo, 'is one of *your* dream memories to compare with my own. If they match, then we'll know it's all true.'

She closed her eyes and pondered things. Hugo waited patiently, not wanting to disturb her concentration.

Before long, she opened her eyes. 'I can barely remember at all,' she said, half apologising for the inconvenience. 'But perhaps there's still a flicker from last night.'

'Tell me.'

She did her best to summon the half lost thoughts. 'I was dreaming really deeply,' she recalled, 'but then I woke suddenly.'

'During REM, no doubt. That's why you can remember something. What was it that woke you?'

She jogged his memory. 'The morning sickness.'

'Of course,' recalled Hugo. 'The sound of you retching woke me too.' In his mind, it all made sense now. 'One moment you were dreaming; the next you were being sick. No wonder my own dream was interrupted.'

His comment left her thunderstruck. 'Last night, when I came back through!' she exclaimed excitedly, the memory returning in a flash. 'I felt so guilty for waking you. Do you remember what you said when I saw you?'

He did. 'I thanked you for interrupting my dream. I thought it was a psychotic one.'

'But do you realise the implications? It wasn't my retching that woke you at all…'

'It was breaking the telepathic link,' he pronounced solemnly. 'That's why I woke up when you did.'

They'd dreamt the event together, it seemed – the evidence was overwhelming now. Dream telepathy was almost certainly real, but it was time to find out for sure. 'Okay,' he said, looking across and sounding business-like. 'Tell me what you remember from last night.'

She hesitated, then looked away and faltered. Something was the matter, and she sank back down on the sofa. 'What's wrong?' he asked her.

'It's the dream,' she quavered, wringing her hands and avoiding his eyes. She'd become emotional and looked on the brink of tears. 'I can't say what happened without admitting something. Something that you don't know about yet.'

At last, she looked his way. 'You see, Hugo, the attacks I suffered as a girl – they had a consequence.'

He knew what she meant by 'consequence' – the maternity ward was fresh in his mind, and he remembered it clear as day. He breathed a long sigh of empathy and then moved from the chair to the sofa. 'It's okay,' he said, taking her hand and squeezing it gently. 'I know about the baby.'

He chronicled what he'd seen in his EEG and it correlated with her memories. 'I'm sorry I didn't mention it when we discussed things earlier. We got side-tracked by your uncle's appearance and never returned to the dreams.'

She didn't care about that but was astounded he knew her final secret.

'You must have dreamt it when I did,' said Hugo.

'But I don't remember,' Elizabeth protested. She breathed in deeply, then blew out slowly. 'It must have been an ordinary dream that faded away.'

'So tell me about last night before that one fades as well.'

Encouraged by his squeeze, she detailed what she could. 'It's very sketchy,' she began, 'but I vaguely recall my first day at school after giving birth. My mum picked me up in her car.' She looked him straight in the eye. 'My adoptive mum, that is.'

*The woman I thought was a midwife.* 'So it's true,' he whispered, dropping her hand when things hit home. 'I dreamt I was in the back of that car. I heard every word that was said.'

And to him, it was more than a faded flicker; it was vivid, and he recollected everything, right up to the moment he woke. Again, he filled her in and watched as her mind made sense of it.

'So now it's over to you,' he said, explaining that things weren't concluded — they hadn't even driven through the school gates before he was woken by Elizabeth's retching. 'That dream was trying to say something,' he continued, 'and *you* have to fill in the blanks for me.'

An idea surfaced in Elizabeth's mind, and her eyes went wide as the thought took root. 'How about we experiment in bed tonight?' she shouted excitedly, grabbing his knees and shaking them.

Hugo wondered where this was going.

She could see he looked unsure. 'I mean – why don't I *show* you what happened? If I concentrate hard before falling asleep, then maybe I'll dream it again. Perhaps you'll see the end of that car journey after all.'

Hugo was enthralled at the suggestion. 'Pure genius!' he marvelled. 'It's got to be worth a try.'

• CHAPTER 48 •

'I had a call this morning,' said Elizabeth's adoptive mother, her hazel eyes shining kindly. 'The necessary papers have all gone through. Next weekend he'll be placed with the new family.'

Hugo heard those words a second time, and now he knew their meaning – Elizabeth's child would be adopted. The baby was born of violence, and a new family would provide the love and affection he needed.

Hugo tried to listen but the view from the window distracted him. House after house rolled past as the elegance of Tunbridge Wells receded. Soon they found themselves in the patchwork quilt of the countryside.

Across the Weald, the rolling fields fanned out, their sprawling hedgerows carving the landscape into stunning a mesh of green. Only at the horizon did the green give way to blue.

*The route they drove was familiar to Hugo: he'd walked it twice before – all the way from the railway station to the cottage. It was so much quicker by car, and they arrived at the village in no time. Hugo had to smile as they were slowed to a trundle at the pond – even back then, the 'metropolis' deserved its nickname.*

*Stepping back in time was disorientating. Everything was familiar but ever so slightly different. All the vehicles were registered before he was born, but it was the hundreds of subtle differences that gave the cumulative effect – a front garden here, or a road marking there – at least the buildings themselves seemed eternal, their timelessness unflinching as he travelled from present to past.*

*Even the rustic coaching inn, where he and Elizabeth had dined a couple of nights before, was just as he remembered it. He hadn't known she was pregnant then, and they'd assumed he was psychotic – so much had happened in the intervening period.*

*Eventually, they came to the T-junction and turned left onto the quiet little lane that led downhill from the bustle. The roadside hedgerows thinned as they descended and before long, the car turned left onto the potholed path he knew so well.*

*The cottage was now within sight.*

*They drew to a halt, and he gazed at the redbrick dwelling, its three-hundred-year-old walls resplendent in the April sunshine. Elizabeth and her adoptive mother got out and walked to the building's entrance. Cloaked as ever, Hugo followed unnoticed.*

*Inside was a curious mix of novel and familiar. The layout was identical, and he recognised most of the furniture – but it was newer and less dated than he recalled from his physical visits. Still, the nooks and crannies were littered with belongings he'd never seen before – a reminder that he was trespassing on a time he was merely a stranger to.*

He followed them to the living room and hovered in the doorway to watch. Elizabeth sat down on the sofa. Hugo didn't recognise the man next to her – he was her adoptive father, no doubt.

He was a kindly-looking gent in his late forties, with a neat black beard that was greying at the chin. His full head of side-parted hair sat above thick black eyebrows and dark brown eyes. He seemed the perfect complement to his curly-haired wife. Hugo felt sad that both these candles were extinguished in the waking world. It reminded him of his own mother's death.

Hugo was becoming wistful, but a noise from upstairs broke his reverie, carried to his ears on a zephyr from above.

It was the sound of a crying baby. He had woken and was balling his eyes out.

The curly-haired woman left the living room and went upstairs to attend to him. Hugo followed her up. Moments later, he was standing in Elizabeth's bedroom.

Except it wasn't her bedroom. Not yet, anyway – for her parents still occupied the master.

He glanced above the bedstead. Hanging on the wall was a picture, but not the masterpiece he was accustomed to seeing – Elizabeth, at this stage, was years from painting the meadow.

*Instead, he saw her adoptive parents' wedding photo; it was smaller, and less striking, than the art that would one day replace it. Her parents were in their twenties then and it looked like they were in love.*

The baby's crying continued while the woman changed his nappy. He stepped closer and stared at the infant, who lay on the changing mat with his eyes screwed shut and his arms waving wildly.

So, this was Elizabeth's son. Tender and helpless, he lay there crying.

But despite being face to face with the child, a more pressing purpose nagged at Hugo. In the corner of the room was an unfamiliar piece of furniture that Elizabeth must have ditched. It was a chest of drawers, and intuition told him that this was the dream's real purpose. He felt impelled towards it, sensing its pull like a tugboat.

Hugo moved closer, desperate to feel the wood against his fingertips. Taking hold of the bottom drawer, his heart began to thunder.

He pulled the handle.

It slid open with silent ease and contained just a single item. He drew the document out and inspected it. It seemed to be rather official...

The little boy's birth certificate.

He looked at the name on the paper – James Ritchie.

James – a name given in remembrance of Elizabeth's late father, Jim. It was a touching tribute to the man she had lost but would always love. Memories of the fire came flooding back and he shuddered at what he remembered.

But the twee sentimentalities of naming customs were forgotten when he saw what was written at the bottom. Even the horrors of the previous dreams paled when he read what it said on the paper.

His heart nearly stopped from the shock. For under the child's name, the date of birth was recorded.

March 23$^{rd}$ – the same date as Hugo's.

And the same year of birth.

He woke and opened his eyes. Next to him, Elizabeth stirred for a moment, then rolled the opposite way and drifted back to sleep.

He sat himself up. Beyond the curtains lay a grey winter morning, and the clock informed him it was already past nine-thirty.

Not wanting to wake her, he slid quietly out of bed. Whatever she was dreaming didn't concern him now: his role as a witness was done.

His thoughts began to calm as he pulled on a pair of underpants.

*Don't panic. A shared birthday is perfectly normal.*

He did the maths – even in the village, there must be five or six people born on March 23$^{rd}$. Extrapolating from that, there would be millions worldwide. So what if the year was the same. *Of course I'm not her son.*

Of course he wasn't! He was raised by his own mother and father in Ealing. Which reminded him: Swann still thought he was in Oxford. He should call him to say what time he'd be back. The day would be momentous enough with the announcement of Elizabeth's pregnancy and his imminent move to Kent. He ought to prepare the ground.

Before going to the bathroom, he stole a quick glance above the bed. The masterpiece gleamed back at him – it was as pleasing now as it was the first time he'd seen it, and far more satisfying than the wedding photo it replaced.

Art was an interest they shared. Hugo was nowhere near Elizabeth's standard, but their meeting outside the National Gallery certainly seemed symbolic. Perhaps it explained their bond as well.

But where did his interest come from? No one in his family had the slightest concern for painting. His father was a sportsman, and his mother had been a keen gardener.

Hugo indulged in neither pursuit.

Was his passion for art inherited? Did it come from a different source entirely – a genetic source? *Don't be so silly, Hugo!*

He wandered through to the bathroom. The air was chilly, and goose pimples sprang from his torso as he looked at his face in the mirror. His blue-grey eyes stared back at him – they were pale and lighter than his mother's had been or his father's still were.

*At least they're not brilliant blue.*

As usual, his pasty white face displeased him but, for once, he was glad of his aquiline nose. He breathed a sigh of relief: it was different from Elizabeth's smaller, neater one. *Thank God I don't look anything like her.*

When he returned to the bedroom, Elizabeth still slept soundly. Even a creaking floorboard didn't wake her when he trod on it. As quietly as possible, he put the rest of his clothes on, then tiptoed down the stairs and opened the front door.

The morning air was milder now that a warm front and cloud had arrived during the night. He didn't even need his coat. Once safely up the path, he fished his phone from the pocket of his jeans. It was time to FaceTime his father.

*And he is my father. Surely, he is my father.*

'Morning Hugo,' said Swann from his living room.

He seemed irritated. A sports programme was on in the background, and Hugo's call was disturbing him.

'What time should I expect you back?' Swann kept his eyes on the TV, not even looking at the FaceTime screen.

Hugo responded curtly. 'This afternoon, I should think.' It was such an important call, and his father's aloofness irked him.

'Try to be in time for dinner,' said Swann. 'I'll be doing a leg of lamb.'

After all that had happened since leaving London, Hugo was through with the pleasantries. 'I can't be too specific with the timings,' he replied bluntly. 'I won't be coming from Oxford – I'm currently down in Kent.'

Swann wrenched his head from the TV and stared at the screen on his phone. 'Hugo, I told you not to see that woman! How dare you disobey me!'

Swann turned the TV off and the noise in the background ceased. 'That's her house I can see behind you, isn't it?'

'It is,' Hugo confirmed, adjusting the angle to show the cottage more clearly. He'd succeeded in riling his father and smiled in satisfaction. 'I had a night in Oxford, then came straight here. I've been with Elizabeth since.'

Swann's cheeks turned red with anger. 'You assured me there was nothing physical between you,' he barked.

Hugo couldn't care less. 'That was just a lie,' he breezed insouciantly. 'Frankly, I'm amazed you believed it.'

Swann's eyes bulged with rage.

'We're a couple, Dad. I suggest you start getting used to it.'

Such impertinence! Swann was apoplectic now, and Hugo rather enjoyed it. The old man turned to regard the shadows cast by the light fitting. They always seemed to calm him.

'You need to come back right away,' remarked Swann. He knew his son was ill, so he tempered his anger in light of the issue. 'You have a serious psychological condition and mustn't exacerbate the risk. Have you taken your medication today?'

'Nope.'

Swann fought to curb his fury. 'Hugo, your illness needs to be kept in check.'

Hugo sneered. His father was so far behind the curve that it was hardly worth dwelling on the mistaken diagnosis. 'I haven't taken my medication because I don't have psychosis, Dad.'

Swann replied immediately. 'I'm afraid you most certainly do,' he said, hiding his disdain by chewing his bottom lip. 'And if you fail to take your medication, things will only get worse. Now please take it before you travel.'

Hugo didn't have time for these lectures. 'Frankly, I don't care about the medication. There are far more important things going on. Elizabeth's *pregnant*. I'm going to be a father.'

He blurted the words and left them to hang for a moment. Never before had he dropped such a bombshell – he wished he hadn't unleashed it, but his blood was pumping insanely.

Swann's cheeks had turned from red to white.

'I wanted to tell you later,' Hugo explained remorsefully. 'But the turn this conversation had taken—'

'Is an abortion date set?'

Hugo sighed. 'No, Dad, it is not. When I said I was going to be a father, I meant just that. Elizabeth is having this baby, and I'm going to be a dad.'

The fires inside him were rising again, and Swann's lip chewing accelerated as Hugo stoked things further. 'She needs me by her side, Dad. I'm moving to Kent and dropping out of uni altogether.'

Swann's next words seemed ominous. 'Get your stuff together, Hugo. We'll talk about it when you arrive.'

'You won't change my mind,' he snapped. 'The bond between us is rock solid. There's so much you don't know about yet, which is why I'll be bringing her with me—'

'ENOUGH!' boomed Swann, banging his fist on the side of his chair. 'You come on your own, or you don't come at all!'

Hugo's anger turned to spite. 'Well, if that's your attitude to the news you're becoming a grandfather, I think I'll stay down here.'

The obligatory rant was quick to follow and it came in a full-on diatribe. 'Just you do that,' raved Swann, jumping to his feet and pacing about his living room. 'Stay down there and throw it all away. Sacrifice your education, your future – sacrifice it all for this nonsense. This childish...*INFATUATION.*'

Spittle hurled from his mouth and splashed against the screen as he raged. Hugo thought he'd finished, but Swann continued relentlessly. 'Your priorities are all wrong. You'll see for yourself when you're working minimum wage in a dead-end job. Why don't you try listening for once in your bloody life!'

Hugo shot straight back. *'You're* the one who ought to listen,' he retorted, glancing back at the cottage in case Elizabeth was watching. Thankfully she wasn't. 'You've no idea the things we need to talk to you about. But you would if you bothered to listen instead of ranting all the time like a fucking know-it-all.' It was the first time Hugo had ever sworn at his father. 'And now *I'm* the one having the rant,' he complained. 'And all because *you* refused to listen. Perhaps we're alike after all, you and I.'

'Rubbish!' erupted Swann. 'I'd never have talked to my father like that.' He turned away in disgust. 'You're no son of mine.'

It was uttered under his breath and was said in exasperation.

But Hugo went white with shock when he heard it.

'What did you just say?' Hugo's voice was a breathless whisper.

Swann stayed silent.

'The mask has slipped, hasn't it...' Hugo was thinking out loud and barely knew he was speaking. 'I was adopted. All this time, I was adopted.'

Swann's demeanour had changed. Suddenly he looked like a defendant in the dock. 'I wasn't speaking literally, Son. I only meant—'

'Let me put it to you differently,' said Hugo, cross-examining his father like a barrister. What an irony that Swann had hoped he'd become one. 'I'll make it a simple question – was I adopted as a child? It's a straightforward yes or no.'

There was no way out. Swann, who'd always valued truth, was cornered. 'Yes,' he admitted with a haunted pain in his eyes. 'We adopted you when you were a baby.'

The old man looked vulnerable. Hugo had never seen him cry, but for a moment, he thought he might. 'This isn't how you were so supposed to find out,' he quavered. 'I'm so sorry, Son. Let's talk properly this afternoon. You, me and Elizabeth. It's fine for you to bring her.'

Hugo's head was spinning. *Elizabeth! The baby!*

Swann owed his son an explanation. 'We were advised to bring you up knowing you were adopted,' he began sorrowfully. 'But your mother insisted on doing precisely the opposite. She couldn't have children of her own – she was pretending to herself as much as to you.'

Hugo nodded in vague comprehension, but his eyes were skyward with dizziness.

'We decided to tell you when you turned eighteen, but she passed away so close to your birthday. I couldn't bear to burden you in your grief, so I decided to wait until you were twenty-one and had finished your degree.' Swann's voice was tremulous. 'I spent months agonising, turning it over in my head. I know you think I've been distant lately – perhaps you'll understand why now.'

Swann broke down momentarily and dabbed his eyes with his shirt sleeve. Hugo was overwhelmed as his father's grief poured forth – he did have a heart, after all.

But to Hugo, the damage was done. 'What do you know about my birth parents?' he demanded.

Groaning in the depths of his misery, Swann felt a duty to answer. 'We knew nothing about your father,' he lamented. 'But we understood your mother was very young. Probably a mid-teen.' Again he dabbed at his eyes. 'There was a suggestion – and this is difficult to say over FaceTime – but there was a suggestion she may have been raped.'

*It's all right, Dad – I know who my birth parents are.*

'Hugo...' Swann remained distraught, but at least his words came cogently. '...Regardless of biology, you'll always be my son. I love you very dearly. I know I don't say it enough, but—'

The line went dead. Hugo had ended the call.

Then, with a flicker of guilt, he blocked his father's number.

# DREAMS

Once again, Hugo stood in Elizabeth's bathroom, sweat glistening on his forehead, fingertips prickling from the stress.

For the second time that morning, he gazed at his features in the mirror. The same pair of blue-grey eyes stared back, but now the penny had dropped. They weren't the brilliant blue of Elizabeth's, but he had seen those pallid orbs before. They were the eyes of his father – his real, biological father.

They were the eyes of Uncle Pete.

That incestuous monster who'd ruined his niece's life – who'd forced her to bear his son.

And *he* was that son.

His aquiline nose was the same as well. Pete was both his father *and* his great uncle. He thought back to Elizabeth's rape and quickly counted the months – he'd probably witnessed his conception on that beautiful midsummer evening.

A sickness erupted inside him, and rancid vomit slopped into the toilet bowl as he thought of Jim and Sandra. They'd been his grandparents – relatives he'd seen in his sleep but never in person. They were also his great aunt and great uncle, given Pete's relation to Sandra.

The repugnant legacy was too disturbing to bear. Unlike his grandparents, he'd bumped into Pete for real. It was just a fleeting glimpse, but the man in that little green car was his biological father.

Again, he emptied his stomach.

His incestuous origin was repulsive, but something sickened him further – the incest that *he'd* committed. He and Elizabeth had made love. His own mother, not that he knew it at the time.

And now she was pregnant with his offspring.

Another child born of incest – it would be more inbred than he was. The birth had to be stopped.

A knock at the door startled him. 'Is everything all right?' asked Elizabeth. 'You sound terribly ill.'

His retching must have woken her. What a role reversal after the morning sickness! Hearing her voice was like a dagger in his heart. He still loved her – not as a mother – but as a woman.

'I'm okay,' he rasped. 'Just give me a few minutes.'

He collapsed on the floor and sat against the wall, grabbing some toilet tissue and dabbing the sweat from his forehead. His hands were shaking from the adrenaline.

'I'll make you a nice cup of ginger tea,' she said. 'It'll help to settle your stomach.'

He listened as she went downstairs, then burst into silent sobs. God bless her – she still had no idea. How on earth would he go about telling her? How could he even broach it?

He opened the bathroom door and headed down when he heard the kettle boiling. Needing to collect his thoughts, he made straight for the front door, hoping to slip out unnoticed.

But Elizabeth saw him and raised an eyebrow. 'Where are you going? Your tea's nearly ready.'

'I just need to get some fresh air. I'll drink it as soon as I'm back.'

• CHAPTER 49 •

Hugo stepped outside.
The milder air was a physical comfort, but the pleasant conditions didn't soothe his thoughts. His head swirled like a maelstrom.

He stuck his hands in his pockets and walked to the end of the path. Turning right, his journey up the lane was lugubrious, his features fixed in a downward glaze. Slowly, he walked to the T-junction and paused when he reached the row of cottages. That little green hatchback – the memory of it haunted him. *This is where I met my father. My great uncle, too.*

He shuffled off and turned right again at the junction. As usual, the road from Tunbridge Wells was busy, but he trudged through the oncoming traffic until he reached the village. The pavements began at the outskirts, and he traipsed past the houses that lined them. When the road narrowed, the cars were slowed to a halt; so, too, was Hugo, for he had finally arrived at the pond.

He sat on one of the benches and looked at the weeping willows, their pendulous branches rustling in the breeze. What would he say to Elizabeth? His world had collapsed that morning, and hers must be brought down with it. She'd suffered an appalling childhood and had attempted suicide in the autumn. At last, she'd found some happiness – but it needed to be ripped right from her.

A mother and daughter wandered past his view. They ambled along in their own little worlds, oblivious to Hugo's heartache. How he envied their ignorance!

He closed his eyes, tilted his head back and started to meditate deeply. Slowly, everything faded – the village, the pond, the willows – all began to recede as he descended deeper and deeper.

But a loud noise broke his concentration.

It was the FaceTime ringtone.

He drew the phone from his pocket and looked at the name on the screen.

*Alice.*

Of course! Yesterday's chat seemed inconsequential now. They'd been so close to solving his dreams, but things had developed since then. Still, he wondered what she'd found out, and he answered the call with a greeting.

Alice was sitting at her desk. She looked perplexed but her bright eyes flashed like fire. 'I worked through most of the night,' she said. 'I have a coherent theory – but there's a problem. And I can't quite explain it.'

It was then that she noticed how vacant he was. 'Jesus, Hugo, are you okay? You look like someone's died or something.'

Her prompt released his emotions, and he started to sob in front of her. 'No,' he whimpered, his bottom lip trembling. 'I'm not okay at all, Alice.'

Hugo confided in her – from Elizabeth's morning sickness and the interrupted car journey, right up to last night's experiment and the date he'd seen on the birth certificate – he told her everything. Including the argument with Swann.

'So, you see,' he wailed, raising his hand to his mouth, and shaking his head. 'My real name is James Ritchie. I'm an inbred, Alice. A fucking mutant! And now I've fathered a baby with my own fucking mother!'

Alice could barely believe it. His tale shocked her deeply, but what he said corroborated her findings – the cards had fallen into place, and she *could* explain things after all.

'Everything ties together,' she whispered, the horrible truth now plain.

'What ties together?' he implored. 'Tell me what you've found out.'

She looked at him empathetically. 'It's called psychological symbiosis. It's something I came across in the Michaelmas Term when doing an assignment on oneirology.'

'Oneirology?'

'Sorry – that's the technical term for the study of dreams.'

Hugo's memory flickered. 'I think I remember you doing it,' he recalled, taking a dispirited glance at the pond. 'It was around the time we broke up – I was doing a Chaucer essay...'

She nodded. 'You were also drilling a hole in your eyebrow and getting a silly haircut.'

He touched his stud and smiled faintly. Her joke helped stymie his tears, so she carried on giving him the details, reading them straight from her notes. 'Psychological symbiosis relates to an infant's first few months and the bond it shares with its mother. It concerns the way we identify as self-aware 'I' subjects, which takes a long time to develop. There's a lengthy process of individuation that begins in our earliest months...'

She told him that babies under five months could not distinguish between their own reality and the experience they have of their mothers.

Hugo looked confused. 'Hold on,' he pleaded, 'you're saying a new baby shares its *mother's* reality before developing its own?'

'That's its *perception*, yes,' confirmed Alice. 'But here's the crux – in your case, the symbiotic link was broken before the developmental process could finish. In fact, it had barely begun. Elizabeth birthed you, but your care was almost immediately transferred to her adoptive mother.'

She watched his unblinking eyes stare at the screen as he listened. She needed to get to the point. 'Soon, you were adopted out of the family altogether. When symbiotic links are broken like that, the natural process of individuation has to occur differently.'

He was impressed with her lofty analysis but still didn't see the connection. 'So what's the story with me?' he asked. 'How did breaking the link affect my individuation?'

She gazed at him ruefully for this bit. It was a shocking revelation, so she proceeded sympathetically. 'Side effects,' she explained. 'There's an umbrella term to describe them.'

'Go on.'

'It's called psychological *psychosis*.'

His jaw dropped at the irony.

'You see, Hugo, you *do* have psychosis – just not the kind you were diagnosed with.'

'Wow,' he commented in a faraway voice. 'You've certainly done your research.'

'I've got my notes in front of me,' she admitted gently, holding them up to the screen so he could see them. She could tell he was suffering, so she paused before proceeding.

He was ready a moment later. 'Okay,' he breathed, 'hit me with the details.'

She took another glance at her notes before resuming. 'The process had been dormant since you were removed from Elizabeth's care. To individuate, you had to use different mechanisms to compensate for the disrupted functions.'

Hugo stared at the screen.

'If you hadn't met your biological mother, you wouldn't have noticed anything different about your own development compared to other people's. But because you and Elizabeth came into contact, the unfinished process keeps trying to reconnect – it wants to enmesh your conscious brains as though you were mother and infant. But the process doesn't work with adults, so all you get is malfunctions.'

Hugo's head jerked as the seeds of understanding germinated. 'Malfunctions,' he repeated. 'That's a euphemism, isn't it? What you mean is the dreams.'

Alice nodded. 'Psychological symbiosis is re-establishing itself via the medium of telepathic dreaming. The former is causing the latter, which, in turn, is providing you with snippets of your own identity, many aspects of which are shared with hers.'

He looked at the pond as he turned her words in his mind. Then, ever so slowly, those seeds of his burst forth. 'Okay,' he murmured, 'let me see if I've got this right. Psychological symbiosis was a latent process. But now Elizabeth and I are back in contact, it's been reactivated.'

He paused.

'But a malfunction in this process means we experience simultaneous telepathic dreaming because our brains perceive our separate realities as the same thing.'

Alice was pleased he'd comprehended. 'That's precisely it,' she beamed.

She had solved the riddle of his dreams. Or so it seemed, at least.

Hugo considered the possibility, then screwed his features sceptically. Her theory had sounded so elegant, but he'd spotted a problem that blew it out of the water. 'It's a lovely idea,' he said disconsolately. 'But there's a massive flaw in your hypothesis.'

With eyes held wide, she waited to hear his pronouncement.

'The dreams started *before* Elizabeth and I met. I had my first one in Ealing when you and I visited Dad. I hadn't even seen the news article then, never mind met her.'

He shook his head as the bubble burst. 'How can your theory account for a process already underway?'

'Because your father *had* met her!' This was Alice's masterstroke, and she'd known the answer all along. 'Elizabeth was his patient when you and I visited Ealing. It was the first time you'd seen him since he'd started treating her. Seeing your father was what triggered the process.'

Hugo was taken aback. 'How's that possible,' he asked. 'Are you saying he was some kind of conduit?'

She was saying exactly that, and he could tell from the way her eyes glowed. 'Ever since you and Elizabeth were separated, your brains have been trying to find each other. Think about how Wi-Fi devices connect to a hub. If the hub goes down, the device continues searching. It's the same sort of thing with your minds.'

Brain-to-brain interfacing was the psychological name for it. She'd come across it by chance when the Wi-Fi went down at Wadham yesterday evening. Alice was reduced to working on her mobile using the 4G network; it had annoyed her at first, but the more she'd considered the parallel, the more the theory made sense.

The symmetry between Hugo's situation and the failed technology was striking, so she'd researched the matter in depth. Just like Wi-Fi devices connecting to a hub, Alice had discovered that human brainwaves could connect to the minds of other individuals. Brain-to-brain interfacing was real: studies had confirmed the phenomenon, and it seemed that Hugo's situation provided further corroboration.

'Your father was the common link,' she explained. 'You were able to transmit your individual signatures to one another through *him*. This is what established the telepathic link.'

Hugo understood what she meant. 'Like when a dog owner visits a house with another dog – when he returns home, his own dog can smell the other one on his clothes.'

'That's a weird analogy, but probably a decent way of putting it,' said Alice. 'Effectively, Swann absorbed your signals, then emitted them slowly over time. When you were near him, you could detect Elizabeth's signal radiating from him, and she could do likewise with yours.'

Hugo could barely believe it. 'No wonder I felt so captivated when I saw her face in the news. My mind had the scent and was trying to sniff her out.'

'You've been searching for each other since the moment you were parted. All your father did was kick-start the process. He set in motion a chain of events that are still playing out to this day.'

Hugo pondered the coincidences – *ludicrously improbable* was how Alice had described their chance meeting in Trafalgar Square. And as for falling in love with her...

He was right to suspect a deeper meaning.

'They weren't coincidences at all,' she explained. 'You were destined to meet from the moment your signals locked on to each other. Neither of you *decided* to be in Trafalgar Square that day – it happened because your brains subconsciously drew you to a mutually convenient location.'

Alice changed her expression. 'And that's what explains the bond,' she said, lowering her voice to a solemn whisper. 'Once you'd found each other, you refused to be parted again. That's why your feelings are so strong. The bond was created the moment you met.'

Hugo's features darkened at that. 'I don't understand,' he protested. 'We love each other as a couple, not as a mother and son. How can that possibly explain the bond?'

Alice's face was a picture of pity. 'I do have an explanation,' she lamented, 'but it stands completely separate from last night's research. It's a different phenomenon entirely.'

Hugo's shoulders sagged. 'Oh great,' he sighed dejectedly. 'Two afflictions for the price of one. Go on then, let's hear it.'

She hesitated, then smacked her lips cagily. 'Have you ever heard of something called genetic sexual attraction? It's often abbreviated to GSA.'

He hadn't, but it sounded self-explanatory.

'You often read about it in the tabloids. It can strike when children separated at birth reunite with family members later down the line. Basically, the Westermarck Effect is absent in these people.'

'What's the Westermarck Effect?'

'Sorry. It's a form of reverse sexual imprinting.'

'Meaning?'

'It's a mechanism to avoid inbreeding – it ensures that relatives who grow up together don't find each other sexually attractive. But it doesn't have time to develop when babies are separated early. Biological family members can have strong sexual feelings for each other if they meet up later in life.'

Hugo appraised the concept. *Genetic sexual attraction.* He couldn't deny its plausibility in this case, and he started to cry again. The bond that had seemed so spiritual – mystical, even – was, in fact, the product of ordinary biological and psychological processes.

Crushed by the realisation, he had just one final question. 'So why me?' he sobbed. 'She and I aren't the only mother and son to be reunited. Why isn't this happening all the time?'

She looked at him philosophically. 'Who says it isn't? Think how many age gap relationships there are—'

'I meant the dreaming, Alice. Why doesn't it happen to anyone else?'

She touched her cheeks and blushed.

But the misunderstanding focused her mind on what Stanley Krippner had claimed about the legacy of his dream telepathy research; indeed, his words about mental illness still loomed large in her mind.

'Maybe it does,' she announced, as a lightbulb moment surfaced. 'There was a time when people with symptoms like yours were all assumed to be psychologically unwell.'

She explained how Krippner's work had contributed to better understandings of sleep and mental illness. 'But perhaps it didn't go far enough,' she suggested. 'Think about what happened to you when you went for your polysomnography.'

'I was misdiagnosed.'

'Exactly!'

Hugo's mind began to race. 'And how many others are in the same boat?' he wondered. 'Even as we speak, psychiatrists like my father could be treating people who don't have anything wrong with them. For all we know, telepathic dreaming could be a widespread, natural phenomenon that doctors don't understand yet.'

She gave him a knowing nod. 'And think about the wider implications of brain-to-brain interfacing,' she added. 'It's not just age gap relationships like yours. Haven't you noticed how many similar-aged couples look like each other? Some of them could be long lost brothers and sisters without realising it. I'm sure it's a low percentage, but the numbers are probably high.'

It was a perturbing thought given Hugo's situation, but he couldn't help marvelling at Alice's discovery. 'Do you realise what you've done, Alice? This could change the course of science and medicine.'

Again, she blushed. 'Well, I think I've found my dissertation topic,' she quipped.

Hugo didn't laugh. 'I'm serious,' he reproved her. 'You've knitted together all these disparate strands of research – dream telepathy, psychological symbiosis, brain-to-brain interfacing, GSA, mental illness. Nobody else has achieved this – not even experts in the relevant fields. You're eighteen years old, yet *your* research could revolutionise things.'

'Nineteen in two weeks' time,' she joked. 'I suppose I do need to get things written up. But that's not my priority right now. At the moment, I'm more concerned about a certain friend who needs my support. I can't imagine what you're going through – I hope you know I'm here for you.'

His bottom lip started trembling; it meant the world to hear her say that. 'Thank you,' he whimpered. 'I'm sure you can see I'm struggling. I'm going to need a friend to talk to.'

She nearly cried herself at that. 'Perhaps we should meet in person,' she suggested. 'There's no substitute for a physical shoulder to cry on. And besides, it would be good to see you again.'

'How about I come to Oxford?' he replied. 'We could go for a coffee while Owen is in the library or something.'

Alice grimaced. 'Actually, things aren't going too well on that front.'

She outlined what had happened in her room when Owen had disparaged her dream telepathy research. 'So why don't you come over tomorrow?' she offered. 'We can spend the whole day together?'

Finally, Hugo smiled. 'I'd like that,' he said, her compassion giving him strength. 'You're such a dear friend, Alice.'

'And you'll always be more than a friend in my eyes. You're the kindest, sweetest person I've ever met. You don't deserve all these awful things happening to you.'

Her words lifted the heaviness from his shoulders. 'In that case, I'll see you tomorrow,' he said. 'But I'd better go and speak to Elizabeth now. And after her, to my father.'

He puffed his cheeks at the task ahead.

Alice gave him an empathetic gaze. Her support was a lifeline to him – thank goodness he'd see her tomorrow. And how he valued her friendship!

When they hung up, Hugo waited a moment and wondered what he'd say to Elizabeth. He knew he was in for the most difficult conversation of his life, and he couldn't procrastinate forever. After one last look at the rustling willows, he rose from the bench and meandered up the road to the cottage.

• CHAPTER 50 •

Hugo found her in the kitchen.

She was preparing breakfast by slicing some rolls with a breadknife. 'Your tea's gone cold,' she commented, 'but I can make you another cup if you want one.'

She didn't look up but continued slicing the rolls. Hugo's haunted expression went unnoticed in the doorway.

'How are you feeling?' she asked. 'If you can manage a bacon butty, I'll have one ready in no time.'

How was he feeling? It was such a simple question, but it knocked the wind out of him. All he could do was stand and gaze at her. She remained oblivious to the horrors he'd discovered. Delineating them was anathema to his instincts, but he knew he had to go through with it.

'Elizabeth,' he murmured, casting his eyes to the floor. 'I need to talk to you about something.'

'Go ahead,' she breezed, her mind still focused on breakfast.

She hadn't a clue what was coming. He screwed his features in silent torment; then, after a moment's pause, he looked up. She still had her back to him and had moved from slicing the rolls to buttering them.

It was time to bite the bullet.

'It's the *dream*,' he said with an insistence that turned her head. 'I felt so sick because of it. That's why I went outside. To come to terms with it.'

Now she perceived his turmoil and swivelled her body to face him. She met his gaze with a worried frown and leaned herself back against the worktop.

He took a deep breath before continuing.

'Can you remember anything from last night?' he asked.

She shook her head. 'Not a thing.'

Her dream had faded immediately. She stared straight at him with imploring eyes, wondering what he'd reveal.

Again, Hugo cast his gaze to the floor in shame. 'I saw the end of that car journey,' he mumbled. 'Oh, Elizabeth...'

He tried to summon the strength.

'What?' she demanded. 'It can't be that bad – just tell me what happened, Hugo.'

And so he told her everything. He chronicled what he'd witnessed with precise elucidation, imparting the specifics just as they'd happened in the dream. Elizabeth knew he was born in March but hadn't been told the date. When he exposed the match with the birth certificate, she dismissed it as pure coincidence.

But there was no gainsaying the FaceTime conversations, first with Swann and, later, with Alice. Elizabeth listened – half in horror, half in disgust – as reality dawned in her mind. His tale was incontrovertible: the young man standing before her was the son she'd birthed as a teen. Hugo, she realised, wasn't really Hugo at all...

*He was James!*

She stood there cold for a moment, her emotions delayed by shock.

Then, they erupted, and she started to shake from the flood. Grief, despair, anger, shame, disgust – she felt them simultaneously, and they burned like a fire inside her.

She spun back around and collapsed on the worktop, bent almost double and overcome with grief and tears. Hugo watched her descend into full-blown panic – there was nothing he could do but let it play out in front of him, the staccato beats of his heart the only movement in his otherwise frozen body.

The shock took time to subside, but when it did, despair rushed in, seizing Elizabeth's mind and toying with it. Trembling like a frightened fawn, she stood before him, broken. Her life seemed cursed after all.

When she was finally able to speak, Hugo stepped from the doorway and entered the kitchen to talk.

'The child cannot be born,' he told her. 'The kindest thing is to abort it.'

'No,' she whispered, her head bowed low and her eyes tight shut. She appeared to be concurring, but when her eyes opened, they displayed a look of fury. '*No!*' she hissed. '*You will not take my baby!*'

Startled by her venom, Hugo stood confused. 'Elizabeth,' he stuttered, 'you can't be serious. Think of the poor child.'

He detected a flicker in her eyes. Was it defence that stirred inside her?

Defence was there all right, but something else sprang forth from the twitch he perceived in her features. Something that looked like…

*Hatred.*

And then hatred lunged at him, fists closed, arms aloft. 'YOU WILL NOT TAKE MY BABY!' she screamed, beating her arms against him like a rabid animal.

'Elizabeth! What are you doing?'

'*I lost a baby before!*' she yelled. '*I won't let it happen again!*'

The blows were raining down, so he grabbed her forearms to halt them. 'Stop it!' he shouted, struggling to control her thrashing limbs. 'It's a fucking inbred, Elizabeth!'

His comment stoked the hatred. Was it Hugo she was attacking, or was it her Uncle Pete she saw in the son now standing before her? It didn't particularly matter – the onslaught kept on coming. 'I *will* be a mother!' she bawled as his efforts to restrain her failed. 'YOU WILL NOT TAKE MY BABY!'

Her eyes went wide with rage, and she went for his throat and gripped it. He grasped her arms and tugged them hard, but her hands still clutched at his neck. The forces caused them to swivel and exchange position. Suddenly, Hugo's back was flush against the worktop, her palms compressing his Adam's apple, her fingernails tearing his skin.

'I'm having this baby!' she yelled. 'I'm having it, you *bastard!*'

She thrust her body forward, restricting his movement and leaning her weight against him. Only his arms were free, and they desperately yanked at hers in a vain attempt to free himself.

Outbursts like this weren't new to him – he'd witnessed one before, and the memory flashed in his mind. But even when he'd revealed that Swann was his father, she hadn't resorted to physical violence. This time, things were different, and her grip grew tighter and tighter.

He knew her rage was shock-induced. She didn't *mean* to hurt him – but he was running out of breath now. 'Elizabeth...' he wheezed, 'I can't breathe...Please, stop it!'

Flailing for support, his right hand motioned backwards. But instead of grasping the worktop, his fingers brushed against something left on the surface.

They clasped around it, reflex-like.

With all the strength he could muster, he used his left hand to push the raging mass in front of him. She shifted back from the force and then started collapsing forwards. To break her impact, he drew his right hand up from the worktop.

She fell onto it heavily and groaned, her hands relinquishing their grip on his neck.

Hugo's throat was free, and he gasped for air like a drowning sailor.

Elizabeth staggered back. When Hugo refocused, he saw a swell of red on her clothing. He watched it spread across the fabric, then spatter to the floor and start pooling. His right hand was still flush against her belly. As she retreated back some more, the length of the blade was revealed.

Hugo blanched with the shock. It was the knife he'd grabbed from the worktop – the one she'd sliced the rolls with. As she'd fallen forward, he'd plunged it into her abdomen and pierced her liver.

She stumbled further back, then collapsed to the floor in a heap. When she hit the ground, she banged her head with a hideous crack. Hugo's senses were scrambled and he froze solid. He stared at his glistening red hand, then moved his eyes to Elizabeth. As her breath began to rasp, blood spewed and spat from the gaping hole in her torso.

It was so surreal – almost like one of his dreams. *This cannot be happening for real.*

Still clutching the knife, he moved and crouched by her side, cradling her head with his left hand. 'I'm so sorry,' he garbled. 'It was an accident. Just an accident...'

Brushing the hair from her face, he watched as blood oozed from her mouth. Her cheeks were becoming pale, and her eyes had started to glaze over. In a panic, he reached for his phone to call 999, but his hands were shaking so much he dropped the device and watched it career across the kitchen floor and away from him.

'Leave it,' she whispered, her voice now weak and shallow. 'It's too late.'

# DREAMS

She started to close her eyes.

'*NO!*' he bellowed. 'Stay with me! Don't you dare close your eyes!'

But she didn't heed his commands. Instead, she looked at him weakly – the hate that had burned just moments ago had turned to love once more.

Hugo repeated his pleas. 'Don't you die!' he implored in vain. 'Don't you dare do it!'

But all he received was the faintest shake of her head.

'I love you, Hugo,' she whispered softly.

And those were her final words. Her breathing faded to nothing and her stare became vacant. With a curious flick, she closed her lids – like theatre curtains concluding a performance, they veiled her eyes for one last time. She looked more at peace in death than she ever had in life.

Crouched above her exanimate body, the shock hit Hugo hard. He let out a great wail, then stood up and backed away.

Trying to make sense of what had happened, he paused and waited in the doorway. Alice's words rang loudly in his ears: *you're the kindest, sweetest person I've ever met*.

And now he was a killer.

The slayer of his lover.

The slayer of his own *mother*.

His head was spinning, and his legs felt heavy. Fearing he might collapse, he placed his hands on his knees and bent himself double. He tried to be sick, but his stomach was empty from earlier.

He dry-retched. Then he did so again.

The sight of her lifeless body was asphyxiating. It was as though a pair of hands remained clasped around his throat. He had to get away from that kitchen. Away from that pool of blood. Away from that...

*Corpse!*

He staggered towards the front door and opened it.

The air outside was sweet, but his body was pumped with adrenaline. There could be no standing still, no space for calm inclinations or clarity of thought.

Instead, he started running.

God-knew where he was going, but he had to escape that cottage. It was some time before his final destination revealed itself.

• CHAPTER 51 •

Hugo closed his eyes as a breath of wind kissed his cheek. The morning was mild yet replete with cruel torments. The meadow's long grass and wildflowers were a dim and distant memory now. No insects hummed their busy tunes amidst the foliage; no choirs of birdsong erupted from the hidden depths of the bramble thickets. Save for the chattering corvids, the meadow was shrouded in silence.

Deep in thought, he sat on the grass and gazed at the stream, its listless flow perturbing him. Eyes wide and semi-hypnotised, he watched a mallard by the far bank as it pottered in search of food. Yet Hugo barely noticed nature's desolate emptiness and unforgiving hardships. Instead, his blue-grey eyes stayed fixed in a forward focus, mesmerised by the ceaseless flow of the stream.

He'd been sitting on his own for a while now. His heart had long since slowed, and his hands were no longer trembling. In a morbid trance, he sat motionless, his mind overloaded with grief. He glanced at the leaden sky above: it was still dry, but the rain threatened to start at any moment.

Hugo didn't care.

How had it come to this? His life had become a waking nightmare more terrible than his dreams had ever been. Perhaps he was psychotic after all.

He looked at the knife in his right hand. Its blade was stained red with the blood of the woman he loved. He conjured her image in his mind and sobbed as he pictured her lifeless body, lying where it fell in the kitchen.

He thought back to their meeting in Trafalgar Square and the meal they'd shared in the pub. He recalled his first night at the cottage and the single bed he'd slept in. The very next day, they'd made love at the meadow. He almost started to smile at the joy the memories brought him.

But then he remembered the truth. His real name was James Richie: he was Elizabeth's son, her own flesh and blood. He was an inbred – an inbred who's slept with his own mother.

And now her life was over.

So, too, was his – he would be charged with murder, no doubt. Despite the circumstances of the tragedy, there would be no escaping the law. Who would believe his tale about the dreams? He was officially psychotic, diagnosed professionally; he'd be denounced as a dangerous killer and sentenced to a secure hospital for the rest of his days.

As his thoughts began to crystallise, an appalling symmetry hit him: he was sitting in the very spot where Elizabeth had stumbled into the water on the day she'd tried to kill herself.

His heart started to pound at the thought.

Slowly, Hugo stood up. Again, his fingers started to tremble as his body prepared for action.

He extended his left forearm. Suspending the knife above it, he pushed down hard with a grimace, pulling the blade towards him and slicing the skin with ease. Endorphins shielded him from the pain.

He'd severed his radial artery. Blood poured to the ground and reddened the mud beneath him. Swapping the knife into his other hand, he then made a cut to his right wrist, a shallower one given the injury to his left. He watched transfixed as blood now dripped from both arms.

The sensation was curious: a euphoric, drug-like rush that transported him to the brink of ecstasy. But the pleasure was short-lived, and moments later, the pain kicked in.

A mixture of pain and panic.

His body was failing through blood loss.

Weak and light-headed, his vision started to blur. Fainter and fainter he felt until he sank to his knees with the dizziness.

His world was turning black, and he sensed he was toppling forwards. Resigned to his fate, he didn't try to break his fall. He was about to succeed where Elizabeth had failed on that fateful day in the autumn.

Hugo fell with a splash.

*I love you too, Elizabeth,* was his final lucid thought. Then there was nothing. Only the stillness of his body as the stream flowed languidly around it.

The disturbance startled the mallard. It quacked and flapped its wings, then continued its paddling and pottering, hoping to find that bit of winter food.

## ABOUT THE AUTHOR

C. D. Fox was born on 1st August 1980 in Bromley, southeast London, but grew up in a Rutland village near the market town of Stamford, Lincolnshire. He attended Stamford School and the University of Sheffield before embarking on a career in Education and has earned two master's degrees from the Universities of Warwick and Oxford, respectively. He enjoys playing cricket during the summer holidays when he gets a break from teaching. Other hobbies include reading, gardening, and walking in the countryside. He has lived in Oxford since 2011.

Lightning Source UK Ltd.
Milton Keynes UK
UKHW050832071222
413491UK00007B/154/J

9 781913 142247